Praise for Jacquelin Gorman's

THE SEEING GLASS

"Like any good memoir, this one is about remembering. . . . For anyone
who longs for the personal, *The Seeing Glass* delivers."
—*USA Today*

"A terrifying bout of blindness stirs up recollections of a dark family
story in this moving memoir. . . . The author's memories of . . .
[her brother] Robin's short and tragic life are artfully woven into the
story of her own blindness. . . . [T]wo memorable stories in one."
—*Kirkus Reviews*

"This is a powerful book . . . "
—*Library Journal*

"This touching, lyrical memoir . . . sidesteps cliche . . .
with impressive skill, viscerally evoking her situation without ever
surrendering to self-pity."
—*Entertainment Weekly*

"[A] bittersweet memoir of personal terror, weakness, strength and
the healing power of love."
—*The Times Record* (Brunswick)

"The author's late brother, called Robin after the color of his
eggshell-blue eyes, was one of the first children on record in whom
autism was diagnosed, in the early nineteen-fifties. This profoundly
moving book, distinguished throughout by clarity and compassion,
describes how, years later, Gorman—during a siege of optic disorders
that rendered her temporarily blind—began to piece together
recollection of Robin's life. Through that dark glass she was able to see
him as he was: luminous, beloved, troubled, but unbowed."
—*The New Yorker*

JACQUELIN GORMAN

THE SEEING GLASS

A MEMOIR

RIVERHEAD BOOKS

NEW YORK

RIVERHEAD BOOKS
Published by The Berkley Publishing Group
A member of Penguin Putnam Inc.
200 Madison Avenue
New York, New York 10016

"The Fly," "The Canary," and "The Sea Gull" reprinted from *Verses From 1929 On* by Ogden Nash. Copyright 1940, 1942 by Ogden Nash. By permission of Little, Brown and Company (Inc.)

First Riverhead hardcover edition: June 1997
First Riverhead trade paperback edition: June 1998
Riverhead trade paperback ISBN: 1-57322-679-3

The Penguin Putnam Inc. World Wide Web site address is
http://www.penguinputnam.com

The Library of Congress has catalogued the Riverhead hardcover edition as follows:

Gorman, Jacquelin.
The seeing glass : a memoir / by Jacquelin Gorman.
p.   cm.
ISBN 1-57322-061-2
1. Gorman, Jacquelin, date.   2. Blind women—California—Biography.
3. Blind women—California—Psychology.   4. Adjustment (Psychology)—
California.   5. Autism—California.   I. Title.
HV1792.G67A3   1997   96-53345   CIP
362.4'1'092
[B]—dc21

Printed in the United States of America

10 9 8 7 6 5 4 3 2 1

THIS BOOK IS DEDICATED WITH LOVE
TO MY FATHER, AUBREY GORMAN,
WHO MADE ME A DREAMER AND A WRITER.

CONTENTS

I. ICE TRAIN   1

II. THE GRIEF SPECIALIST   67

III. GOODBYE FIRST   123

IV. THE SEEING GLASS   197

When the loop in time comes—
and it does not come for everyone—
The hidden is revealed,
and the spectres show themselves.

T. S. ELIOT
"The Family Reunion"

THE
SEEING
GLASS

I

ICE TRAIN

ONE

JANUARY 17, 1994

It is 4:31 in the morning, and we are wide awake. My husband and I are sitting in bed, only inches apart, shouting to make ourselves heard above the rumble of moving earth and the sound of shattering glass. We were supposed to be prepared for this. All Californians are supposed to be prepared for earthquakes. But we are not.

The power is out. We are in total darkness. We haven't kept a pair of shoes by the bed so that we can walk across a floor littered with shards of glass. We don't own a radio that operates without electric current. Our flashlights don't work, because the batteries have died. We can't find any extra batteries. But we are not screaming about those things. We are shouting the names of our children, a seven-year-old and a four-month-old infant, asleep on the other side of the house.

We call their names over and over, hoping they will shout back. Kelsey! Benjamin! No answer. Kelsey! Benjamin! Over and over, until our voices wear down to a whisper.

Native Californians have been told throughout their lives what to do in case of an earthquake. The Earthquake Preparedness Manual fills the first ten pages of our telephone directory in huge bold print, instructing people to go to the nearest doorway or heavy table or desk and stay underneath it until the shaking stops. *Drop. Cover. Hold.* Drop to the floor, cover your head. Hold on to something solid. This drill has been practiced so many times, in schools, in offices, and as part of a "Family Disaster Preparedness" plan at home that it should come as a reflex. But the drills are never rehearsed in total darkness.

At this moment, all over Los Angeles, people are failing the ultimate test. Many will be killed because they acted instinctively, trying to save their loved ones before themselves. There are others whose first instinct will be to turn over in their beds and shut their eyes tight, trying to put the nightmare back where it belongs—under the covers, under control. Better, they think, to die with their eyes closed, not seeing what's headed toward them.

Kenny is out of bed and is plunging forward in the darkness to find them. I can hear him stumbling down the hallway toward their rooms, cursing as he trips over all the things that have fallen out of shelves and drawers. I decide that I will wait five minutes. If he does not come back with them, I will go after him. I don't think beyond this five-minute plan.

I hear him stumble again, fall down, and pick himself up. He is taking deep, loud breaths, as if he could blow away all the unseen obstacles between him and his children.

"Jackie!" he calls out. "Help me. I can't see anything."

We have made a crucial mistake. The wrong parent is going down the dark tunnel that is our hallway. It should have been me. I am the one most prepared for this moment, for the strange, other world of terrifying darkness. I have been blind before.

I go over the terrain in my mind, a visual dry run, before I get out of bed. Memory is my guide. Twenty-two steps. Turn right. Three steps to Kelsey's room. Doorknob on the right. Six steps to her bed. Drop. Cover. Hold. Eight steps back to the doorway. Ten steps from Kelsey's room to Ben's room. Doorknob on the left. Four steps inside to Ben's crib. Drop. Cover. Hold.

"Kenny, wait for me," I shout, counting my steps under my breath.

Automatically, I assume my blind walker's stance. I raise my arms at my sides like wings, fingertips grazing the walls for balance. I am stepping slowly and carefully, exaggerated movements, as if the ground were quicksand, ready to suck me down, capture me if my feet stop for a moment too long.

My fingers feel for familiar landmarks as I walk, a mental list that I check off with my hands. The old routine steadies me. Sliding-glass-door handle, shutters, plant, top of chair, picture . . . no picture. Only the metal picture hanger.

Suddenly, I feel a sharp stabbing pain in my right toe. A piece of glass. I reach down to touch my foot. The cut is clean and shallow, a tiny scratch. I feel only a drop of blood, like a pinprick, but I know its fresh red shade. This red, bright, fire-engine red, is the first color my eyes lost and the last color my eyes restored. Red is the color for warning signals, for danger ahead. I hate the color red.

My favorite color is blue. Blood held inside the body is blue, but once it hits the air, it turns this awful red, then finally black. Blue for safety. Red for danger. Black for death. Moving feels blue. Stopping feels red. Dying feels black.

How could I forget this? That colors can be touched. Shades within a color have texture, tone, and temperature like human skin. I will never forget how red feels. I will never forget how I feel when I can see the color red and how I feel when I can't. It has been almost three years, but my heart remembers every single detail of that siege of blindness. My body and brain propel me forward, down the hallway, toward my family, my future, but my heart is looking back.

TWO

Kenny and I are standing in the pediatric recovery room, gripping each other's hands over the unconscious body of our four-year-old daughter. Parents are not allowed in here, as a general rule. A few minutes earlier, one of the nurses asked us to come in because they were having trouble bringing Kelsey out of anesthesia.

"She is not responding to us," the nurse said. "Maybe the sound of your voices will bring her back sooner."

It takes us a few minutes to find our voices when we first see her. She is stripped naked from the waist up, her ribs ladderlike under her skin from the recent loss of weight, her chest covered with heart monitors. There are bandages thrown hastily on the floor around her gurney. I have spent enough time in hospitals to recognize this scene, but Kenny is alarmed.

"Where did all this blood come from?" he asks.

"I'm afraid we had to suction her," the nurse answers. She kicks the used pieces of wet gauze aside. She sounds defensive. "Her sinuses were still draining blood, and some of it was restricting her breathing. After all, she was in there more than three hours."

As if we, her parents, had not been counting every minute.

Kenny is smoothing Kelsey's curls away from her forehead. "But look at her lips! And her face! They're all bloody!"

Another nurse comes over, sensing trouble.

"Jackie, look at her," Kenny says, pushing the other nurse's hand away as she tries to clean Kelsey's face with a wet cloth.

I lean over to examine her face. Up close, I can see that her lip is swollen, but I can't see any blood. Her face looks and feels wet. She looks sweaty.

"Her lip must have been cut from the intubation," the nurse mutters under her breath.

Now I understand what has happened, but to have it happen to my own child is unnerving. I shudder at the violence of the operating room. Even after years of working as in-house counsel for a large hospital, years of advising physicians and nurses as to the best way to handle such accidents, I am shocked.

It's all covered in the patient consent-to-surgery form—all the mishaps that could occur under the phrase "emergency procedures necessary to preserve life." It can range from bruised faces to broken ribs from CPR. I can't even remember signing it this morning.

Kelsey moans. Kenny whispers into her ear.

"Hello, Perfect," he says. "Daddy's here."

Her eyes are still closed, but her body twists toward the sound of her father's voice. She's coming back.

The auditory sense is the beginning and end of consciousness. A person can hear even if they have lost the strength to open their eyes. I learned that when my mother was dying.

So where is my voice for my daughter? Why can't I just whisper to her? Why can't I tell her I'm here? Why does my head hurt so much?

I reach out to the nurse, grabbing her arm. Her flesh feels cold, like the room. I can feel the bone underneath her skin. She is so small and thin that my fingers close around her wrist.

"Please, could you help me?"

She yanks her arm away.

"Help *you*?"

"Yes—I need some aspirin. Please, I have this terrible headache."

Kenny looks up at me. I can't see his expression but I can see his head shaking in disbelief.

"How could you possibly be thinking about yourself and your headache at a time like this?"

His rebuke cuts through me like the sharp knife piercing the right side of my head. I have rarely heard Kenny raise his voice to anyone. He has never before, in twelve years of marriage, raised it in anger to me.

In fact, we have been speaking in near whispers in our house for months as we guided Kelsey through painful diagnostic tests and complicated treatments in an attempt to find out why she could not stop coughing, why she could not seem to breathe right. Kelsey has offered us her own explanation.

She thinks that there are all sorts of little people inside her, running up and down her ribs as if they were monkey bars. They don't mean to hurt her, she says. They just forgot to put their soft tennis shoes on.

"Mommy, those little people with hard shoes are bouncing around the inside of your head," she told me last night when I first complained of my aching head. "Tell them to change into their slippers now—it's time to go to sleep."

The room blurs as my eyes fill with fresh tears remembering my failure last night to take care of my daughter properly. My little girl is sick, she needs me, and all I can think about is myself and my own pain. Still, if I could just get some aspirin, I could think more clearly.

"Please," I repeat to the nurse. She motions to me to follow her as she walks toward the exit doors of the recovery room. I rush after her, desperate for relief. I don't even look back.

The nurse pounds the electronic button, and the doors swing open to the family waiting room where we sat earlier. She puts her hand at the small of my back and shoves me forward. She is amazingly strong for a small person. It takes me a moment to realize what she is doing: she is throwing me out. I am being bounced. They are taking away the privilege of staying with my daughter.

"You can come back when you get ahold of yourself," she says, as the doors swing shut.

I stare at the closed doors.

I didn't say a word to Kelsey. She never knew her mother was there. I didn't tell her I loved her. What kind of mother am I?

I sit down on the floor next to the doors, and wait for them to open again. I will storm through them, and I will stand beside my family. It's my right as a mother, not a privilege. I'll remind them of this fact. I practice my indignant speech, waiting for the doors to fly open.

But as soon as I hear the doors move, before I can get on my feet, I feel an arm encircle my shoulders, and hear Kenny's voice, soothing and low.

"Kelsey is awake. She's going to be coming out in just a minute."

He's holding me now with both arms.

I pull away so that I can see his face. I keep blinking, as if I have just opened my eyes after diving into deep water, except this water is not cool and clear like a swimming pool. It is murky like ocean water, filled with sand and salt and gray particles that filter out the light from above the surface.

"Everything is going to be all right," Kenny says, his voice confident and strong.

I can't make out the expression on Kenny's face. I want to read his face, figure out if he is just saying this to make me feel better, or if he believes it himself.

I realize that my headache has disappeared, but the realization makes me more afraid. If the headache is gone, then why can't I see the face of the person I have known and loved all these years?

"Mommy," Kelsey calls out as an orderly pushes her little gurney through the electric doors. I rush to her side. "Where were you, Mommy?" She reaches for my hands. "You promised."

She's right. I had promised to be there when she woke up.

"Of course I was there, darling."

She shakes her head. "No."

"But I *was* there," I say, struggling with the words to explain something I can't understand myself. "I was there, and then I had to leave for a minute, so the nurses could help you, and make you better."

"You left me, Mommy," she says, closing her eyes. "Please, don't ever leave me again."

"I won't, darling. Mommy won't leave you again."

I bring my face closer to hers, rubbing my eyes, trying to bring Kelsey's face into focus, as I crouch beside her gurney in the crowded elevator. But this only makes my contact lenses slide up into the recesses of my eyelids.

Kenny must think I'm crying, because he has handed me his handkerchief. I hold the flimsy cloth against my eyes gratefully, as if it were a healing compress. I can smell his aftershave, that same menthol smell that trails him all over the house. Early this morning, before we left for the hospital, I smelled it when I buried my face in the dog's fur. And later, I caught it in Kelsey's hair as I held her head tight against my chest, bracing her for the preop shot of tranquilizer. This scent lingers on all the creatures he has touched. I inhale it deeply, as if it were pure oxygen.

The elevator bell rings, and we must move quickly to get off before the doors close. I walk on one side of the gurney and Kenny on the other, as an orderly wheels Kelsey into the pediatric ward where she will stay overnight. I keep bumping into the walls of the long hallway.

"Careful, these walls tend to jump out at you," the orderly says to me, chuckling at my clumsiness.

I grab the metal retaining bar with both hands and keep my bruised elbows bent close to my body. I wish I could climb in there with Kelsey and lie beside her, swaddled in flannel blankets, but I hold on to her bed and let it tow me along.

Finally, we arrive at her room. Kenny and I try to go through the narrow doorway at the same time and nearly knock the orderly down.

"Okay, let's get our jobs straight," he says, with the dramatic, resigned sigh of a man who has choreographed this scene a thousand times. "Dad, you get the bed ready. Mom, you take this, and I will handle the rest."

My fingers close around plastic. He has handed me a coil of Kelsey's intravenous cord. He picks Kelsey up in his arms, and I follow him, closely attached by this plastic leash. Kenny is already over by the bed, following orders, turning down the sheets. The orderly sets Kelsey down gently on the bed. She heaves a deep sigh and rolls over onto her side.

"Go back to sleep, sweetheart," Kenny says. "Daddy's going to stay here with you all night long."

"No!" I shout. This is not the plan we agreed upon. "You know it's my turn." This is *my* watch. He took the night shift last night, after my headache kicked in. He never slept. He resisted Kelsey's pleas for water after midnight. He crawled inside her mist tent every hour to change her nightclothes.

We kept a pile of his softest old T-shirts beside her bed. Kenny used up the entire pile, covering her with clean cotton, over and over, as she coughed and vomited until daybreak. So now it's my turn. But Kenny is just standing there, mute.

"I am going to lie all night on this bed with her," I say. "I will hold her when they draw blood . . . when they give her breathing treatments. And I'll watch her antibiotic bag, and call the nurse before it runs dry and bruises her arm . . . I . . ." I am searching for the right words. What else can I say that will convince him that I can be trusted, that I will not let our daughter down again?

"I'm a telephone call away," he says finally. "You promise to call me if she needs me?"

I can hear the doubt in his voice, although I can't see the expression on his face. It makes me doubt myself. Suddenly I want to say something else. What I want to say is that it isn't just Kelsey that needs him. *I* need him. I need him to stay with me. But I don't say any of this out loud.

"We're going to be just fine, Kenny."

I sit on the end of Kelsey's bed, my posture straight, trying to look like a soldier on duty. I wave at him as he leaves.

As soon as he is gone, I crumple down beside her, my head on her pillow. Her body is so still it scares me. I put my hand under the covers, on her chest, still sticky with the contact jelly of the monitor equipment. I spread my fingers wide, touching as much of her as possible. I will take the place of cold machines and monitor her vital signs through touch.

I press my hand flat against her skin, and hold my breath. I watch the outline of her upper body but I see no sign of movement. I thrust my other hand against her open lips.

And then—finally—I *feel* it, the whisper of air on the back of my hand like a warm breeze. At last I feel her small rib cage gently rise and fall in an even rhythm.

The little people inside her are finally asleep. For the first time in many months, Kelsey's damaged respiratory system is behaving exactly the way it should, like any other healthy four-year-old child's. Her breathing is effortless. This white noise of my daughter's perfect breathing wipes out all the other sounds of night on a pediatric respiratory ward. I drift into sleep like a baby listening to a favorite lullaby.

THREE

I awake to the alarm of Kelsey's screams. She's sitting up, her nose still loosely bandaged, and she's wrestling with a monster. At least it appears that way to her, and to me at first. I grab Kelsey and hold her still, blinking into the dark, before I realize that it is a male night nurse attempting to put a breathing mask over her face.

"I'm sorry. I must have scared her," he says. "I was trying to give her a treatment without waking her up."

I look up at him. He is well over six feet and seems as wide as he is tall. I'm having a hard time discerning his face in the darkness. The only light source is the crack of hallway light that spills through the door. As he moves back from Kelsey's bed and is outlined in this light, I realize that his skin is very dark.

"Monsters!" Kelsey is screaming.

I hug Kelsey closer, embarrassed by the implication of this outburst.

"She has nightmares," I explain.

He smiles, but he takes a step back from the bed, and holds the mask out to me.

"I think it would be better if you give her the breathing treatment," he says, "and I'll stay out of the way."

He flips a switch and the mist full of bronchial medicine pours out like fake fog on a movie set. I hold the mask against Kelsey's face. Kelsey leans farther into me, breathing deeply, still sobbing involuntarily, taking big gulps of the wet air. I look up and see that the man has disappeared into the night.

"That nice man wasn't a monster, honey," I say loudly, hoping he is still within earshot. "He was trying to help you feel better."

She nods her head up and down, and closes her eyes.

"Mommy's here," I say. "I would never let anybody or anything hurt you."

She squeezes my hand, her eyes still closed. After a few minutes, she loosens her grip, and her body relaxes into sleep. The machine shuts off, and the mist disappears.

"Sleep now," the nurse says, rolling the nebulizer cart away.

But I can't sleep. I'm wondering why I still feel afraid, even though the surgery is behind us.

"Mom, this is the most scared I have ever been," Kelsey had said this morning before we left for the hospital.

"What are you afraid of?"

My hands were trembling as I pulled out a fresh pair of pajamas for her to wear. I held the pajamas to my chest and waited for her answer.

"I'm afraid I will go to the hospital and never come back."

I didn't dare turn toward her then. She would have seen her own fears magnified to gigantic proportions on my face. This fear, of not coming back, is a realistic fear; I have seen this happen to other children. I have defended malpractice suits where the hospital took custody of a young life for routine surgery and did not give it back. I've argued about fate, about circumstances beyond a physician's and hospital's control. I have written briefs that clarify that the legal system cannot always provide a remedy for every injustice, or hold a hospital or doctor accountable for every surgery that ends in death.

The courts cannot make life fair, I used to say in my most lawyerly, sensible voice. That was years ago, before I became a parent. Before I understood that there is no such thing as "routine surgery" whenever that surgery is performed on someone you love.

I remember my first preview of this lesson. The admissions nurse had called me to say a patient scheduled for surgery in ten minutes was on his way up to the legal department. He had refused to sign the consent form. Before I had a chance to discuss it any further with the nurse, the patient had entered my office.

He sat down in the chair across from me. In one hand, he held a small vinyl overnight bag, the handles tied together with red yarn. He was dressed in a gray warm-up suit, and his face almost matched the color of the sweatshirt. He was perspiring, and blinking his eyes at me. In his other hand, he held our standard consent-to-surgery form, and he had circled the sentence that stated that it was possible to die from complications of general anesthesia.

"I am disagreeable to death," he said simply.

"You disagree with death?"

He nodded.

"Yes, I disagree with the idea of dying here in this hospital," he explained. "I can't sign a paper that says I accept the fact that you might kill me. I can't."

"I'm sorry, but . . ." I began, starting to explain that it was a precaution that all hospitals had to take.

"Don't be sorry about it, just do something about it," he interrupted. "The admissions people said the legal people wrote this thing. You are a legal person. Please strike that one sentence about my death. Then I'll sign."

I sat back and looked at him carefully. He appeared nervous, but mentally competent. Definitely a mature adult, somewhere in his mid-fifties. I was not informed about the nature of the scheduled procedure, and the nurse did not refer to him as a high-risk patient.

I picked up the form, marked out the offensive line, and initialed it as approved by legal. Later, this almost cost me my job. I had inked out the hospital's protection from a wrongful death suit. Although the form was signed by the patient, this was not a legal release of professional liability under the law of informed consent. In fact, it was the opposite. It was a declaration of complete refusal to consent to the risk of death.

I learned that lesson again with Kelsey. Even a child as young as four knows that the possibility of dying is unacceptable. I had to turn away from my child when she confessed her fears. I didn't want her to see my face when I lied to her.

"Kelsey, darling, Mommy and Daddy will never let you be taken away from us forever."

"I *knew* you would say that," she said, impatiently. "But I want Mommy and Daddy to take the *feeling* away."

"What feeling?"

"That creepy-crawly feeling inside. I'm scared of the doctors, scared about everything."

"Honey, we'll try to take that feeling away. But no matter what, as soon as you wake up, it will be gone, because it will be over and you won't have anything else to be afraid of."

"Good," she said, believing me.

I used to believe my mother too when I was four. When I was Kelsey's age, I was often afraid. Fear struck under cover of darkness. It invaded my body, tortured me from the inside with its fast-moving poison. Fear would slither around my heart, squeezing it too tight, then move up to my throat, filling it with the weight of tears I was too scared to shed. Finally, it would settle down in my stomach and empty it completely. I always threw up when I was most afraid.

I was afraid of many things. Usually, these fears had their own season. In the summer, I was afraid of swimming because I was afraid of drowning. In the fall, I was afraid of going back to school because I was afraid of losing last year's place, first place. In the winter, I was afraid of ice-skating, afraid to let go of the side rail, and have my feet slide out from underneath me. In the spring, I was afraid of climbing trees and falling off the weaker, higher limbs. But my biggest fear tortured me all year long. I was deathly afraid of the dark. If a noise woke me during the night, I'd stay awake until morning, sitting guard upright in bed. I'd beam my eyes around the room, like roving lights, searching for movement. I blinked and blinked, until I was sure I saw them, shadows against shadow. Monsters. Then I'd begin to scream.

It would take my mother a few minutes to stumble in from her sleep and hold me until I stopped screaming. My throat would be raw by this time. My baby sister, Sally, who slept in the top bunk because she never had nightmares, would groan in her sleep.

"What are you so afraid of?" My mother asked me the same question every night in a voice worn tired of asking, but still soft and calming.

I always gave the same answer. "I'm afraid the monsters of the dark will take me away."

Mom would kiss my forehead, as if to kiss away the very thought. Then she would give me her same answer.

"The dark will never take you away from me. There are no monsters strong enough to take a child away from its mother."

For a short, blissful time, I believed her, just as Kelsey believed me. By the time I was seven, I discovered the truth. There *were* monsters out there, and my mother was *not* strong enough to win the war. She would have to give me up, a hostage to darkness, no matter how much she loved me. She had done this before, been forced to give up one of her children. And she had loved him too.

I learned to read stories when I was four, before I started school. I read every fairy tale I could find in the house. By the time I was six, I had read enough books and studied enough illustrations to connect the story world to everything that happened in my world. I saw every real person and thing in my life as having a parallel character and fate in a story. My brother, Robin, was Peter Pan. Robin's image would fly into my brain with the night and break through the locked windows of my dreams, like that ghost of a boy who flew into Wendy's room.

But as I grew, I learned that I was not Wendy and Robin was not Peter Pan. I could not sew my brother's shadow back onto his lost self, and he could not fly to safety. I was too young and too afraid to do anything but watch as the darkness took him away. And later, all I could do was remember exactly how that ghost of a brother looked before he disappeared.

Kelsey shudders in her sleep, and I draw up the sheet and hold her close. But it's not enough. I get up and turn on the ceiling lights and flood the room with their unnatural fluorescence. Kelsey sighs and turns her face into the pillow. She is familiar with this routine.

I used to fool myself into believing that my fears would never affect her. I told myself that it might be comforting for a child to have a mother who kept the lights on until dawn, who intimately understood what frightened her. I know now it's not true. It would be better for both of us if I were the kind of mother who wasn't afraid of the dark.

FOUR

The next morning, Kelsey is discharged. We have to walk through the cystic fibrosis ward on our way out. At one point during Kelsey's illness, the physicians were convinced she had CF, an incurable, debilitating disease of the lungs. This route home is like walking through a hell we have narrowly escaped. When it came, the diagnosis itself—pertussis, or "whooping cough"—posed further complications. Kelsey had been unable to take the protective booster shots against the disease due to an allergic reaction in infancy. By the time it was diagnosed, her lungs were saturated in fluid and partially destroyed, and immediate sinus surgery was needed to open up her breathing passages. Kenny and I had spent enough time in waiting rooms with terribly sick children to understand how lucky we were to have a child with a medical problem that could be solved.

Kenny tightens his hold on my arm. "Don't look," he whispers. But I do. I always look.

Fortunately, I can't see these scenes clearly. I didn't put in my contact lenses this morning; my eyes were sore and swollen from lack of sleep. I'm wearing an old pair of glasses, all scratched up and dirty from years of neglect. It's like looking through fogged-up windshields.

I hear loud angry cries. We are passing by the nurseries first. Blurry mother-shapes are bending over plastic bassinets, murmuring reassurance. Raging little baby-shapes scream louder and harder, already beyond the comfort of a mother's voice and touch.

In the next cluster of rooms, I hear children's voices. They are shouting. The toddlers are too young to communicate their feelings in coherent sentences. They speak in moans and cries and grunts, interspersed with an occasional one-word command, like "Stop!" or "Don't!"

We pass the rooms of the older children. There is the jumbled sound of televisions blaring, but the last few rooms are eerily quiet. These private rooms are awarded to the long-term patients, very old children, veterans of their own private wars. Their doors are closed. Their parents are not here to keep them company at this early hour. They are back on the home front, getting the luckier, healthier siblings off to school.

"You look terrible," Kenny says, as we reach the elevators.

"Thanks."

"I'm sorry, but you look as if you didn't sleep all night, and your right eye is all red."

Kelsey peers around in her wheelchair. She holds out her hand. I reach out to clasp it, but my hand clutches air, and I fall forward. I catch myself by grabbing on to the handle of the wheelchair and I lean against it.

"What's wrong?" Kenny's voice is concerned, but with an edge to his concern, as if he is really saying, What's wrong with you *now*? His reserves are low. I don't want to admit that I don't know what's wrong, so I avoid the question.

"I'm so tired I can barely stand up," I mumble.

"Mom, I've got an idea," Kelsey says.

This is her favorite phrase nowadays. Kenny says she is like Ford, always having a better idea.

"I'll trade you. Why don't *you* sit in the wheelchair, instead of me?"

Kenny laughs.

"No!" I can't believe how loudly I've shouted this out. "No deal," I say, trying to make it sound like a joke.

But it's too late. The image of me in a wheelchair has stuck. I can't shake it off. Another ghastly vision pops up and superimposes itself on top of the first one. It is the panoramic shot, long frame with Kenny added to the picture. He is pushing me down a narrow, dark corridor. There is blackness ahead. He looks up and stops moving. Then he lets go.

"Jackie!"

"Mommy!"

I blink at the sight of them, my husband and my daughter, in front of me, inside the elevator. An orderly is holding the doors open for me. His fingers tap impatiently against the rubber moldings.

"Hurry up, Space-Face," Kelsey and Kenny shout at the same time.

Everyone on the elevator is laughing.

I jump forward with both feet, like a person trying to leap from the dark of her own shadow.

"Safe," Kenny whispers, as the doors close behind me.

FIVE

R ead me a story, Mommy. Please."

"I can't, my eyes are too tired."

"Then I'll read one to you."

Kelsey doesn't know how to read yet, but she has memorized most of the words, and gives a great performance.

"It's a new book. It's called *What's Missing?* Daddy got it for me."

"That's nice, sweetie."

"This is a book that I can read by myself. Just by looking at the pictures," she says, lying down beside me on the bed, propping the picture book on her stomach.

She goes to the first page. There is a picture of a mother pushing her child in a swing set. But the swing is missing. The child sits on air.

"What's missing?" Kelsey asks.

She turns the page with a loud, dramatic swish.

"The swing!"

And there it is—the same picture, but the swing is in place, no longer invisible.

"I love this book," Kelsey says.

She leans back, her head fitting neatly under my chin, and keeps up the same pace. Every picture is missing something vital in the little girl's life—an ice cream cone, the bicycle, the ball, the teddy bear. Kelsey flips the pages, her timing so practiced that she screams out the answer as though she really were reading it instead of merely seeing it.

My head is throbbing with pain again. I take off my glasses and rub my eyes.

"Don't you like my reading, Mommy?" Kelsey asks, her voice thick with disappointment.

"Yes, I love your reading," I say.

It's just the book I can't stand. I really find this book disturbing. This is life in reverse, with time acting like a giant eraser, rubbing out the favorite parts of a child's life. It makes me want to cry, this stupid book.

I want Kelsey to stop turning the pages. I already know what I am missing right now. My own mother. I miss her more than ever. She should be in this picture with me and Kelsey. If she were still alive, she would have flown to California, and she would be upstairs making something wonderful, something like roast chicken and baked custards and lace cookies that would fill the house with the smells of my childhood.

"Mommy, why are you crying?" Kelsey asks.

"I'm just very sad."

"I don't want you to be sad."

"I know, sweetie. My eyes hurt."

"That's okay, Mom. I can read you these pictures. You don't have to look at them. Close your eyes. It will be like a bedtime story. You can fall asleep while I read." She is thrilled with her new talent.

I close my eyes and try to train my mind on the sound of her voice. It is such a simple joy to see her healthy again. I marvel at her resiliency, only twenty-four hours out of surgery and just like new.

"This next picture has the little girl walking," Kelsey says as she turns the page and holds the book up to my nose.

It is a blur of blue and green colors. "See, Mommy, she is holding a leash, but there is nothing at the end of the leash. What's missing?"

She turns the page.

"The puppy!" She's laughing now. "A little brown and white dog is there now, Mommy. The puppy was missing."

Peanuts. This terrible book has made me think of my first dog and tears escape my eyes. That's it.

"Let's put this book away, Kels."

"Okay." She wipes the tears from my face. Her hands smell like vanilla cream cookies. "I know what will make you stop crying, Mommy. I'm going to get you Uncle Og's book. Those stories always make you laugh."

She runs off. The cookie smell stays behind.

Fortunately, I don't have to read the Ogden Nash poems. I have memorized most of them since I first learned to read and discovered that my favorite great-uncle, my grandmother's brother, wrote books of poetry for children.

"Here it is, Mommy. Let's read the ones about bugs and birds."

Lucky break. Those are his shortest poems. I know most of them by heart. "All right," I say to Kelsey. "You tell me what the picture is, and what the first letter of the poem is. It's a game. I'll keep my eyes closed, and see if I can guess."

"Good idea," she says brightly. "Here is a drawing of a black bug with wings, and it starts with *F.* What is it?"

"The Fly," I answer. *"God in His wisdom made the fly, and then forgot to tell us why."*

"Good for you," she giggles. "Now, here is a drawing of a bird, and it's yellow, in a cage, with feathers flying all around it. Starts with big letter *C*."

I remember my older sister Polly's canaries, and the cage always smelling terrible. *"The Canary. The song of canaries never varies, and when they're moulting, they're pretty revolting."*

"I don't get that one—too many big words," Kelsey says, turning the page. "Okay, here's another bird drawing. And it's white, and it's flying over the beach. And it begins with *S*.

"The Sea-gull," I say, hesitating. I am trying to remember this one. Seagull rhymes with . . . Oh, yes.

"The Sea-gull. Hark to the whimper of the sea-gull: He weeps because he's not an ea-gull. Suppose you were, you silly sea-gull. Could you explain it to your she-gull?"

"Silly sea-gull," Kelsey says, lisping through her lost front tooth. "Silly sea-gull, silly sea-gull," she keeps saying, as I drift off to sleep.

SIX

The seagulls have woken me up again, calling my name over and over, calling me to come outside. I sit up and watch them through the window. I love the way seagulls fly, their wings always pointed to the sun, making the letter *V* as they climb higher and higher. My favorite quiet game is to think of all the pictures that go with alphabet letters. A big *V* is the shape that Canada geese make when they fly together. But a little *v*, which is soft and curvy, looks like a baby seagull flying all by itself over the water. "Virginia" and "vacation" start with *v*, and they go together, since we come to my grandparents' house here in Virginia every summer vacation.

I can't stop thinking about letters, even now. It's like magic when they aren't squiggles anymore, but stand for things, like birds and places. I was thinking about the letter *v* in the car all the way from Baltimore. We were talking about our favorite summer smells, and I said I liked vanilla best, like the way my grandparents' kitchen smells after Lucy sets the custards out to cool in the pantry.

I love letters ... and words that rhyme. I've decided that I want to be a writer when I grow up. I want to make words go together in just the right way so that everyone will understand what I am thinking, because I'm too shy to tell them out loud. My father's Uncle Ogden is a writer and he's very shy too. My mother says I got it from him, and that I have it so bad it's like a disease.

"Jackie! Jackie!" the gulls scream at me in their hurry-up voices, and I hope they will wake somebody else up so I can go outside.

I look over at the bed next to me. My baby sister Sally is still asleep. All I can see is her yellow hair spread out on the pillow, and one puffy little hand covered with white goo sticking out of the covers. She got sunburned when we went fishing yesterday because she kept holding her toy bunny over the side of the boat so he could see, even though I told her he can't see anything with his fake glass eyes. When the water got bumpy and waves splashed over the side of the boat, Sally got scared and dropped the bunny into the water. Horace had to stop the motor and catch her bunny with a fishnet. Sally cried all the way back because her hand got sunburned and her bunny's fur was all wet and smelly. She was hollering loud enough to scare away the fish, so we came home early without catching anything.

Today, no matter what, I'm going to catch some crabs. I want to get out before Sally wakes up and starts talking. She talks all the time, every minute she's awake and sometimes even in her sleep. I like things quiet. I want to go down to the dock before everybody else wakes up so I can listen to the sounds of nobody talking. I want to hear the water slapping up against the dock, the splash of fish, and the sound of the boat lines squeaking as they rub against the wood pilings.

The trouble is, we have two rules about going near the water. Number one: We have to wear a life preserver, all the time, no matter what. Number two: We have to go down to the dock with a grown-up. So I have to wait for someone to wake up and take me down.

At last I hear the back-porch screen door slam. I pull on my shorts under my sleepshirt and run downstairs and outside, closing the screen door soft and slow, so it won't wake Sally up.

All four small life preservers are lying out on the grass where we left them after the boat ride. That means it isn't Polly or Robin who have gotten up already. I look down to the boathouse and see that the door is open.

Only one person is allowed in the boathouse and that's Horace.

I love Horace. Horace can do anything. He takes care of my grandfather's boat and fishing stuff, and fixes all the broken things in the house. This summer he has to do a lot of fixing of the things Robin breaks, before anyone else finds out he broke them. Horace loves Robin more than all the rest of us put together.

I grab a life preserver and pull it over my head as I run across the grass. I run past my grandmother's garden, around the big tree with green, red, and white flowers that makes me think of Christmas even though it is hot and sunny. I hug the life preserver tight so the metal buckles won't flap back against my face as I run. My nose and chin are tucked inside the life preserver. All the smells of summer are in there—fish guts, and crab juice, and bloodworms. It makes me run faster. I don't want to be late for the first crabs. In the early morning, the crabs are sleepy, a cinch to catch. But as soon as the sun gets too hot, they crawl to the cool squishy bottom of the river.

I run around the boathouse, and look at the dock stretched out into the deep water. My feet land on the first wood plank and it is still cool. It must be very early. I run ahead to get the crab net.

I see two long skinny legs lying across the dock sideways.

Robin has gotten there before me! He must have forgotten his life preserver. He is twelve years old, and he's the best crab catcher in the family, even better than Horace, who taught us all how, like he taught my mother when she was a little girl. I walk up to Robin quietly and watch, trying to keep really still so I won't scare away any crabs. I'm very good at being quiet. I got the Best Rester award in my class this year. Polly and Mommy and Daddy laughed about my Best Rester pin, but I love it. Sometimes I even let Robin wear it.

I can only see Robin's back and neck, which are burnt and puffy like Sally's hand, and his swimming trunks. I stand on tiptoes so I can see him better. I see the bony backs of his ankles, and the top of his heels hooking his feet down the side of the dock so he can lean so far over that his head touches the water's edge.

The handle of the crab net pokes up from the water, swinging back and forth. No matter how hard he tries to stay still, Robin's hands always flap around. When Polly told me that Robin was named after a bird, I used to think it was because his hands were always flapping like wings. They flap even harder and faster when he is afraid or excited. When he is happy, his whole body shakes, like he's got a chill right after hopping out of a warm bath.

Robin gets upset when we don't understand what he's saying. He tries his hardest, but he just can't say things right. He will say the same words we all say, but somehow they come out backwards or too fast. Sometimes it makes Sally and me laugh, but then Polly gives us an angry look. We don't mean to hurt Robin's feelings. It's just that he acts like he's starring in his own Jerry Lewis movie.

But the one thing we can never laugh at Robin about is catching crabs. He has his own special tricks. Very quietly, I lie down beside him so I can watch him more closely. I knock his arm by mistake, but as usual, it seems like he doesn't even know I'm there.

He doesn't even knock my arm back harder the way Sally or Polly would. Robin doesn't get mad like that. He never fights with us, even though he's the biggest and the strongest kid in the family and the only boy. He never hits or bites or gives Indian burns. But when Robin gets really mad, he acts all crazy and makes us afraid.

Crabs are the hardest things to see when they are in the water. But once you pull them out, you see the bright blue on the tips of their claws. In the water, they are the exact same muddy color as the river bottom, so you have to stare at one spot and wait and wait until you see a claw move. That's what Robin is doing now, staring at one place in the water. In his other hand, the one without the crab net, he is holding a piece of broken glass between his face and the water.

Robin always carries around bits of plastic in all different colors, and sometimes glass too, if he doesn't get caught. But I've never seen this piece he's got now. It's dark yellow-brown, like iced tea. He puts the glass so close to his face the end of his nose rubs against it. I can't lean over far enough to see through this glass without falling in the water.

From where I am, I can't see anything in the water except the barnacles stuck on the piling. They are white and crusty, like popcorn. Crabs always go straight for the barnacles. Robin is keeping the net close to the barnacles so when he sees a crab, he'll pull it up fast, catching the crab on the move, before it even reaches the piling. That's the hardest way to catch a crab. It takes a lot of practice and really good eyes. Only Robin can do it that way. I have to do it the easier way. I wait longer, until the crab has already gotten himself stuck to the piling and is too busy eating the barnacles to see my net coming.

Suddenly there's a big splash. Robin pulls the net up fast out of the water. He jumps up and holds the dripping net high above the water. There are *two* big crabs in it, stuck together. A double-decker!

"Look, Horace, look!" he shouts.

I stare at that double-decker—I can't believe he saw them.

"Robin catch crab!" He is screaming now, he's so excited. I bet they can hear him all the way up at the house. "Robin—me—catch!"

"Yes, son, you did!" Horace laughs as he comes out of the boathouse to look. He is smiling at Robin and clapping his hands. "I heard that splash, and I knew my Robbie had caught himself the first crab of the mornin'!"

Robin is having one of his giggle fits. He is shaking all over with happiness. He hops from one foot to the other, as if the dock is a hot plate. Drops of water fly from the net, and one lands in my eye. It stings and I rub it.

"Miss Jackie, your brother is the winner today in the crab race," Horace says. "And there you are, still rubbin' the sleep outta your eyes. Lookit your brother—he's done made himself his very own special glass, his seeing glass for crabs!"

I try to open my eyes to look at Robin, and look at the glass, but my eyes hurt too much to see him. I keep rubbing them, but they still sting. The last time my eyes hurt like this was last summer when we went swimming in the river, and I swam into a big stinger. My face blew up like the belly of a blow-toad, and I couldn't open my eyes for the longest time.

SEVEN

I am rubbing my eyes when I wake up. There is a sticky wetness on my cheeks. I must have been crying in my sleep. It has been such a long time since I have seen Robin's face, even in my dreams. My eyes are throbbing like they did the night before.

I get up, go into the bathroom, and bring my face close to the mirror to examine my eyes, to see if I have some kind of infection in them. Without my contact lenses in, my reflection is blurry and out of focus. I find my glasses on the floor by the bed, and go look again.

I still can't see anything wrong with my eyes except that the right one is wet, my eyelashes clumped into points as if I'd just gotten out of a swimming pool. My left eye looks dry. I hold a washcloth against my right eye. It must be some kind of infection, but at least it hasn't spread to the other eye.

"*Sangre!*"

The scream startles me. It is Teresa, our housekeeper. I hadn't seen her until now. She was in the bathroom, putting away clean towels.

"*Sangre!*" she screams again.

I have no idea what she's saying, but her screams are frightening me. I press the washcloth tight against my face, like a shield.

She reaches for me, pulling my hand away gently. She starts to scream again when she looks at the towel.

"Blood!" she shouts.

Now *blood* is a word I understand.

"What blood? Where?" I shout back at her.

She points to my eye and the towel. I look, but I don't see anything. I go back into the bedroom. Teresa follows me, and stands there staring at me as I lie down, with the towel by my side. She stands at a distance, as if I have been possessed. I start to call out for Kenny, and then remember he is out playing golf. My eye hurts even more now.

I hear Kelsey calling me from her room. All this screaming must have woken her up.

"Teresa," I say, trying to sound calm. "You must go and take care of Kelsey. I don't want her to see me."

I grab the phone to call friends. I give up after I reach the second answering machine. I'll have to drive myself over to the Urgi-Care Clinic. I take a baby pillow off the bed and hold it against my right eye. The cushion makes it feel better, like a big soft bandage. I sit there for a few minutes, taking deep calming breaths.

I feel our dog, Jake, licking me and sniffing around the pillow. Maybe it *is* blood, because dogs can smell blood. Then something occurs to me: Jake sleeps on the bed with us. Maybe he got his paw in my eye. He's often scratched my cheek before. Maybe he cut the outside of my eyelid and I can't see it in the mirror because my eye is open when I'm looking at it.

This theory calms me down. I grab the car keys, shout to Teresa that I am going to see the doctor, and head out the door.

The clinic is only four blocks away. I stare straight ahead, still holding the baby pillow against my injured eye. I drive too slowly, overcompensating for my disability, like a drunk. At the traffic light, I notice my left hand gripping the wheel so tightly that my knuckles are white.

I take a deep breath. Just a scratch. I might need an antibiotic ointment. Maybe some sutures to stop the bleeding. I flinch thinking about getting a shot of novocaine in my eyelid.

I keep taking deep breaths. I look up and realize that the light is no longer red. I step on the accelerator. There is frantic honking all around me. What is happening? I hit the brakes and screech to a stop just before a car coming from the right almost runs into me.

"Red light, you idiot!" somebody screams from a convertible. I'm sure it wasn't red, but maybe I'm so scared that I'm not thinking straight. One more block. I drive into the parking lot for the clinic and go to the very end of the lot, which is vacant. I don't trust myself to park between other cars.

As soon as I walk over to the reception desk, I am asked if it is an emergency. I take the pillow off of my face. The receptionist gasps.

"Come right through the door," she says.

She ushers me into an examination room and tells me that the doctor will be in immediately.

"How on earth did you drive here by yourself with one eye covered up like that?" the doctor asks as soon as he walks in.

"Very badly," I answer.

He laughs. He comes over and stands in front of me. He crouches and brings his face so close to mine that when he laughs, I can smell the peppermint from his toothpaste. He moves closer, aiming a small flashlight into my right eye.

I hold my breath. I have that self-conscious feeling I get when I'm having my picture taken. I can't imagine what I must look like to this man. Slept in my clothes. Never washed my face, brushed my teeth or hair, clutching a baby pillow that it took this doctor three tries to pry from my eye.

"All right," he says cheerfully, gliding back from me on his rolling stool. "I've examined that eye thoroughly, and there is no sign of any serious injury. The outside of your eye is red and irritated. Probably from rubbing it so hard with that pillow. My guess is that the blood must have come from a small capillary vessel that burst during the night. But it is no longer bleeding."

"You mean there's nothing to worry about?"

"Well, nothing serious that I can see. However, we'll test the vision, just to be on the safe side."

"I think I'm having trouble with colors," I say.

"Oh, really? Are you color-blind?"

"I never was before this."

"What color is my shirt?"

"A medium brown," I say.

"Really?"

"That's what it looks like to me," I say.

"It's a very bright red," he says. "You have lost the color red."

He says this like the color red is something very important, something I should have taken better care of. It has never occurred to me that it is possible just to lose a color. I understand that a person can have trouble distinguishing one color from another, but not lose an entire part of the spectrum.

"What does that mean?"

"Let's test your distance vision and then we'll talk about the possibilities," he says in a clipped voice, without a trace of the laugh I heard only a few moments before.

He hands me an oversized plastic spoon. I put my glasses back on.

"Cover your left eye, and read the chart with your right one," he says.

I cover my left eye and stare straight ahead with my right eye. There is nothing in front of me but a fuzzy gray cloud. It's as if a dirty blanket has been pulled down over me. I drop the plastic spoon and it clatters to the floor.

"Oh, God!"

"What's wrong?"

I can't answer him. I don't know what's wrong. I tear off my glasses and look at them, thinking that maybe the right lens got chewed up by the dog, or covered with carpet lint or something. But both lenses are clear.

I cover my left eye again, this time with my hand. I look straight at the doctor as I do this. He disappears into a gray fog. I pull my hand away as if it has been burned. He comes back into view. No, it can't be. I do this over and over, slapping my eye in a panic. Every time I cover my left eye, the doctor disappears, and every time I uncover it, he reappears out of the gray mist like a character beamed in from *Star Trek*.

Finally, I look up at him, and this time I cover my right eye. I look at him only with my left. I can see him perfectly.

"I'm sorry. I can't see anything with my right eye," I say.

He stares at me for a few seconds.

"You're absolutely sure?"

"Yes," I say, my voice now so high and squeaky with panic that I barely recognize it.

"Cover your left eye one more time," he orders, as if he is talking to a child. "Now. How many fingers do you see?"

I drop my hands into my lap and look at him with both eyes. He is standing there waving two fingers in the air. He looks frantic, and that unhinges me further. I'm starting to lose my patience. I want him to be in control here. Somebody has to be in control and it certainly isn't me.

"I have to tell you one more time. I can't see you or your fingers with this eye!"

"I'm sorry," he says, his arms now at his sides.

I look at him, waiting for his next move.

All my life I have trusted doctors. My grandfather, my uncle, friends of my parents, and now many of my own friends from high school and college. I spent two years practicing health care law in a large hospital where I defended the staff doctors in malpractice suits, negotiated their contracts, and worked with them to develop hospital policies and procedures. I served on committees with them, gave them updates on California cases, even dispensed advice to them on the telephone.

Sometimes it was like working on a hot line. Physicians would call me from the trenches, wanting an instant legal analysis, an airtight opinion. One moment, it was a call from the emergency room. Was the hospital required to report a stomach filled with cocaine balloons to the police, or were they obliged to protect patient privacy and overlook the evidence? The next moment, it was a call from the operating room. Did the consent-to-surgery form for a routine hysterectomy also include the right to put back a tooth knocked out by the intubation, or would the patient sue for assault and battery? I always tried to give them enough information to be helpful. I respected their knowledge and their experience. Underlying this respect was the expectation that when I came to them with my medical problems, they would put out my fires too.

"What are you going to do to fix my eye?" I ask.

He steps back as if I have slapped him.

Then he says something that I have only heard doctors say

when their deposition is being taken. And even then, it is a remark made when the patient is already dead.

"I'm sorry. But this problem is beyond my expertise."

"What?" I am stunned by his sudden loss of confidence.

"Do you have a regular internist?"

The handoff.

"Yes," I stammer, trying to remember his name. "Bill Lang," I say, finally.

"Great!" His face brightens. "I know Bill. We interned together. I'll call him. You're in good hands."

He is grinning at me, clearly relieved. The intercom buzzes. It's the receptionist.

"Doctor, we really need you out here. We are backed up, and people are getting angry."

She sounds pretty edgy herself. He looks at me, shrugging his shoulders. People need him. I am beyond his expertise.

"I'm going to have to see a few other patients," he says. "I want you to call somebody to come get you. Use this phone. I'll be back and we'll talk some more. Just a few minutes."

He is dumping me, but at least he's trying to be gentle about it. He reaches over and puts the telephone receiver in my hand.

"Call your husband. If he's not home, call a friend. We'll call Bill Lang together," he says over his shoulder as he walks out the door.

I put the receiver back. No. Kenny should be back from his golf game by now, but I do not want to give him this kind of news over the phone. I can't stay here one more second. I have to go home. I pick up my glasses, my purse, and my mother's baby pillow. I walk out the door. There is nobody in the hall and the door to the other examination room is shut. I go back into the waiting room, and out the door to the parking lot. I hear the receptionist calling for me, but I keep moving.

I drive very carefully, very slowly out of the parking lot. It's my husband's birthday. It's my daughter's first day home after surgery. By now they will have noticed I am missing, and they will be worried. I have to go home.

EIGHT

Kenny's face is pale when I walk in the door.

"Thank God," he says.

He's holding the telephone receiver against his chest, and now he lifts it to his face but keeps his eyes fixed on me, as if he expects me to disappear.

"Bill, she's right here. Yes. I'll put her on."

"What the hell's happened?" Kenny whispers to me as he hands me the phone. "Teresa was crying and carrying on about blood all over your face. I see a bloody washcloth in the bathroom and then some Urgi-Care doctor calls here. He says you ran out on him, and he called Bill, and now Bill's talking about taking you to the hospital. For God's sake, what happened?"

I take the phone, and cover the mouthpiece with my other hand. "I don't know exactly what's wrong," I say to Kenny.

Our voices always change decibel levels when there is an emergency. My voice rises to an unbecoming screech and Kenny's lowers to a heavy whisper.

"Hi, Bill. Sorry to ruin your weekend like this," I squeak.

"Jackie, I need you to tell me in your own words what's happened. I want every detail. You told them at the clinic that you thought your dog might have scratched your eye, and they tell me you can't see anything out of that eye. Why didn't you call me right away?"

I take a deep breath. Bill Lang is not an alarmist. That's why he's my doctor, because he's easygoing and slow to leap to horrible conclusions. But he's not sounding like himself either. He's talking double-time, his voice picking up speed with every word. We are all sounding more and more like we're rehearsing a scene out of *Dragnet*.

"Well, it didn't seem worth paging you on Saturday. I really didn't think it was that big a deal."

"Did you have any trouble at all with your vision before this morning?"

"I don't think so. I mean I had headaches, and it seemed as if my eye was throbbing, you know."

"I don't have your chart in front of me, but I don't remember you having a history of migraines, right?"

"Right."

"Have you had any trouble with your balance lately?"

"What do you mean?"

"Like stumbling—missing a step, or something?"

"Well . . ." I roll this over in my mind. Bumping into the walls of the hospital, clutching Kelsey's hand and falling. Was that a vision problem or a balance problem? I tell him about this and I can hear him taking notes.

"Then all this dizziness, this blurry vision, this growing loss of coordination has been going on for at least a few days?"

I'm feeling suddenly very stupid. Growing loss of coordination? He's making me sound as if I've had a stroke.

"Well, I haven't had very much sleep," I say, defensively. "I just thought it was fatigue."

He doesn't say anything for a few seconds.

"Let's not worry about that now. Here's the plan. You'll have an MRI of your brain done over at the hospital. Then, you'll have that eye examined by an ophthalmologist. Then I'll give you a complete physical, blood tests, all that—you are probably overdue for one anyway—and then. . . .Well, we'll take it from there."

I try to process what he's just told me. Brain scan first. Doctors always rule out the worst stuff first. What's he looking for in my brain? Is that why Kenny looks so pale? What did Bill tell him before I walked in?

"Bill, I won't be able to get on the MRI schedule for days. Why don't we start with the eye doctor tomorrow?"

There is an uncomfortable pause.

"Jackie, we need to do these things right away. Today." He is speaking slowly and deliberately now, as if I am hard of hearing. "I've already gotten a radiologist and a tech to come in for the MRI. We'll do the lab work right at the hospital. And I have a good friend, an ophthalmologist, who is going to open up his office tonight. You can stop there on the way home from the hospital."

"All of this *today*?"

I can't believe he has already booked me for all of these appointments without checking.

"Is there any reason why not today?"

"Well, no, except that I'm so tired. Really, I need some time to think this over and—"

"Jackie, you don't have any more time," he interrupts. "We can't fool around. You've lost one eye already."

I am silent as I try to process this stunning pronouncement.

"I'm sorry, Jackie. I don't mean to upset you further," Bill says. "It's going to be all right. *It is*. It's just that we need to get moving."

"I know that, Bill. But it's all moving way too fast for me to absorb. I just need a minute to catch my breath here."

"The MRI can be done as soon as you get to the hospital. Do you have someone you can leave Kelsey with for the rest of the day?"

"Yes, I'll ask our housekeeper to stay late."

"Could she also stay overnight if she needs to?"

My stomach lurches. "Well, yes, I suppose."

"Good. I'll meet you in radiology. It's on the second floor."

"Yes, I remember."

"And, Jackie—please let Kenny do the driving."

In the car, Kenny repeats the conversation he had earlier with Bill, word for word. I'm momentarily relieved. Whatever is happening to me, it's not so bad yet that he is keeping secrets from me.

"I asked him about the brain scan," Kenny says. "What he was looking for exactly. Bill explained that a brain tumor might be pressing against the optic nerve. He said that's the first thing they'll look for in the MRI."

"But how can I have a brain tumor growing so quickly? How can that be possible? I can't believe this!"

I close both my eyes and put my head in my hands.

"Honey, listen to me," he says softly. "I asked him that too. The fact that it has happened so rapidly could be encouraging. It's probably not . . ." He hesitates. "Anyway, the point is that they can remove a benign tumor and your vision would probably come back soon."

I lift my head up suddenly. "Are you talking about brain surgery?"

"Well, I guess so, but Bill said that it's not as bad as it sounds. It happens more often than we think."

"Once is a lot more often than I have ever thought about something like this happening to me."

We drive into the front gate of the hospital. It is the same hospital where I worked before Kelsey was born. Kenny and I stop at admissions. I recognize the admitting clerk.

"Dr. Lang is waiting for you. He wants your husband to stay here and fill out the forms. You are to go straight to radiology," she says. Then she smiles, uncertain of herself. "Welcome back—I guess."

"Thanks, I guess." I try to smile back. "Don't keep him too long under all that paper. I need him."

She nods her head.

I walk through the main lobby toward the elevators. The chairs, always overflowing with people, are empty on this Saturday afternoon. Only emergencies are handled now. This whiff of reality stings my face like an icy wind. I hold my hand against my lost eye.

The radiology tech is still switching on lights and pieces of equipment when I walk in. Bill is pacing, with papers in his hand. As soon as he sees me, he walks over to me, and immediately pulls my hand gently away. He lifts my chin up and stares at my right eye. I stare back at him, hoping to figure out what he's thinking from the expression on his face, but I can't.

He looks exactly the same. At the hospital, the nurses had given Bill Lang a very high rating for being "easy on the eyes." One nurse said he was a dead ringer for a Jewish Tom Selleck, tall and dark, without the movie-star blue eyes and dimples. Bill has deep-set brown eyes and a down-turned mouth, beneath a heavy mustache. The mustache makes him look serious all the time, so that when he smiles, it comes out of nowhere, without warning. He has a face that doesn't betray what that serious brain is thinking, a perfect doctor's face, a mask.

"Maybe you would feel more comfortable if I go ahead and bandage that eye, for now," he says.

"No, it doesn't hurt anymore. It's just . . ." I can't explain how it feels. It isn't pain. It isn't discomfort. It's the feeling that I don't want anyone looking at an eye that can't hold its own and look right back at them. "Actually, maybe a patch or something might make me feel better."

"Sure. I'll go get some gauze. By the way, the pupil is quite enlarged—probably very sensitive to light. Here's the MRI consent form to sign. Can you read it with one eye?"

I look over the form briefly. It sounds very familiar. By the second sentence, I know why. I wrote it.

"No problem," I say, scribbling my signature at the bottom.

"Will the patient be needing the injection?" the technician asks Bill.

It's as if I'm not in the room. My heart skips at the thought of a shot. Where? In my eye? In my brain?

"Oh, Jackie, I forgot to mention that we might need to inject a dye into your arm during the procedure. It will give us better contrast shots. Highlight certain sections."

The tech is rubbing his hand up and down the inside of my arm. His hands are cold, and I shiver.

"I don't like her veins," he says with a petulant sigh.

"They're small, I know," I say, feeling like I have to defend or explain them. "My mother had the same kind," I add, realizing as soon as I say it how irrelevant it is at the moment to these two people.

"I'll get a pediatric-needle IV kit at the lab," Bill says.

"Good, we'll need it." The technician frowns at my arm. He still has not looked at my face. I try to read his badge, but the name's not familiar.

"How long have you been working here?" I ask him.

He stares at me. I'm trying to sound more friendly than curious. I want him to like me. I also want to be sure that he is in a good mood, and knows what he's doing. I'm haunted by a case I read about in which a lab tech had a fight with his girlfriend, came to work, and during a routine preop blood test, stabbed a child through the main distal nerves. That was the last time the child ever felt anything in that hand again.

"I used to work here, myself," I say. Suddenly I want this guy to be my best friend. I know that he will be the one in that room with me, the one to stick the needle in, the one to put me in the machine and get me out right away if I beg him to, but first he's *got* to be listening to me.

"Yeah, so I heard," he says, still not looking at me. "Hospital lawyer. That's how come they could pull me in on Saturday. You're a VIP around here."

Great, I'm at the mercy of a technician who hates lawyers. Where is Kenny? What's taking him so long? I don't want to go in that room with this guy by myself.

"Actually, I don't practice law anymore," I say, backpedaling. "That was ages ago. I'm a full-time mother, now."

Kenny walks in while I'm saying this.

"And a writer," he adds.

The technician looks interested.

"Really? What are you writing?"

"She's writing a novel," Kenny says. "A murder mystery set in a hospital. It's all about mistakes, and the people in hospitals who make them."

Oh, Kenny, thank you.

The technician loses his smirk. "We'd better get you ready. I don't want to make any mistakes," he says, glancing at Kenny.

"What's it called?" he asks as he walks me into the MRI room.

"What?"

"Your novel."

"Held Harmless," I say.

"Like the hospital admitting form says? The hospital will be *held harmless* for any patient injuries?"

"Yes, that's it exactly," I say. "Most people don't get it right away." This is shameless flattery, but also true.

"Great title," he says. At last, he is smiling. He reaches out his hand and introduces himself.

His handshake is firm and his skin is cool and dry. In comparison, my hand must feel like a used tissue.

I get on the metal table, and he rolls me into the tunnel-like machine.

"See you in a few minutes," he says, patting my ankles, as he leaves the room.

Half an hour later, he comes in, and rolls me out.

"So, how was it?" he asks.

"I would really like to rewrite that consent form," I say, my head pounding.

"That bad?"

"No, just very different from the way I described it in the form. I mean, it's missing some important things—it doesn't give enough information. Like the loudness of those clangs and pounding. And I underestimated how hard it is to stay still, and how creepy it is to have your head all enclosed, and only be able to see your feet in that mirror, like the rest of you doesn't exist. And. . . ."

I stop babbling when I hear him laughing.

"Maybe lawyers should be required to go through all the procedures they write consent forms for," he says. "It certainly might cut down on law school admissions."

"True," I say. It might not be a bad course requirement for radiology techs either, I think, but keep it to myself. I realize that the MRI pictures haven't been developed yet, and we might have to do this all over again. I need to keep him in my corner a little while longer.

Bill is waiting on the other side of the door.

"Hurry," he says. "I've given Kenny the directions to the ophthalmologist and he's out front in the car waiting for you. I'll walk you out there."

As we walk into the lobby, I am shocked by the darkness outside.

"How did it get to be that late?"

"It's not late for a hospital," Bill says. "I've got a night-shift radiologist on call from ER reading your films right now. I'll call you later."

"Thanks, Bill," I say. "You're the best." I go out to the car, and slide into the front seat. "Bill said he'd call with the MRI results later. He's great."

Kenny doesn't answer. I look up at him. I look straight at his profile with my good eye. His eyes are fixed ahead and his lips are pressed tightly together. These are signals I can read even with one eye working.

"What's wrong?"

"Well, I told 'Dr. Great' that I would say a prayer that there wouldn't be anything on the films. You know, no sign of a tumor."

"Yes?"

"Well, then he tells me I'm praying for the wrong result. He said he's hoping that that's precisely what they'll find."

"Hoping they *do* find a brain tumor?"

"Yes. He said that was better than the alternative. He said just to pray for that, and he wouldn't say anything else. Nothing. So, I just went to the car. I'm sorry."

What could be worse than a brain tumor?

I think this over from a doctor's perspective. And then I understand, with the kind of understanding that goes straight from my brain to the bottom of my stomach. The worst thing for a physician to find is something they can't do anything about.

NINE

We are on our way to see an eye doctor. I know the correct term is ophthalmologist, but I've always called them eye doctors. My grandfather was one. He was chairman of the ophthalmology department at Johns Hopkins Hospital in Baltimore, where I grew up. When he died, they built a research center in his name. Bob Hope, whose eyes my grandfather had "saved," flew in from California to give a speech at the dedication ceremony. I was eight years old. I adored my grandfather, but it wasn't until Bob Hope talked about him that I fully understood what he meant to so many other people.

"If it were not for the Woods Research Laboratories, my husband would be blind," my physics teacher had said to me in high school. The look on her face when she told me this was one of reverence. She was under the impression that I had inherited my grandfather's scientific genius. She would soon discover otherwise. But if she was disappointed, she never showed it. She beamed her approval at me every time I raised my hand in class, even if it was to ask her to explain the directions to the Bunsen burner one more time.

"What are you thinking so hard about?" Kenny asks.

"I was thinking about Doc."

That's what all of his grandchildren called him. It didn't seem odd to me when I was a child not to call him Grandpa or Grand-daddy. We thought that Doc was the first and most important part of his name. Since he never asked us to call him anything else, he must have thought so too.

"That's a great idea," Kenny exclaims. "We'll call Uncle Alan tomorrow. The Woods name will get you into all the best ophthal-mologists in the world. This is wonderful!"

My uncle, Alan Woods Jr., my mother's only brother, was also a surgeon at Johns Hopkins and a professor at the medical school. He must know all the best doctors in California, but the thought does not reassure me. I am afraid that even my grandfather could not have saved this eye now.

I tell Kenny this while we sit in the dark lobby of the building waiting for the eye doctor to open up his office.

"So, don't you see, Kenny," I say with a whine in my voice. "There's no use in having this doctor—any doctor for that matter—examine an eye that is already gone."

Kenny reaches over and holds me close.

"Don't *you* see, Jackie?" he whispers in my ear. "You still have another eye."

For a long time we hold each other in the dark of that waiting room, and it feels as if we are the only two people awake in the world.

"I'm ready for you now," the eye doctor says finally, opening the door to the examination room. Kenny goes over, shakes his hand, and introduces us, but the eye doctor does not say his name. He mo-tions us into the room impatiently. He seems to be in a hurry, al-though it is past nine o'clock on a Saturday night, and certainly he doesn't have any other patients to see. I sit down in the examination chair, lean forward, and put my chin on the little paper chin rest.

The eye doctor shines a light in my right eye. Tears flood down my cheek.

"Well, I can see that your eye has already been dilated," the eye doctor says with a sigh.

"What?"

"The pupil in this eye is already dilated. Did another doctor put drops in it already?"

"No."

"Oh," he says, sighing again. "Well—that certainly shows you."

"Shows me what?"

"The fact that your pupil has dilated spontaneously shows exactly why you are blind in that eye." He turns off the light. He has looked into my eye for maybe thirty seconds, long enough to pronounce the verdict. *Blind.* This is the first time that word has been used in my presence. It is a devastating word to hear. It makes me appreciate Bill Lang's euphemism. "Loss of vision" sounds serious but temporary, with the implication that what is lost may be found again. But blind is permanent. Blind is too late.

My grandfather never spoke that word out loud as far as I can remember. "Those eyes have gone where the woodbine twineth," he used to say when he was discussing an unfortunate case. He was, in his time, the most skilled eye surgeon in the world, but it was the rare operation that could bring an eye back once it was already gone. He pioneered research into various drug therapies to prevent blindness. He believed in avoiding loss before it happened.

I have lost vision in one eye, but I still have the other one, I tell myself this over and over, repeating it silently in my mind, like a soldier marching. *Left eye left.*

"See for yourself," the eye doctor says to Kenny. "Anybody can see this. No need for me to come down on a Saturday night to figure this out."

Kenny comes over and looks into my right eye as if he is looking at it for the very first time. And he is. I realize I have had it covered with a bandage ever since the hospital.

"God, it's totally black," he says. "Her left eye is blue and her right eye is black."

"Yes, that's because the pupil is so enlarged it has taken over the normal color of her iris," he says.

Kenny looks at me again and his face brightens. "But her other eye is fine. It's blue, as always. That means the other eye is not having any problems, right?"

The eye doctor sighs, and walks over to his desk. "Personally, I have never seen a case of this symptom presenting bilaterally," he says flatly. He says this in the same monotone he used for the word blind. Good news and bad news delivered with equal detachment.

"So, that means it won't spread to the other eye?" I ask.

"No. It's not *that* kind of problem," he says.

"Then *what* kind of problem is it?" Kenny asks.

"Let's go out in the hallway for a minute, and talk."

I start to get up and go with them and then I realize that he is going out in the hallway to get away from me. I give Kenny a warning look. He puts a tissue in my hand.

"I'll be back in a minute," he whispers. "I have to go to the bathroom anyway."

They close the door behind them. I start to shred the tissue into pieces. I hear the sound of the eye doctor's voice but not Kenny's. I can't make out the words. Then I hear a door close. The eye doctor comes back in and sits at his desk. He writes something in his chart. It's as if I am sitting in the blind spot of his rearview mirror.

"Where's Kenny?" I ask.

He looks up from the chart.

"Your husband? He's in the bathroom."

At that moment, we hear the sound of Kenny retching, over and over, and then the sound of the toilet flushing. Kenny and I both have emotional alarm systems directly wired to our stomachs.

"What did you tell him? What did you tell my husband out there?" My mouth is sour, and the words sound as bitter as they taste.

He takes off his glasses and rubs his eyes, as if he hopes that will make me disappear.

"I'm sorry," he says finally. "But your husband asked me a question and I answered it. That's all."

"What was the question?"

"Well . . ." He hesitates, putting his glasses back on. "He specifically asked me why your right optic nerve would blow all of a sudden like this. I told him I believed it was a symptom of an underlying neurological disease that had been going on for quite some time. Blindness in one eye is just the first presentation of a symptom. One of many, I might add."

"What?" I ask. "What disease would cause this to happen?"

As soon as I ask it, I know that I have made a mistake. It is what they tell you never to do in law school. Trial Law Examination. Never ask a question of a hostile witness that you don't already know the answer to.

"Multiple sclerosis," he says. "Severe optic neuritis—that is, swelling of the optic nerve—is almost always associated with the disease of multiple sclerosis. I think it's time for you to see a different kind of doctor. A neurologist. I'm sure your internist can recommend a good one who treats multiple sclerosis patients—to the extent they can be treated."

This new piece of information has knocked me speechless. No

wonder Kenny is throwing up in the bathroom. I don't have any firsthand knowledge about multiple sclerosis, but all my visual images are associated with wheelchairs and lack of bodily control. I keep remembering Bill's earlier questions about loss of balance and coordination. So this is where that road was leading. Blindness was just a pit stop on the road to multiple sclerosis.

The telephone is ringing. We blink at each other for several awkward moments, like a game of chicken, before the eye doctor picks it up.

"It's for you," he says, after a moment. "It's Bill Lang."

"Jackie, I've just talked to the radiologist. There's no visible sign of a mass or tumor anywhere in your brain. However, it does show that your right optic nerve is swollen and dysfunctional—a neurological problem."

"Multiple sclerosis, right?"

"Uh-oh," he says. "Who told you that?"

I don't say anything, but keep staring across the desk at the eye doctor. He keeps his head down, as if he's not listening to our conversation. His hair is neatly combed into a wide side part which, under the glare of the desk lamp, rises like a surgical scar across his skull. Everything seems to have taken on the unnatural and unflattering sheen of an operating room light. Bill's voice, full of energy, sounds like it has been piped in from another world. I can't hold the phone close enough.

"I'm sorry that he told you that . . . that . . ." Bill is stalling, trying to avoid repeating the name of the disease. "Possibility," he finishes. He takes a long breath, before continuing. "MS is merely one possibility we have to consider, but I wanted to examine you first, before we went in that direction."

I am listening very carefully to his word choices. I note that he has reduced several syllables of the diagnosis to initials, as if by stripping it of formality, he can also disarm its potential threat. It's an-other trick they teach you in law school. If you are a defense lawyer, call the defendant by a nickname or first name to make him seem like a regular guy. So, the little wave of MS barely moves me, as I take hold of the other word and lean on it for a moment. *Possibility*. This word keeps me afloat.

"You mean I may *not* have MS? It's not definite?"

I think I'm shouting for the eye doctor's benefit, but it is also good news. Kenny hears me as he comes into the room. He goes back out immediately and picks up the extension in the hallway.

"We can't make a definite diagnosis, yet," Bill says. "The only way we can determine if you have MS is by looking at the spinal fluid. And it's still not a final diagnosis until you present with a second symptom."

"So we just sit tight and wait for something else to go wrong?" Kenny interrupts.

"No, absolutely not. Listen, at this point, I want to do my own detailed workup, and then, if necessary, we would have a neurolo-gist take a look."

"What would he be able to find that you might not?" I really don't want to meet any more doctors right now.

"Well, a neurologist would have the equipment to determine if a second symptom was on its way."

"On its way?" we ask simultaneously.

"Well, yes. A specialist in neurological disorders might be able to detect slight loss of strength or sensory ability in the toes or fingers or something. Some neurological change that was so subtle the pa-tient doesn't even notice it yet."

He's talking about me. I am the patient not noticing it yet. What was it? What was missing that I didn't realize was missing—yet?

"Bill, do you think I've been having a problem with this right eye for a long time, longer than even a few days?"

"Yes, Jackie, I do. I think you may have started to lose vision in that eye months ago, but the left eye has been compensating for it."

"And that would explain the headaches."

"Yes—the headaches are a symptom of eyestrain."

"Eyestrain," I say.

The word evokes a memory I cannot summon. "Eyestrain," I repeat, trying to bring the memory forward.

"Yes, Jackie," Bill says patiently, "but we have to figure out what caused the eyestrain in the first place. Now, Kenny, this is what we need to do . . ."

Their voices start to drift away from me. They are sounding more and more distant and I'm having trouble understanding what either of them is saying. It's like trying to eavesdrop on a conversation taking place just far enough away to make out the voices and the serious tone, but not the words.

They keep talking about me, beyond me, trading thoughts, and I look up long enough to see the eye doctor glaring at me, waiting for me to stop using his phone.

"Hey, guys," I say, my voice cracking, giving away how tired and scared I am. Kenny and Bill stop speaking right away, a guilty silence, as if they had been caught saying something unflattering about me, rather than simply caught forgetting I was still on the line. "It's late. Let's all go home."

All this talk isn't leading anywhere I want to go. I want this long day to end. I want to go home and go to sleep.

When we get home, I fall into bed. I don't want to take my clothes off and change into nightclothes. I just want to go to sleep, without moving, without thinking.

"Eyestrain," Kenny is saying. "That's all it is—just a simple case of eyestrain. Your eyes just need a long rest."

"Yes," I mumble.

I hear him go into the kitchen and get something. I lie on the bed faceup, my baby pillow across my eyes. Teresa has washed it for me. It smells like bleach and it reminds me of the hospital. I examine the pillow. I can only see some faint beige droplets, as if weak tea had been spilled. I don't see a trace of red, even with my good eye. She must have used an entire bottle of bleach to get the bloodstains out.

"Here," Kenny says, as he takes the baby pillow out of my hands and lays a cloth against my eyes.

"What is that?" I shriek. It's freezing cold and wet.

"Ice," he says. "It works on my tennis elbow. I thought maybe it would reduce the swelling of your eyes."

Eyestrain. Now I remember. *Ice train*.

I see my brother Robin as a young child, leaning over his electric train set. He is laughing as he puts a cube of ice into the back of the baggage train. The hot metal hisses and spits like an angry cat, making him laugh harder, rocking back and forth with delight.

"Ice train!" I say out loud, laughing at the memory.

I tell Kenny the story. I was in second grade and had been having such severe headaches that I had begged to go home early from school. It was an unusual complaint for a young child, particularly one who loved going to school, and so our doctor came to the house that night. He diagnosed my problem as eyestrain due to nearsightedness. A few weeks later, I got my first pair of glasses.

"But what about ice train?" Kenny asks, still not getting it. He only met Robin as an adult, and doesn't know about all of his childhood speech difficulties.

"Well, Robin got the words confused. He somehow thought we were talking about an ice train. He tried to build me an ice train. We played with it for as long as we could, until the ice melted and the transformer short-circuited."

There is this moment of silence which, like a strong scent, always trails the mention of my brother's name in any conversation. Robin's name overtakes every word that had hung in the air before.

"I think that it would be better not to talk about all this right now," Kenny says softly.

"All this?"

"Well, you know . . ." He hesitates. "All these sad Robin memories."

"But this memory is happy," I say, eager to tell him.

"So we can talk about it tomorrow," Kenny says, yawning. "You need to get some sleep."

He reaches over me to turn off the bedside lamp.

"Please don't," I say, suddenly afraid. I don't know what it is that I am afraid of, but I am gripped with fear.

Kenny sighs. He hates going to sleep without total darkness. He sleeps best when it is cold and pitch-black, his head under the pillow to shut out all light. When we are away and the bed is next to a wall, he chooses that side, and sleeps with his face pressed into the crevice. I am the opposite. I want the bed to be in the center of the room, set adrift like a sailboat, the walls as far away as possible. Sleep is an uncharted journey for me, the destination always a surprise. I am still the Best Rester. My preference rules.

And for the third night in a row, I go to sleep in my clothes, with the lights on, watching and waiting for whatever comes across my narrow view.

TEN

Robin opens his mouth wide, as if he is about to scream. He doesn't have the piece of glass anymore. He only has the net in his hands and this awful look on his face. What happens next is even more awful. He drops the net, and throws himself off the edge of the dock. He makes a huge splash, like a belly flop. It must have hurt. Before I can even blink, Horace jumps in after him.

I am the only one left on the dock. I'm too scared to run to the edge to see them. Robin doesn't have a life preserver on and he doesn't really know how to swim any better than I do. He can't even doggy-paddle.

Suddenly there is another splash and they spring out of the water, coming up for air. Horace keeps trying to grab Robin and hold his head up out of the shoulder-deep water. If Robin would let Horace hold him up, he would be all right.

Horace is holding him tight in a hug, but Robin is faced the wrong way. I can see Horace's strong dark arms wound tightly around Robin's thin white chest, and for a second I'm scared he is going to break my brother's ribs in half, accidentally. But Robin keeps squirming out of Horace's arms, because he is almost as tall as Horace and so skinny. As soon as Robin gets loose, he starts flipping over, in forward somersaults. He keeps dunking his head under the water.

"I'll get the glass for you, Robbie!" Horace shouts. I've never heard Horace shout before. "Let me get you outta the water first!"

Now I understand. Robin must have dropped his piece of glass when he caught the crab. As soon as he used his crab-net hand, he forgot about his crab-finding-glass hand. That's one of the problems with Robin.

"Your brother has more problems than an arithmetic book," my grandfather always says, shaking his head whenever he sees Robin do something odd like walking down the steps backwards. "That boy can't think straight." That's not the way I see it. Robin's biggest problem is that he thinks too straight; he can only think about one thing at a time. Once he starts thinking about the second thing, he forgets about the first. That's why Robin was never allowed to hold Sally when she was a baby. Mommy said he would drop her—just drop her right where he was—if he saw something else that he wanted to hold more.

I don't worry much about Robin hurting Sally or any of us. What scares me is that he wants to hurt himself all the time. Like now. It's a good thing that Horace is so strong. He's got Robin over one shoulder, the way firemen carry children down ladders from burning houses. He's walking in slow giant steps over to the mud-bank.

But it's no good. As soon as he gets on land, Robin squirms out from Horace's arm and starts running up the dock. He is running toward me, he's going to knock me over because he's acting so crazy. It's like he doesn't see me. I jump out of the way as he runs past me. Then he stops at the very end of the dock.

"No!" he shouts over and over. "No! Gone for no good!"

He's screaming about the crab net he dropped when he jumped

into the water to find his piece of glass. The net is empty. His crabs have gotten loose. They are gone.

Robin's face is all crumpled and red. He is about to cry. Now I'm more scared than when he was in the water, because when Robin starts to cry, it's the worst thing of all. It's like the tears are killing him. It's like he wants to jump out of his skin to get away from his tears. He is slapping his face hard, slapping away the tears.

Horace is running toward us, his trousers all muddy, his wet shirt stuck to him. He found it. He's got the yellow piece of glass in his hand. But Horace is too late. Robin is lying facedown on the dock, banging his head against the splintery old wood.

"Gone for no good!" he shouts each time he lifts his head to bang it down harder. "Gone for no good!"

Horace is trying to pick Robin up, but Robin is all wet and muddy too, with no shirt on. Horace still can't seem to get a good hold on him. At last, Robin stops all at once, like one of his toy cars when the battery dies. He's just lying there facedown. He's not moving at all now. His hands are curled into tight fists, and his face is flat against the dock.

Horace picks him up and sits down on the dock, his legs crossed Indian style, with Robin in his lap. He rocks him back and forth in his arms like a baby doll. I can't see Robin's face—it's pressed against Horace's chest—but I do see a big red stain start to creep up Horace's shirt.

My chest hurts when I see the blood and I feel like I can't breathe. I want to tell Horace about the red stain, that Robin has hurt himself bad, but I can't make enough air come out of me to force the words out.

Horace hugs Robin tighter, and I watch the red stain spread, but Horace still doesn't see it. He is looking straight up at the sky.

"Dear Lord," he prays, his eyes closed. "Please help Your poor lost boy."

I look up where Horace is looking. We wait for a long time, but nothing happens. I know that Horace believes God is always around us out here. That's the very first thing he says when we go out in the boat—"We're in God's outdoors now."

If God is really out here, He didn't hear Horace. Robin is still not moving. Horace continues to rock him with his eyes closed. He is crying. I have never seen a grown-up man cry. He's so quiet about it, the way he is about everything. His tears are huge and roll slowly down his face, dripping one by one on each shoulder. His wet eyelashes are clumped together. They look like the points of stars.

Only something really terrible would make brave Horace cry. I once saw him get a fishhook stuck through his hand, and he never even made a sound, or changed his expression.

"Horace," I whisper. "Is Robin going to die?"

Horace opens his eyes and blinks at me a few times. He must have forgotten I was there. That happens to me a lot, because I can stay quiet and still for hours. After a while grown-ups forget I'm there. I like listening to everybody else talk. I like watching them do things. That's why Daddy calls me his little sponge. When people tease me for being so quiet, Daddy tells them that I am sponging it all up. He says I soak up every word and every sight like water, then save them all in my head in case I need to remember it later.

But I don't want to remember any of this. If Robin is going to die right here, I don't want to watch it happen. I know I should turn around and run back up to the house, but for some reason I can't move. I can't even look away; I keep staring at Horace's shirt stained deep pink. Finally Horace looks down at himself and sucks in his breath sharp and loud like a train whistle.

"Oh, my poor boy, what have you done to yourself now," he cries out.

Horace slides his hand in the space between his shirt and Robin's face. When he brings his hand back out, it's sopping with bright red blood.

"Miss Jackie," Horace says, looking straight in my eyes. "Run up to the house with your fastest legs and get your grandfather down here."

I start running as fast as I can. Horace always knows what to do. If God isn't going to help Robin right now, then Doc can fix him. Maybe he can even fix that hurt place in Robin's brain that makes him act so strange. My mother told me that Robin has a bruise inside his head that will never get better. But I don't want to believe that.

I am thinking about this so hard that when I reach the screen door on the porch, I pull back on it with my whole body, and it smacks me in the face.

"Doc!"

He is sitting on the porch, staring at me with a surprised look on his face. He's got a fishing rod across his knees that he is putting new line on. He stands up and runs over to me, and the rod falls from his lap and hits the floor with a bang.

When I see that, I think about Robin dropping his crab-finding glass in the water, and I remember what I came up for. Suddenly I can't stop crying, even to tell my grandfather what is wrong. Doc is holding my face in his hands, wiping my tears away with his thumbs. The skin on his hands is rough but not too rough, and it feels good rubbing against my cheeks. His worried face is right up next to mine and he's looking at me through thick glasses that make his eyes look so big. I love Doc so much I want to crawl into his arms and let him hold me for hours, like he does out on the boat. I'm the only granddaughter he holds that long, because I keep so quiet and still. I don't wiggle like Sally or even cough, no matter how much the smoke from his cigarette tickles the back of my throat.

"Jackie, has Robin hurt you?" Doc asks, in the softest voice I have ever heard him speak. Doc always growls his words. It scares a lot of people, even Horace and Lucy sometimes, but not me; it tells me I'm in a safe place. I have never been scared of anything in this house, as long as Doc is around. Until now.

I don't understand his question. Robin didn't hurt me. He could never hurt me or anybody.

I can only get two words out at first.

"Robin's hurt." My voice is high and squeaky like Minnie Mouse's. I am crying so hard the words come out choppy. "Horace says . . . come down . . . right away. . . . There's blood."

Doc lets go of me so fast I almost fall backwards. He goes inside to get his doctor's bag, then he's out of the house, running down to the water. I turn around and look across the lawn toward the dock through the porch screen. The screens are black, with tiny holes that make everything I see through them look dirty gray and blurry. I should open the door and run out after my grandfather, but I'm afraid of what I might see if I get any closer.

II

THE GRIEF
SPECIALIST

ELEVEN

It's time to see some specialists," Bill Lang is saying. "There is nothing unusual about any of your blood results, no sign of an active virus that might have attacked your right optic nerve. That's what I was hoping to find, of course. Something simple."

"What kind of specialist?"

I hate anything having to do with the word special ever since they started using it to describe my brother. *Robin has special needs. He has to go to a special school with special teachers.* Now it's called special education, but there is nothing special about any of it. It's the perfectly healthy child who is special, who gets to live the privileged childhood that is denied their "unlucky" sibling.

My mother always knew in her heart that something was wrong with her firstborn and only son. He was defective, imperfect as an infant, with deep red triple forceps dents in his swollen head. But the scars were soon covered by a cloud of soft blond curls, and for eighteen months of his life, he was perfect. He grew into a beautiful toddler, though his startling blue eyes never seemed to look directly at anyone.

His development was slow, and then it became clear that it had stopped altogether, that it had actually regressed. The few words he had spoken at one were never heard again. By the time he was two and a half, he could not speak or hold a spoon. The specialists were called in.

I have told Bill Lang all this before as part of my family's medical history, but I feel compelled now to repeat it in detail. I know that autism is now classified as a neurological disorder and that my loss of vision is presumed to be a neurological defect.

"And that's where the similarities end," Bill says. "You have suddenly developed this condition at thirty-six, with no history of eye trouble other than nearsightedness. Your brother was born with autism, even though the diagnosis was late."

"Actually, it was early," I say, remembering what my mother had told me when I needed to give information for prenatal counseling. "Robin was one of the first children to be diagnosed as autistic." Dr. Leo Kanner, the chairman of child psychiatry at Johns Hopkins, had taken him on as a favor to my grandfather. It was called Kanner's syndrome in the early 1950s. It was renamed infantile autism a few years later.

The diagnosis was so new it wasn't in the dictionary. When I looked it up as a child, I thought I must not have heard the word correctly, so I found the word that sounded most like "autistic" and that fit my brother. Robin was *artistic*. Of course—I had always known that. He loved making and building beautiful things of his own invention. He was obsessed with bright colors. He would stare through the stained-glass windows in church during the service, and then keep his nose pressed against them from the outside while we went to Sunday school with the other "normal" children.

He always had a camera in his hands, ever since I could remember, always taking pictures. He would stay up late at night, studying his pictures with a flashlight and a broken magnifying glass

THE GRIEF SPECIALIST   71

of Doc's that he had found in the trash. He could never get enough of the way the world looked.

"But aren't there other things that are the same about these diseases?" I ask. It has occurred to me, more over these last few days than ever before, how alike Robin and I were when we were very young.

"There are no similarities between multiple sclerosis and autism, Jackie. Just two unlucky breaks."

"But, I was thinking about the fact that—"

"I don't want to cut you off, but I've made you an appointment with a neurologist at four o'clock this afternoon. He may have to do some more invasive tests, but I think he can find the answers to these questions better than I can."

I look up at him. I am being handed over again. I'm about to tell him that the relay torch doesn't like being passed along so abruptly, but what's the use of complaining when I know that he's trying his hardest to do what is best for me, and there's nothing else he can do. As an internist, he's a generalist. And I need a specialist. I go out to the waiting room and hand Kenny the address of the next doctor.

In the car, I can't stop thinking about the obvious connection between the two neurological disorders. Both diseases are unpredictable and incurable. Far less is known about them than is needed for adequate treatment. But that's not what scares me the most. Researchers have never found out what causes either disease. They don't know for sure why one person in a family develops autism or multiple sclerosis and the others do not. This is the hardest part for me to accept. If the specialists don't know where and how it all starts, how can they predict my fate any better than my brother's?

"I know you're scared," Kenny says, trying to interpret my silence. "But remember, you had a needle like that when you had Kelsey. The epidural—exact same thing."

"What needle? What are you talking about?"

"The spinal tap. Didn't Bill tell you? He told me that it wouldn't be so bad. It wouldn't bother you any more than an epidural."

So that's what he meant by invasive tests.

"It's not the same, Kenny!" My voice is shaking with anger and fear. "The last time I had a needle in my spine, it was easy. They were putting morphine into me, and then took a baby out of me. A nice trade. I'm not getting anything out of this but pain and more bad news."

"I don't think so, Jackie. Think positive thoughts. I really don't think it's going to be as bad as you think."

"Then why don't *you* have the spinal tap since *you* don't seem to be worried about it and *you* are all prepared for it!" With each "you" I spit out, Kenny's shoulders tense up higher and higher toward his ears.

Now that I know that I am half blind, I feel like half a person, and I'm acting like one, a little shrunken version of myself. I am screeching at the person I need most in the world. What's missing? Half of me is missing. The better half, with all the good parts—one good eye, and good manners, and good judgment, and a really good sense of humor. And the more I see of the half that's left, the angrier and angrier I get about what's missing.

Kenny has steered the car over to the curb. We sit there staring at the back of a delivery truck that exhales sooty air onto our windshield like an insult. Kenny puts his head in his hands and sighs deeply. When he lifts his head up finally to look at me, his eyes, the large amber-colored eyes I fell in love with eighteen years ago, are swollen and pale.

"Listen to me, Jackie. Please listen to me. I would take this test, or any other test, for you if I could. It would hurt far less to take that needle in my own back, than watching it go into yours."

I nod my head at him. I believe him, but it's not enough. "But you can't."

"No, I can't. But this is what you must understand. You don't have to take this test or any test, if you don't want to. It's *your* back, and *your* body."

"I know it's mine and it's a lemon. It's falling apart. I'm falling apart. And of course I have to take this test, and all the other tests the doctors order. Because that's the only way we will ever find out for sure what's wrong."

"Jackie, what if they do find something out? Have you thought about that? Then what? And what if it is something like MS, and there is no way to fix it or make it better . . ."

"Kenny, stop it!"

"Jackie, listen to me instead of your doctors, because I love you far more and I know you far better than they do, and . . . Oh, forget it. Let's just go in there and get it over with."

"No. Not yet. Finish what you were saying. And what else?"

"And, whether you want to believe it or not, I am the one who is in this with you. Forever. I am the one who will live with you and whatever else we find out, forever, for better or for worse."

"What a lousy deal it looks like you got. All the worse, none of the better, as far as I can see."

"A lousy deal we *both* may have gotten. We're in this together."

"Sure."

"What do you mean by saying it like that? 'Sure,' with a sneer on your face? Do you think I would ever leave you alone with this?"

I can't say anything. My throat is tight with the tears I have held back. Until he said those words, I didn't understand exactly what it was that I was most afraid of. Beyond the tests and the news, it was this. Being left alone. Like Robin.

I nod my head, tears spilling down my cheeks.

"How could you *possibly* think a thing like that?" He pounds the steering wheel with his fist so hard it makes me jump. "How dare you think so little of me?"

I don't know what to answer. I don't know exactly how we got here. All those months when Kelsey was so sick, needing constant care. Night after night of no more than three hours' sleep. But we never took it out on each other. So why is this happening to us now?

Finally, he says the only thing left to say.

"I love you forever," he whispers, as he wipes the tears from my face with his hands.

Forever. When Robin first learned to write the word forever, he wrote it with a four in it. *Fourever.* It was his favorite number. He wore the number 4 on his clothes, his own wooden hand-carved, hand-painted, yellow 4's with a face cut out in the triangle.

It's true. He will be four forever, my mother said in that sad voice.

I haven't heard my mother's voice in over a year. For the longest time after she died, I was sure I still heard it perfectly. I would ask questions, and for a while, I was sure she was answering those questions, in her own words, in her own voice. But as time wore on, the answers started to come back in my own voice, and I realized they were my answers.

We would ask him questions, when he was four, over and over, ask him all those questions, and we thought he would answer, but the doctors said he wasn't capable of answering, just repeating the ends of our questions. But it sounded so smart to us. No, just echoes, they told us, meaning nothing. His words weren't his own independent thoughts, but a clever repetition of ours. So we stopped asking him. And he stopped echoing. And then he became so silent they thought he should see another specialist, that he might be deaf as well as brain-damaged. All this and deaf too?

But she never gave up on her son. The specialists told her to give him up. My grandfather, her father, a specialist himself, also told her to give him up, to preserve the rest of the family.

Put him away, they told me. But he's my beautiful baby boy, I told them. Put him away, they told me, and forget you have a son.

"Jackie?" Kenny is squeezing my hand to get my attention. "Jackie, we have to get out of the car and go up there. We're late for the appointment. It's after four."

I look up at the medical office building. The neurologist. Four o'clock.

Better late than too late—one of Robin's favorite phrases.

I am hearing ghosts. How can I explain this? Maybe I'm going crazy. Maybe I'm not really blind, but I just think I am. Hysterical blindness. Is there such a thing? I think about this, and realize that I'm hoping I *am* crazy, the way that Bill was hoping I had a brain tumor, because I don't want to face the alternative.

"Kenny, do you think that it's possible that all of this really is in my head, that I'm losing my mind?"

"No," he says immediately. "Bill told me that it's not the kind of thing that happens simply due to emotional stress."

"You mean you asked him that already? You asked him that when I wasn't there? Have you been thinking I'm a lunatic with psychosomatic illnesses?"

"Jackie, calm down, it wasn't like that. It was more about all the stress we've been under with Kelsey sick, the lack of sleep, all that."

"Do you think I should see a psychiatrist? Do you think we can find one that specializes in my problem? So tired she can't see straight. I can look it up in the Yellow Pages. Remember the Grief Specialist? I can ask him for a referral."

"No, anything but that," he says, shaking his head.

Six months after my mother died, I decided to go to a psychologist that specialized in bereavement. I had never been to a therapist before, so I looked in the Yellow Pages, and there was this man's name and his specialty: Grief Specialist.

All I did for those first few sessions was use his box of tissues. It wasn't working. Since I was a writer, he suggested that I go home and write down what I was feeling and read it out loud to him. Start with writing down your dreams, he said. I have nightmares, I told him. Well, then write them down too.

I didn't tell him about the first nightmare. It was the paint-by-numbers kind, so easy I could figure it out for myself. The one where I am alone in the church after my mother's memorial service. It's over, and everybody else has gone home. I get up and try to leave, but the doors are locked. I got it: I was stuck in the grieving process. That's what gave me the idea to see a grief specialist in the first place.

So I wrote about the more complicated nightmare, the one I woke from crying every night, the one that finally drove me into therapy. It was about my last ambulance ride with Mom, the things we said, the way she looked when she was dying, all that. I wrote down every detail, and read it out loud to him, finally finding my voice again.

But my reading was interrupted by this terrible noise. I looked up and saw the psychotherapist crying; actually, he was bawling his eyes out. He had to leave the room and I could hear him in the bathroom crying even harder. I had no idea what to do. Was I supposed to leave? There was at least a half hour left to the session. Was I supposed to knock on the door and apologize? I rapped gently on it, but he didn't seem to hear me over his wailing. Finally, I picked up my purse and my grief journal and left.

He called later and apologized. He said that my writing brought all this stuff back about his dead father, and he had never really grieved properly. I didn't go back.

In the end, he did help me, by getting me writing again. I never had the ambulance dream again. He got me unstuck, but at his own expense.

When I told Kenny this story, he said the Grief Specialist confirmed his worst suspicions about the people who choose the field of psychology. But I don't think the Grief Specialist made a bad career choice. He made a bad word choice. He should have called himself a surrogate griever.

"Jackie, we have to go," Kenny says.

Circle tracks, Jackie. That way the train always ends up back where it started.

I don't remember my brother being happy very often. But he was always happy with his trains, his own kingdom of circle tracks, where every train goes one way and always ends up at the beginning.

"Okay, let's go," I say, getting out of the car.

TWELVE

I'm sorry, Jackie, it seems that we never come together in pleasant circumstances."

"A doctor always makes me nervous when he starts out by saying he's sorry." I am trying to sound lighthearted, to coax a smile out of him. He's the kind of person who projects such sadness that one feels compelled to smile, for his own good. "I'm glad I'm seeing you as my neurologist, rather than a stranger."

He is a small man, with tightly curled, steel-gray hair. His face, every time I have ever seen him, seems frozen in a state of apprehension, as if expecting a blow at any second. He looks that way now, his eyes heavy-lidded, wary. No chance of a smile coming this way in the next decade.

When I worked at the hospital with him, the nursing staff called us the "Twin Angels of Death." Our meeting to confer over a chart was a sign that the patient would soon be declared legally dead under the detailed statutory definition of brain death in California. The laws required that all notes pertaining to the patient's demise be recorded in the chart by the attending neurologist, and our hospital required that the legal department monitor the charting to ensure that the hospital was protected.

I was always relieved to see his name on a chart that I was re-viewing, because it made my job easier. His handwriting was neat and easy to read, an anomaly in his profession. His opinions were stated clearly and objectively. The family's privacy was respected, though the mandatory conversation about withdrawal of life support was noted, and all the papers and test results were filed into the chart and signed immediately. He always made sure the papers were in the correct order. The last document would be the final EEG, a flat one. Each time I saw him, he would always appear smaller than the last, as if worn down by each step toward the patient's inevitable mechanical shutdown.

This was what I had respected most about him. His sobering expression combined with the almost sacred way that he shepherded his silent charge through the "just for the record" arrangements. He never lost sight of what was being lost by others. The sadness never left his dark eyes, but seemed to deepen them with the passing of each patient, until they were nearly black, the color of sorrow.

He leads me through a series of manual tests, like the choreographer of a dance he has watched people stumble through a thousand times. These mournful eyes assess the level of my strength, my sensitivity to pressure, both dull and pinprick, my hand-eye coordination, my reflexes, and my balance. We are both concentrating. He is grading my performance, and I am trying to ace the test. Neither of us says a word to the other. The only sound in the room is the deep breath I release when he calls for the nurse to bring Kenny in and motions to her to remove a tray of syringes and needles that was on a table within sight of my seeing eye.

"Unremarkable," he says. "Totally unremarkable. I am not at all impressed."

When he says this, he looks into my eyes for the first time and smiles. He looks twenty years younger. His teeth are perfect, and I can't help but stare at his mouth.

"That's great news, isn't it?" Kenny says, walking into the room to find us both grinning.

"Yes. Your wife's central nervous system is unremarkable," he says to Kenny. "Except for the neurological deficit in her vision, of course."

Of course. I think about how neurology is one of those fields, so prevalent in the medical profession, that define good news by negative definition. The clinical goal is to be unimpressive and unremarkable. It is similar to the phrase "no finding of malignancy" on a biopsy report. This is my A+ grade. I let this sink into my brain and enjoy its warmth. No second symptom on its way, and no indication that one is coming.

"That means she does not have to worry about MS ever again?"

The Neurologist winces.

"I'm sorry," he says. "MS is not a disease that can ever be ruled out. There is no test that I can give her that will tell me she does not have nor ever will get the disease."

"What about the spinal tap?"

"It's an invasive procedure with possible complications. I would only do a spinal if my initial examination gave me reason to proceed further. And it hasn't. Not at this point in time."

"I don't understand," Kenny is saying. "I don't understand what we are supposed to do now. What do we do next?"

"Well, in terms of further neurological testing, there is nothing more that is called for at the moment." He turns to me. "However, *if* you have any other physical problem besides your eyes, then you need to call me and we'll talk."

I nod. I don't want to stay here anymore. He may change his

mind and ask for that tray back. I slide off the examination table and reach for my purse. I am seconds away from a clean getaway, when Kenny comes over to me, his hand on my back, tugging on my sweater.

"Wait a minute, please," he says, shaking his head. "I'm sorry, but I still don't understand."

"Understand what?"

"I don't understand what it is we are supposed to be hoping for. I know you are saying we simply wait for something else to happen, but how can anyone live like that?"

"All of us live with uncertainty," the Neurologist says. "It's just that in this case we know the names of those uncertainties, but not if and when they will make an appearance."

"But it's all so vague. It sounds like we could *all* get MS. I mean, what you are saying is that *I* may have MS, and have the same chance of being diagnosed with it as she does."

Kenny is standing between me and the Neurologist. I can't see either of their faces, but I see Kenny put his hand to his chest, and I realize that he wants to be in my place, to understand, to close the distance. But he can't, and he must know that.

The Neurologist steps back from both of us. He rubs his forehead as if he has a sudden pain there.

"No—that is absolutely wrong. I can't let you leave this office thinking that. In fact, Jackie has presented with an exceptionally severe neurological symptom that is almost always associated with MS."

"But there could be some other explanation?"

"Not another explanation, but no explanation at all. On rare occasions, there will be an isolated case, episodic blindness, without recurrence. This is called a neurological incident with etiology unknown."

"What?" Kenny is now rubbing his forehead in frustration.

"Unknown origin," I say. My years of practicing health care law, interpreting medical charts have given me a working medical vocabulary. I used to study the medical charts that became malpractice cases like they were murder mysteries. I took them apart and tried to figure out where things went wrong. It was never one thing, but a series of mistakes that fed upon each other in the fertile breeding ground of mistakes, life-and-death mistakes, that make up any large hospital environment. I would ask the same questions that Kenny is now asking, interrogate our nurses, doctors, and staff to figure out how we could guard against a similar setup in the future. It was preventive law, just making its debut behind preventive medicine.

"So right now that's what it is," Kenny says. "A freak thing—a once-in-a-lifetime event that happens. And it didn't happen to the other eye, and lots of people can function perfectly with one eye, even drive, right?"

"Yes, of course. But I don't want to raise your hopes. The far more likely scenario in cases this severe is that a series and variety of debilitating symptoms will follow within the next few years of the first."

A series and variety of debilitating symptoms? Don't ask him, Kenny. Please.

"What is the likelihood that will happen to Jackie? What are the exact percentages of probability?"

The Neurologist looks over at me now, his face contorted, worry lines etched deep into his forehead. I've seen this expression on doctors' faces before, in depositions, when finally the one question they don't want to answer has been asked, and there is no turning back.

"I don't like to give out statistics like that," he says quietly. "I'd rather not say." He's hedging.

But this is not a doctor who is hedging due to legal repercussions. He's not trying to protect himself. He's trying to protect me.

"Doctor, I know that you do not want to venture your own opinion of my prognosis at this stage," I say, letting him off the hook. "And I respect that. So we'll just sit tight. Thank you for your time." I reach again for my purse. This time Kenny does more than tug my sweater. He grabs my arm and squeezes it. He doesn't like what I've done. He wants his numbers. But they are not *his* numbers. They are my numbers and I don't want them. I squeeze his arm back harder, and we stand there like that, glaring at each other, two lawyers, husband and wife, suddenly on opposing teams.

This has always been a fundamental difference between us. Kenny and I both went to law school, passed the bar, and got our licenses to practice law. That's where the similarities between our professional lives end. He had never intended to practice law, but used the degree as a protective coat of armor for a career in business. As a partner in a large independent oil company and a real estate investor, he is constantly assessing legal threats. His legal questions focus on the future, and he never looks back.

My career path was more traditional. I joined a large firm and practiced labor law, defending corporations from the myriad lawsuits that are filed by disgruntled ex-employees in California. Then I went in-house, defending the hospital where this neurologist and I worked together.

When I studied suits brought against the hospital, I would look for the cause of action in the same way a coroner looks for the cause of death in a postmortem. To me, statistics that attempted to predict the future were no better than guesses. The past is fact.

When statistics are brought in during a deposition or trial, they are usually brought in by the losing side.

Kenny pulls out of my grip and turns back to the Neurologist. "Doctor, is there a statistical range of probability for patients that are in Jackie's position to end up with a diagnosis of MS?"

The Neurologist looks over at me again, as if, as his lawyer, I will instruct him not to answer the question. But I can't defend him. I am too busy trying to defend myself. I want to put my hands over both ears.

"Yes," the Neurologist says again, moving farther away from both of us. He is literally backed into the corner of his own examination room, his hand on the windowsill, looking as if he wants to open it and jump out. "Yes," he says again, still looking longingly out the window, "there is a range of probability for a firm diagnosis of MS when this optic neuritis presents."

"What is it?"

"Eighty to ninety percent."

Kenny has grabbed my hand again, squeezing it so hard my knuckles ache. He never expected these kinds of numbers. He never would have asked for them if he had known.

"I'm sorry," the Neurologist says, trying to fill in the shocked silence. "That is what the current literature states. For people like Jackie, in that unfortunate gray area between the first and second symptom, the chances of a later diagnosis of MS are extremely high."

"Thank you," I say. I'm thanking him for his effort, though unsuccessful, his valiant attempt to tap-dance around the elephant in the room. It wasn't his fault that Kenny charged at it thinking he could knock it down to size.

I glance at Kenny. His head is down. His thick dark hair shines like patent leather under the fluorescent lighting. It doesn't look like his hair. It looks like shoe polish hair, with none of its natural copper and auburn highlights. I look at the doctor, and now his head is down too, his prematurely gray hair also dulled. I'm embarrassed to be looking at both of them this way. It's like looking up in church during an especially long prayer to find out that everyone but you still has their head down. But I keep staring at their hair, and I remember what terrible news can do. It made my hair go gray when I was twenty-five. A part like a skunk's stripe grew only weeks after Kenny had called me, over ten years ago, with the news about Robin.

Within a few months, my hair was entirely gray. It was always a shock to catch my own reflection in the mirror. I couldn't stand the sight, so I began to dye it. Not because I was vain, but because it was such a painful, constant reminder of what had happened. Shortly after Mom died, Sally's beautiful blond hair lost its curl, and began to thin and droop lifelessly, like the leaves of a dehydrated plant. Polly's hair too fell out in sympathetic chunks.

The Neurologist is the first to raise his head, and catches me staring.

"I'm sorry I can't be more helpful right now. Jackie, you will call me if you have any other problems, won't you?"

I look over at Kenny to see if he has anything more to say, but he has already gone over and opened the door to leave.

"Kenny?"

"Bathroom," he mumbles, rushing out.

"Of course, I'll call you when something else . . ." I answer, realizing that I have no idea what it is I am supposed to be watching out for. "What will it be? This second symptom?"

As soon as I say this, I know that I have made a mistake. Chances are that I don't want to know what I'm looking for. But it's too late.

"It will not be hard to figure out," he is saying. "In your case, the second symptom would present as dramatically as the first. Total shutdown of another part of your central nervous system. Most likely the spine. In other words, you might get out of bed one morning, and suddenly fall down because your legs won't support you."

My legs buckle instantly. I crumple against the examining table, knocking it loudly against the wall. The Neurologist moves quickly toward me.

"I'm sorry. I shouldn't have told you that. Forgive me. I just didn't want you to worry about all the little things, like your foot going to sleep, and think it was MS. I see that I've upset you. Can I get you some water?"

Water? How about a very strong tranquilizer? I doubt there is a narcotic strong enough to ease this horror. I have this picture stuck in my brain and it won't go away. The picture of me, getting up and then falling facedown on the floor by my bed. Once I get a picture in my head, I can't let go of it. I've got an entire album of real-life pictures I want to get rid of.

"I think it's time for me to go home," I say. "I'm so tired I can't stand up straight."

Kenny and I are silent on the ride home. I try to imagine what pictures eighty to ninety percent conjures up in Kenny's brain. Maybe a block graph with the probability column for a firm MS diagnosis almost completely filled in, shooting like high blood pressure to the top of the scale, blazing red. As horrific a vision as it is, I am oddly comforted by the fact that I can still see red in my dreams and thoughts.

I have lost the color red on anything solid and real. I stare at the stop signs as we go home. The letters of the word STOP are less distinctive against the beige background, but I can still read the word. I don't need the color red to see words in black and white. I can still read with one eye, and reading is an indispensable part of my professional life. Since I left my hospital position over four years ago, I have made my living by writing. I am working on two books at the moment—the novel at home and, as a freelance attorney with my own hours at the law firm, a research supplement of new case summaries for a labor law manual.

There is no reason why I can't continue working on my books. Even if I begin to have trouble with my legs, I can work in a seated position, or even in bed. I would simply need to invest in a laptop computer, and a modem for connecting to the library at UCLA, where I went to law school. I'll save money on gas, parking, and wear and tear on the car. By the time we get to the house, I have succeeded in soft-filtering the horrible picture in my mind.

Hours and hours later, after trying to catch the elusive good night's sleep, I understand how I failed to contain the damage from this afternoon. This neurologist is a very kind man, and a good doctor—good in every sense of the word. But he has made a mistake by delivering this harsh prognosis. He has knocked me flat, made me a prisoner of my own bed.

I resist sleep so I won't have to wake up and face the devastating possibility he's depicted. The sheets are getting heavier and heavier against my legs, like concrete hardening. Even my eyelids are heavy, but I won't let them close.

I can sleep with my eyes open. I can. It was quite a useful skill that I honed to perfection during many of my law school classes. I'll just keep my eyes open and my mind at rest. I won't let anything disappear before my very eyes.

THIRTEEN

From a distance I can see Horace carrying Robin up from the dock. He's walking very slowly. Doc walks across the lawn to meet him. I know Doc is old and must be walking as fast as he can, but it seems like it is taking him forever to reach my brother.

When he sees Doc coming, Horace lays Robin out on the grass, face up, under the shade of a big tree. He puts Robin's head in his lap.

At last Doc kneels down beside Robin, shining his special doctor's flashlight in Robin's face. He puts a big white handkerchief under Robin's nose. Like magic Robin starts to jerk his head up and flap his arms at the same time.

Robin sits up and pushes Doc's hands away. That seems to make Doc mad. Horace tries to hold Robin back, and I can see him talking to Doc, but I can't hear what he is saying. Doc shakes his head, gets up off his knees, and starts to walk back up to the house without his doctor's bag. As he gets closer, I can tell he is angry. His lips are pressed together tight. He has green grass stains on the knees of his pants. I bet this is what made him mad; he hates to get his clothes dirty.

Horace is poking around in Doc's black bag. He pulls out

something that looks like a dirty baseball and then begins to unravel it. It is a kind of big cloth Band-Aid, like the one the school nurse put around my ankle when I fell off the seesaw. Horace is wrapping it around and around Robin's head, and I can't tell, but it looks like he's bandaging up Robin's eyes too. If Robin's beautiful blue eyes are all covered up, how will he ever catch crabs again? Did Doc tell him to do that?

Doc opens the door and slams it behind him hard and loud, like he is trying to wake up everybody in the house. What happened? He stomps by without even looking at me.

I want to run after Doc and ask him what has made him so mad. I am worried that he won't fix Robin now. I want to explain to him that it is all my fault. That Robin was having a perfect morning until I came down and ruined it. I feel like I just swallowed a big pill that got stuck in my throat.

My grandfather has fixed famous people's eyes, like Walt Disney and people in the White House who are friends with President Kennedy. Patients used to come from all over the world to see Doc. He doesn't work at the hospital anymore, but I bet he could find some time to fix Robin's brain so it would work right again.

That would be the most wonderful day in the world, better than a thousand Christmas mornings. It would be like my favorite Shirley Temple movie, *The Little Princess,* when she goes to sleep in that cold attic room, and wakes up to find she has been turned into a princess overnight. It would be like those miracle pictures in my children's Bible. Doc would lay his hands on Robin's head, and a light would shine out of the sky, and Robin's brain would be all better forever.

I think a lot about what it would be like, what our whole family would be like, if Robin suddenly became like every other twelve-year-old boy, like all the older brothers my friends have. I could have friends over to play any time I wanted. Their parents would let them come to our house without first asking if Robin will be there.

My friends whisper into the phone that they can't come over if my goofy brother is around. That's how the nice kids say it. The kids that tease me at recess call him something different. They yell it out loud so even the teachers can hear. REE TARD. Jackie is a REE TARD, just like her REE TARD brother.

I know it's not pronounced like that. It's not even two words. It's called retarded. Polly had me say it over and over so I would know, and then she told me to teach those mean girls a lesson, by saying the word exactly right, because I am much smarter than they are, she said. She told me that retarded isn't even the right word, that there is another new word that describes what's wrong with Robin. The doctors have just invented it, but I can't remember it now.

The first time they screamed REE TARD at me, I told Polly as soon as she came home from school. She ran over to her bookcase, and looked it up for me in her dictionary. There was no picture to go with the word. But Polly said it meant slowed down. She said it's really not such a bad word. It just means that Robin's brain works slower than other people's brains, which is why his tongue moves slowly too.

But I still hate that word. I hate it no matter how it's pronounced. I hate it because people always say it in a different tone of voice. I want that word out of our house and out of our life.

What if the word isn't in the dictionary anymore, is it still a real word? I ripped the page with the word retarded on it right out of Polly's dictionary. She hasn't noticed yet, or she would have come after me. Polly's very serious about her books. She thinks people ought to be turned in to the police or put in jail for writing in books, or tearing pages out on purpose. But I snuck into her room and did it anyway. I wanted to see if, at least around our house, that ugly word could be taken away forever with the trash.

If the word retarded was gone, then Robin wouldn't be retarded, right? My father says good words have power. The right words can change people, even make them think better. That's why we read books. That's why President Kennedy got to be president, Daddy says, because of all his speeches.

So I figure if ugly words can hurt people, then we should just get rid of them. If we all throw them out, then they can't hurt any of us ever again.

I'm crying now as I think about all this. Then all of a sudden, someone is holding me, saying my name over and over. It's Lucy. She's married to Horace, and I love her just as much as him. She loves me a lot too, and my sisters, but Robin the most. She is kneeling in front of me, wiping my face with her apron. I can smell everything she is cooking for breakfast and it makes me feel sick. My mouth gets watery, like I sucked on a lemon.

I throw up in her apron. I say I'm sorry over and over, like I can't say it enough. She picks me up and carries me into the house. We must be headed back into the kitchen, because the breakfast smells are stronger—bacon and buttered toast and sausage. These are usually my favorite smells because my favorite meal is breakfast, but right now, I can't think about eating anything ever again. How could I eat when my brother is spread out on the lawn with his eyes all covered up. And Mommy isn't even there to make him feel better.

My stomach hurts so much, I want to punch it and make it stop hurting. I understand why Robin hurts himself now. It must be because he wants to make his outsides hurt more than his insides so he won't feel his insides hurting anymore.

Lucy has set me up high on the kitchen counter. She is smoothing back my hair, which is stuck to my skin. She washes my face and hands, and then all around my neck with a cold washcloth. She gets a clean dry dish towel and lays it across my legs. I lean my head against her shoulder. She is whispering into my ear. She asks me if I want some orange juice, and I shake my head.

I can hear voices floating through the house now. Mommy's soft voice, Daddy's low voice, and Doc's gruff one are all talking at once. Lucy hears them too but she doesn't think we should be listening. She kisses me on the forehead, and takes off her dirty apron. She washes her hands, then goes back to her cooking. She hums a nice church kind of song, but she hums it louder than normal. Now I know she doesn't want me to hear what the grown-ups are saying.

Lucy stops humming for just a second, but it's long enough for both of us to hear Mommy crying and nothing else. Robin must be hurt very badly. And it must be what I thought. It must be that Doc is mad at him for not wearing his life preserver and he made Horace cover up his eyes as punishment, so he couldn't catch crabs or have fun anymore. Nothing could be worse than being sick or punished and having to stay still a really long time.

Daddy told me that Uncle Ogden got an eye sickness when he was seven years old, almost the same age as me. Uncle Ogden had to lie quiet in his bed with the windows shut and the lights out for months because the light hurt his eyes. Daddy's grandmother, Uncle Ogden's mother, read to him all day long. I wonder if this is why he got to liking the sound of words so much.

Lucy has stopped humming, but I still can't hear any words outside the pantry door. Mommy's crying makes me want to cover my ears with the dish towel. Mom cries a lot about Robin. She cries when he breaks things. She cries when he bangs his head on the

floor. She cries when the mean kids in our neighborhood tease him. She cries every time she finds out that another one of our friends won't come over to our house because their parents are scared of him.

It seems like the only thing about Robin that makes Mom *not* cry is the color of his eyes. Everyone—even strangers—says that he has the most beautiful blue eyes in the world. I think so too. They are light, see-through blue, like a piece of sky.

My grandfather walks into the kitchen.

"Horace is going to stay with the boy a little while, Lucy," he says. "He won't let anybody else touch him."

Lucy nods. Doc hasn't seen me yet. I want to ask him what he's talking about. Is it Robin who won't let anyone touch him, or is it Horace who won't let anyone touch Robin?

"The boy's all right *this* time, Lucy," Doc is saying. "He didn't even get hurt that bad. But he could have hurt little Jackie. He had this sharp piece of glass with him. What do you think he's doing with something like that down there? The boy's dangerous—to himself and everyone else."

Lucy shakes her head. I have never seen Lucy disagree with anybody, but she is shaking her head hard, and her arms are crossed over her chest, in a big *X*. She has a pained look on her face. She told me that her stomach's been hurting too. Poor Lucy.

"He's not a bad boy, Dr. Woods," Lucy is saying. "He's a good boy. He's got a good heart too. He'll get better with time."

"No, Lucy, he's growing bigger and bigger, and crazier and crazier."

Doc is speaking slow and clear, in a voice like the one my teachers use when we keep giving the wrong answers. "By next summer," Doc says, "he'll be taller than Horace. We can't keep him safe here. We can't keep any of the girls safe while he's around."

Lucy is wiping off her face with a pot holder. It's as hot and smoky in this kitchen as it is in the underpart of the fishing boat, where the toilet is, when the motor's been running too long.

"We have room for him, Dr. Woods," she says, after she puts the pot holder back down. "Horace and I have room for him."

Doc sighs. He looks at her for a second and doesn't say anything. "No, Lucy. That boy's too much of a burden. You got your own family to look after."

"The Lord won't give us a burden too heavy to bear, Dr. Woods."

"No, Lucy," he says, louder this time, shaking his head. "Don't bring God into all this. It's a little late for that. God stopped looking after that boy the day he was yanked into this world with metal pliers."

Lucy's face crumples up like she's about to cry.

But Doc doesn't see. He has turned around.

"He can't come down here with them again, even in the summer," he says. "We have to preserve the rest of the family."

I've been listening but I don't get what he's saying. I must have heard him wrong. There is no way my grandfather would say such a thing—that Robin could never come back down here. That would mean none of us could come down here again. Mommy and Daddy would never go on a family vacation without Robin.

When Mom told me about the bruise on Robin's brain, she said it didn't change the fact that Robin will always be my brother and I will always be his sister. Doc will always be our grandfather, but it seems like he doesn't want to be Robin's grandfather anymore.

I don't think Lucy understood what Doc was talking about any better than me. She is still looking at the doorway, staring at the empty spot where Doc stood just a few moments before.

I want to run to the bathroom, but I can't move my legs. I have been needing to go pee all this time and I can't hold it in anymore. I didn't want to move and let Doc know I was there. I was scared I'd wet my pants, but I was more scared of my grandfather's words, scared of them more than anything else.

FOURTEEN

The next morning, I get up and walk into the kitchen for a cup of coffee while Kenny is in the shower. So far so good, I tell myself. But only seconds later I realize that I have congratulated myself too soon. Jake's soft furry head is on my lap, sniffing furiously. I reach down, expecting that I have dropped some cereal in my lap, and find that my pajama bottoms are soaking wet.

I run to the bed and pull back the covers. There it is. An enormous wet spot. For the first time in my adult memory I have wet the bed. *Is this it?* Is this the second symptom?

"It's not," Kenny says, when he gets out of the shower. "Jackie, I'm sure there is another reason for this."

"What? How could I have done such a thing? Why didn't I wake up?"

"You were so tired, you must have fallen into such a deep sleep, and this just happened. It's perfectly natural."

I don't believe him. This is mortifying. I'm looking at this handsome, sweet man that is my husband and all I can think is how pathetic for him to sleep with a wife who needs to wear diapers to bed.

The phone rings. I pick it up.

"Jackie, it's Dad."

"Daddy." My voice sounds too high.

"How are you, Button?"

"Not so good right this minute."

"I'm just calling to say that my plane lands at four o'clock this afternoon. Tell Kenny not to pick me up. I'll take a cab straight to the house."

"Oh, Daddy! Of course we'll pick you up at the airport. I can hardly wait to see you."

"Everything's going to be fine," he says. "I've talked to Uncle Alan. He's given me all the right names and numbers. I'm bringing them with me."

"Names and numbers?"

"Of doctors. There are a few good ones out there, but Alan seems to feel that the best thing is to bring you back to Hopkins. He can get you into the top guy in neurology, and of course, the ophthalmology department."

"Dad, I'd rather stay here. I have good doctors here."

"But they're California doctors."

"Of course they are. I live in California."

"But that doesn't mean you have to be stuck with California doctors."

This makes me laugh. "Dad, I was just having a very bad moment but you called and turned it around. Thanks."

"Well, I'm leaving for the airport in half an hour, but tell me what the moment was about, and maybe I can help."

I hesitate. Everyone in our family has a carefully ingrained discretion about bodily functions. My mother taught us to run the water in the sink when using the toilet. A lady was never to discuss certain things in mixed company.

"Well, it's kind of personal."

"Female problems?" he asks.

"No, not really. It's just that . . . it appears that somehow I wet the bed last night, and my doctors told me if anything like that happened, any sudden, unexplained loss of muscular control, that—"

"Listen, sweetie. Listen to me." Dad's tone is serious. He has a voice that never ages. When he would call me at college, my roommates always thought he was a boyfriend. Even now, he sounds impossibly like a man who has never known a moment's sorrow in his life. And nothing, absolutely nothing, could be farther from the truth.

"I'm listening."

"Anyone who has lost half their vision, has excruciating headaches, a daughter who has been desperately ill for the last six months, and then gets told they probably have some god-awful disease would have peed in their pants long before this."

"Oh, Daddy, I love you."

"Try not to be afraid," he says. "I'll see you this afternoon."

Try not to be afraid. Fear can do this. It can pull humiliating tricks on the human body. I took a skydiving course once. And just before they put us on the plane for our first jump, they told us to go to the bathroom and empty our bladders, or fear would empty them for us.

We'd laughed nervously, but we all went to the bathroom, except for one guy, who was sure he had nothing to worry about. When he landed, he picked up his chute and held it across his body, his face crimson.

"Kenny," I say. "I don't think I wet the bed because I was tired. I was scared out of my mind."

"Those nightmares about your brother," he says.

"They aren't nightmares. They're dreams."

"But they're upsetting. You need to stop thinking about sad things in the past and focus on the present, Jackie."

"But that's the nightmare, Kenny," I say. "I don't know what's happening to me right now. I don't know what's going to happen. It's like that nightmare when you are falling and falling and you don't think you'll hit the bottom, and . . ."

"And then you wake up, and you're fine, right? Doesn't it always end that way?"

I look at him. He sounds exactly like Dad. He won't give in to my fears, and won't even acknowledge that he has any himself. I did exactly what my mother said I would do. I married a man just like my father. Relentlessly optimistic at the most difficult times.

Later, we pick up my father at the airport. I sit in the back seat and stare at their profiles when they turn toward each other. They look nothing alike. I'm not totally Oedipal. I didn't marry a man that looked like my father, just one that acts like him. Their builds, their coloring, and their facial features are completely different, although I think they are the two handsomest men I have ever known.

Dad is tall, well over six feet, and lanky, with long legs, like a marathon runner. He has fair skin that sunburns easily and warm smoky blue eyes, a shade between my dark blue and Mom's light blue. He has a huge dimpled smile that lights up his face. Kenny is five foot nine, muscular, and compact. There is no sport he can't play well. He has olive skin and hazel-brown eyes that are large, deep-set, and intense. He also has an easy smile, with a flash of a dimple on the left corner. When he is not smiling, his lips are full and down-turned, adding years to his otherwise boyish looks. He is not smiling now.

We drive straight through Manhattan Beach, the town we have lived in for over a decade. The car idles before a crosswalk, and we watch a young man in his twenties, shirtless, chest muscles oiled and glistening in the afternoon sun, walk his bike in front of us, a surfboard attached to the back.

"Does anyone have a day job in this town?" Dad asks. He always knows how to get a laugh out of us by reminding us of the absurdity of our California lifestyle.

"No," Kenny says, finally breaking into a smile. "They're all waiters, bartenders, and night-shift people. Sometimes they dress up for the occasional audition, for which they need the right tan."

"I thought so," Dad says, laughing.

We watch several women in thong bikinis walk past. This still surprises me. I grew up on the other coast. They have cover-ups back East. And only once you are on the beach—exactly at that spot on the sand where you've spread your towel and are ready to lie down and bake—is it permissible to take off your cover-up. At least it was like that when I lived there. In any case, there is no such thing as a cover-up in Southern California.

Dad takes in this uncovered view and sighs.

"What do they do with old people in Manhattan Beach?" he asks. "Just haul them off the strand if they are caught outdoors during the day and shoot them?"

Kenny laughs again but doesn't rise to the bait.

"No, Daddy," I say. "Nothing that obvious. They're evicted when they turn forty. Then they have to move to some other place more accepting of wrinkles and gray hair. Like Pasadena or something."

We are driving along the Pacific Ocean now. It is on my right side, my blind side, as we head south. I have to turn my head to see the water. The waves are perfect. As we drive, we see car after car parked on the side of the road, with surfers outside their cars, stripping quickly and putting on their wet suits. Some of them are already suited up, waiting to cross the road, their hands across their foreheads, shading their view, staring at the ocean—the surfer's stance. They can stand like this for hours.

The sight of the ocean has always comforted me. I remember how grateful I was that Mom died at home, on the Eastern Shore, with her face turned toward the water. I take some deep breaths and then look at the back of my father's head. All those years of childhood car trips between Maryland and Virginia come back to me when I see the back of his neck, the way his hair still sticks out over his collar unevenly.

We pull into the driveway. Kelsey is waiting at the window, waving her hand wildly. Teresa opens the front door, and Kelsey flies into her grandfather's arms.

"My little champion," he says. "My little champion hugger."

I didn't realize until this moment how much she missed him, and how much he missed her. I am shocked to see him stagger under her small weight, as if she has almost knocked him over. But he steadies himself on the top step, and Kelsey clings to him, her legs encircling his waist, her arms clasped tightly around his neck.

My father doesn't let her out of his arms for the longest time. This man who flew a fighter plane when he was eighteen, watched so many people he loved die violent deaths during the war, this oak tree of a man can still be shaken to his roots by the embrace of a child. I stare at them, wanting to hold this picture in my heart forever. But it's getting dark, and Teresa has turned on the inside lights, which makes the house look inviting, the windows glowing bright yellow, like a child's drawing of home.

FIFTEEN

It's still dark outside, even though it's morning. Mommy woke us up very early, even before the seagulls woke me. We are going back to Baltimore. The station wagon is packed. Mommy carries Sally, still sleeping, down the steps. Why are we leaving so early, before breakfast even? I want to ask them, but Mommy and Daddy are so quiet and tired that I better not. We get into the car. My grandparents are still asleep. I won't get to hug them goodbye.

The car is going down the long dirt road that I love best about driving to this house. I can smell the honeysuckle bushes on either side of the road through the open windows. It smells like cotton candy at a fair, only better. If summer could have only one smell, honeysuckle is the one I would pick.

That was one of the questions we played when we were driving up the road to the house a few weeks ago. What summer smells like. Polly's favorite summer smell is lemons. She puts lemon juice in her hair to make it shiny. Daddy said he loves the smell of Lucy's bacon in the morning, when we all sit down on the big porch for breakfast. Mommy's favorite smell is this beautiful white flower that looks like a rose but grows on thick branches without any thorns. I can't remember the name, but whenever I touch its soft white petals, they turn brown, and Mommy gets upset. Sally hasn't picked her favorite summer smell yet. And nobody asked Robin, but I guess he would say it was that gas smell of the fishing boat when it first starts up, and puffs of smoke blow out. Robin always takes a deep breath of it, and says, "Good for Horace. Boat not broken. Good for Horace," with a big smile.

Daddy slows down the car as we get to the gate, then brings it to a stop. Horace is waiting by the gate, even though its white wooden doors are already open.

He winks at me as soon as he sees me wave at him. Polly and Sally are asleep. Then he walks around the back, and knocks on the window. Robin is sitting with his transistor radio against his ear. He is facing backwards, in his own seat, behind all the suitcases. He reaches up and puts his hand against the window, and Horace lays his hand against Robin's with the glass in between. Their hands are big and wide, just about the same size.

"Robin fall, Horace catch," Robin sings over and over to some song he must be listening to as he rocks back and forth. Horace can't hear him through the closed window, but he nods his head and smiles, leaving his hand pressed against Robin's.

Then he comes around to my father's side and shakes his hand. "Thank you for everything, Horace," Daddy whispers.

Horace nods. Then he looks over at my mother and his face becomes sad.

Mommy is crying, but she's crying so softly I hadn't heard it before. But now I see her shoulders shaking. Horace walks quickly around the front of the car and puts his arm inside the window on my mother's side.

She doesn't pick up her head, but she leans her whole body

against Horace's arm, her head resting in the crook of his elbow. Horace gently lays his other hand on the top of her hair and strokes it as if *he's* really her father and not Doc.

"It's gonna be all right," Horace says, in that same voice he uses with Robin, a voice so warm and comforting you could crawl inside it and never want to come out. "Everything's gonna be all right."

Mommy lifts up her head then, and looks at Horace. Her face is covered in tears.

"No!" It's almost a shout, the way she says it, but Horace doesn't seem to mind. "It will not ever be all right, Horace. Nothing will ever be all right again."

Horace squeezes my mother's hand in both of his. He doesn't say a word, just holds her hand for a long time.

Daddy starts the car up again, and Horace steps back. Mommy is crying even louder now that Horace has let go, louder than the car's motor, loud enough to wake up Polly. Polly looks at me with a surprised face. She pokes her elbow in my side. She wants me to tell her what's going on.

"I don't know what's going on. I really don't," I whisper.

It's true. I can't figure it out. I have never seen Horace hold my mother like that, like she was a scared little girl, and I can't believe that she talked back to him that way.

"What's wrong, Mom?" Polly leans forward. She tugs gently on the collar of Mommy's blouse from behind. Polly is very tall and ladylike. She is taller than my mother because she has giraffe legs. She can talk to Mommy just like a grown-up friend.

"Nothing, darling," Mommy says, in a tired, sleepy voice. "Goodbyes are always hard. You know that. Go back to sleep. You too, Jackie."

Polly sits back, shrugs her shoulders at me, and does just what

Mommy told her. She goes back to sleep. I close my eyes so that Mommy will think I'm sleeping, because that's what she wants, but I'm only pretending. I'm hoping she will start to talk to my father and I can find out what's really going on.

But they don't say anything. Not one word. All I can hear are the sounds of Robin humming to himself. I open my eyes and turn around. There he is, his face pressed up against the back window, making sweat marks on it with his forehead. His humming is very squeaky, and it stops and starts over and over again. He sounds like a record that's stuck in one place.

Mommy has her eyes closed. Everybody is sleeping now except Daddy and Robin and me. Robin has turned his radio up so loud I can hear it through his earphone. He's still looking out the back window, but now he's got a blue piece of plastic spread across it.

I squirm around to see. The piece of plastic is big enough for me to see everything behind us in a different color blue—all the cars, the trees, the road. Blue always makes Robin laugh, as he is now.

"Daddy, why does Robin like to look backwards so much?"

I always save up my Robin questions for Daddy when we are alone. I look into his eyes as he watches me in the rearview mirror. They are a darker shade of blue than Robin's.

"I'm not sure, Button," Daddy says. "But I think it's because Robin likes to see where he has already been."

"But I think it's more fun to face forward, don't you? Why doesn't Robin like to look at where he is going and see new things?"

Daddy scratches an itch on the back of his neck. He always does this when he's thinking very hard.

"Button—sometimes—for some people—it is just easier to look backwards than to look forward."

He is speaking slowly and carefully, like he knows each word must take its time sinking into my head, because it is a hard idea for me to understand, almost as hard as an arithmetic problem.

"But why?"

Daddy sighs and looks past me in the mirror at the back of Robin's head bobbing up and down. "Maybe it's because we can never be sure about what's in front of us, but we always know what's behind us. And not knowing what's coming up next can be very scary for some people."

"But how will they ever know what's coming next, if they aren't looking in the right direction?"

"Well, sometimes, you just have this feeling it isn't going to be good, so you don't look ahead. You are just too scared to look."

I really want to understand this, so I try to think about the most scared I have ever been.

"Like when I hear the scary music at the movies and I hide my eyes because I'm scared of what's coming—like monsters and coffins?"

"Yes."

Suddenly my mother cries out, like she's having a nightmare. She sits up straight. "Oh, dear God, Aub," she says. "That's what Dr. Kanner called that place. A living coffin! That's what he called Rosewood."

My father rolls his eyes back at me for a second, just long enough for me to know that I better be quiet and not ask any more questions. Mommy is crying again. And somehow, although I don't know exactly how, this time it's all my fault.

I reach under the seat and take out my box of Crayolas and my new Snow White coloring book. I start to fill in the window box flowers in the dwarfs' house. I try to find as many bright colors as I can. I pick a pink. Rose pink. Rosewood. It sounds like such a pretty place, like a wood full of roses. I imagine a wood with the ground covered in petals of all different colors, a rainbow floor.

I sort the crayons by color. First, I count all the blue crayons. There are eleven kinds of blue in this box, more than any other color. I go through them one by one, looking for my favorite, robin's-egg blue.

SIXTEEN

The next morning, my father looks straight into my eyes.

"I'd forgotten how dark blue your eyes are," he says. "A real navy blue, like the ocean on a cloudy day."

"Dad, that's not my normal color. The right eye, my bad eye, is darkened because the pupil is so big."

"You've always had dark eyes." Dad shrugs his shoulders. "Those doctors haven't known you as long as I have. Both your eyes look exactly the same to me. Huge and dark and full of serious thoughts."

"Oh, Daddy. What do you know? You're my father. You only see me the way a father always sees a daughter. You thought I was pretty even when I was twelve, with crooked teeth, funny pointed glasses, looking like I should have been walked around on a leash."

"No, you were pretty when you were twelve years old," he lies.

We get in the car to drive to my next appointment with another specialist. He's a retinal specialist in Beverly Hills. The optic nerve connects the retina to the brain, so if something is wrong with the connecting part, doctors want to rule out the possibility that the "connectee" is also involved.

"Dad, drive the coastal route instead of the freeway. We have time. Turn left here, and right at the next light. Is it red?"

My father reaches for my hand and holds it. "Yes, it is, Button." His hands, like Kenny's, can warm my cold ones in seconds. "Your Uncle Alan is color-blind in the red-green categories, and it's never bothered his driving," he says.

"Really?"

"Yes. He told me that yesterday. He said to tell you to focus on the position of the lighted circle, instead of the color. He has a trick. Top—stop. Low—go."

I laugh as I repeat this to myself.

"Well, he's from your mother's side of the family. He didn't inherit the Nash gene," Dad says, laughing with me.

"No, he didn't." Then I remember something I had wanted to ask Dad, about family and genes.

"Daddy, I've been having dreams about Doc and Virginia and Robin, and I was wondering if—"

"Oh, that reminds me, Button. When you mentioned your grandfather—I was thinking about him too. Doc had his cataracts removed in 1941, back when it was a primitive operation, and—"

"Dad, I don't have cataracts. It's a neurological problem," I snap, irritated because he cut me off as soon as I mentioned Robin. He always does this. It's impossible to finish any sentence that starts with my brother's name.

"That's not what I was getting at," Dad says, persisting. "The point I was trying to make is that Doc operated for years after his own cataract operation, and nobody could believe that he would ever be capable of doing the kind of surgery that requires perfect focus for tiny details."

"How did he manage it, then?"

"He prescribed himself a kind of occupational therapy to strengthen his eyes. Of course, he chose to take his rehabilitation all summer down in Virginia. He spent hours on those thousand-piece wooden puzzles to get his eye for color and shape back, and then picked hard-shell crabs to fine-tune his hand-eye coordination."

So that explains why there were always puzzles all over the house, and why we could never catch too many crabs.

"Doc believed in the law of compensation, one part of vision compensating for a lost part, the way parts of one lung will expand to make up for a damaged part. If there is something still left to work with, it can be done."

"Well, Doc was a genius. He could do anything he put his mind to."

"You can too," he says.

"You are saying that because you're my father. But I know better. My brain doesn't get stronger when I get sick, it turns to mush. You should have seen me in the neurologist's office. All he had to do was mention the possibility of losing the strength in my legs, and they gave out from under me. I'm weak as water."

"Water isn't weak. It's strong. It can erode land, destroy it, with time and constant force."

"I'm sorry—I know myself better. I can't be that strong, particularly when I'm scared. Like right now—I'm scared that as soon as this doctor says one word about my retinas, they'll disintegrate."

"That's ridiculous. You're setting yourself up. Stop that. This doctor won't find a thing wrong with your retinas. And you won't have anything at all to be afraid of after this."

"You stop that, Dad. There's *always* something else to be afraid of, you know that."

"Only if you have an overactive imagination."

"I've always had an overactive imagination."

"Well, you don't need to bring it with you into the doctor's office," he says, as we pull into the parking lot.

As soon as we walk in the door, a nurse comes out and announces that they need to prep me for the injection right away.

"What kind of injection?" I ask, the panic audible in my voice. "Why do I need it?"

"It's the best way to look at the retina. It's a special dye that goes into your arm, but lights up the vessels in your eye. Just a regular IV."

She leads me down a hallway and points to one of those chairs that all labs seem to have. It's a student chair with a desk surface attached, except it's my arm that is supposed to lie across the desk, not a notebook.

"Great veins," the nurse remarks, tapping the inside of my elbow with a long fingernail. "I love it when my day starts like this." She laughs softly to herself.

I look up at her to see if she is being sarcastic.

"Are you serious? Most nurses hate my veins."

"Honey, have you taken a look at the other patients out there in that waiting room? They are all over seventy. Usually that's when the retina starts to go. You've got young veins, girl! I'll only need to stick you once. There! You're golden."

I barely felt a prick. I look down and she has an IV up and running. Suddenly I feel warm all over, as if the stuff is boiling through my blood.

"Getting the hots already," she says casually.

"I'm on fire," I say.

"Good—let's get you in the exam chair while you're still cooking."

She rushes me into another room. It looks just like every other eye doctor's office. I sit down, and automatically put my chin in the cup. I close my eyes, and when I open them, I am looking straight into another eye. Dark brown, with lush, feminine lashes that curl up at the tips.

"I'm sorry, did I startle you?" he says. "We have to be quick. The dye is so strong we can't give you a long-lasting dose. Open your lids as wide as possible and don't blink."

He shines a flashlight into my right eye. I expect it to hurt, but it doesn't. He then turns to my left eye, and it immediately begins to fill with tears.

"It's the right eye that's the problem," I say, sniffling.

"Yes, so I've been told."

He keeps looking in my left eye. Tears are streaming down my face, down the sides of my neck, making my skin both sting and itch at the same time. I squirm in the chair.

"I'm sorry, just a few seconds more, I promise."

He twists his head sideways—first one way, then the other. He did not spend this much time on my bad eye.

"Did you come here by cab?"

"What?" Why does he assume I could not have driven myself? I have already asked about the DMV requirements for keeping my license—there's a minimum standard of 20/40 in one eye. I presumed that even if my right eye never came back, I would always be able to drive, and in Los Angeles that is a matter of survival.

"I need to know if someone is here with you. Someone who can drive."

This question must be routine in his profession. Most of the patients he sees can't see him as well as I can. But the way he asks the question is too urgent. He isn't talking about getting a ride home.

"My father's with me," I say, inexpressibly grateful for this fact. "He's out in the waiting room."

"What's his name? I'd like to speak to him," he says, turning off the light and handing me a tissue.

"Mr. Gorman. Same as mine."

"I'll send the nurse out to get him. You just relax. The hot flash should be over shortly. You seem to be having a skin reaction to the dye. It's not unusual, but that may take a while longer to go away. If you still have problems when you get home tonight, take an antihistamine."

When you get home tonight? It's still morning. Where else am I supposed to go before I get home?

I hear my father's voice and the doctor's voice in the hallway.

I want to get up and open the door, and tell them to stop talking about me, but my skin is still burning. This hot flash is more like a lava flow under every inch of my skin. I touch my cheek with my finger and it feels like a topographical map. Hives. I've only had hives one other time in my life and it was my wedding day. I'm trying to think about what all this means, when the door squeaks open.

I look up. I can see my father in the doorway floating toward me through a blur of tears.

"What's going on, Dad?"

"What's happened to your face?"

"Allergic reaction to the dye. What did the doctor say?"

"Well, the nurse came out and called my name, and then said that the doctor wanted to talk to me about my wife! That sure threw me. The nurse thought that you were my *second* wife! Only in Los Angeles. And by the way, I figured out where all the old people they chase out of Manhattan Beach go. They end up in this guy's waiting room. Looks like an AARP convention out there."

"Dad, please."

"What?"

"You haven't answered my question. What did the doctor say?"

He sighs.

"Oh, you know. Doctors. Nothing wrong with your retinas, so he's referring you to another guy. Somebody downtown at USC."

"Why? What are they looking for now?"

Dad is making a froglike sound in his throat. I recognize this danger signal. It's a sound Dad makes when he is extremely agitated. He's not telling me the whole truth. The rest of it, what he is supposed to tell me but can't tell me—those unspoken words are lodged in his throat.

"Dad? Are you going to tell me what's going on?"

"We have to leave right away, Button," Dad says. "This other doctor is double-booked, and we have to get down there in thirty minutes or we miss him. It's four freeways to get there from here. Four freeways! And exit names that nobody in this office can spell or pronounce. Can you believe that?"

The other warning sign is when he starts talking about banal things like directions or weather, as if they were the most fascinating topics in the world. Full-scale cover-up.

He grabs my arm and pulls me out of the office, his grip strong and determined. We get in the car and head straight to the nearest freeway entrance, tires screeching like a drag racer's. This morning he drove Kenny's car carefully. Now he's driving it like a maniac, ignoring the traffic signals that we argued about earlier.

"Dad, slow down or the CHP are going to stop you and give us a ticket."

"That would be a help," he says, breathing hard. "Maybe they could give me decent directions."

Several freeways later, we finally slow down in front of a tall white building.

"Is this the Doheny Clinic?"

"Yes," says the parking attendant. "Do you have an appointment? You can't park here unless I verify an appointment."

"Emergency visit," my father says. "He said he would see us as soon as we got here." Dad is handing her a white business card.

"Hurry, then," she says. "Park in the handicapped space."

"Dad, what is the emergency?" I ask, as we go into the elevator from the parking garage.

"Oh well . . . I just said that to get a good parking spot."

"Dad, who is this doctor we are seeing now?"

"He's a real specialist," Dad says. He's tapping his foot nervously as the elevator climbs to the top floor, where it seems all the godlike physicians have their offices. "He only takes special cases referred by other specialists. You're lucky he can see you today."

"I don't feel so lucky."

Dad doesn't comment, but his foot is tapping faster and louder.

The elevator doors open; I hear "Gorman" being shouted from across the room. The waiting room is as big as a small auditorium, with at least five separate seating areas. The first thing I notice is that everyone sitting there has gray hair. Most of them are wearing dark glasses, very dark glasses, too dark to see anything through, the kind of dark glasses that only blind people wear.

"Gorman? Is Gorman here yet?" The voice is booming.

"Yes," my father and I answer together, loudly.

The nurse grabs me by the arm, and pulls me through another door. How did she know I was the patient and not Dad?

"It's written all over you," she says, when I ask. "Big strawberries blooming on your face from the retinal dye. Now I'm going to put some drops in both eyes. This is going to cause some discomfort. Hold still and lean back now, please."

My right eye explodes with pain, as if she had poured acid

into it. Reflexively, I push her arm away, so that she can't do the same thing to my other eye. But she's too quick. She grabs me by the back of the neck, her hand like ice, and forces a drop in the other eye.

"Stop it!" I scream.

"What's wrong? What's happening?"

It's Dad's voice, but when I turn toward him, I can't see him. I can't see anything.

"Dad, I can't see you! And it hurts so much!"

"What have you done to her?"

"It's just the medication. She's fine. The doctor will be here shortly. The patient has to keep still."

This is an unnecessary order. How could I get up and move anywhere, when I can't see an inch in front of me? I clutch the arms of the chair. I feel completely disoriented. I lean forward and bang my forehead against sharp metal. I reel backwards.

I hear the sound of a door opening. Someone is touching my forehead.

"I'm sorry," the voice says. It's a nice voice, with a slight British accent. "I see you've hurt yourself. They should never put this machine so close to your head."

A soft cloth is pressed against my forehead. I reach up to touch it and touch his hand instead. We both keep our hands there for a moment, awkwardly, like new friends hugging for the first time, each one wondering when to pull away. He gently slides his hand out from underneath mine, and pats my hand in place.

"Keep my handkerchief as long as you need to. The bleeding has stopped. It was just a surface scratch."

"Thank you," I say.

I don't know what I am thanking him for exactly. But something about his manner, his calm tone of voice, brings me back to my best manners. I am embarrassed remembering the wrestling match with his nurse a few minutes ago.

"You're welcome. Now I'm going to examine your eyes. Please don't move unless I tell you to."

"I won't," I say. "I learned my lesson."

There is a clicking sound, like a combination lock turning. My eyes are still burning, but it is bearable now. I try to put the hand-kerchief over the eye he will not need to examine.

"Hold still, please."

"I'm sorry. I'm trying."

"Thank you for your patience," he says. "I know it's already been a long day. Now, I'm going to look at the other eye, and then we'll talk."

The stinging has stopped as suddenly as it started, but I still see nothing except darkness. My eyes feel frozen and numb, like they have been placed on ice. I hold my breath and try to stay still. I can't see exactly where he is, but I know he is within arm's reach because he is holding my chin up with his fingers. It is an odd feeling, like I'm a puppet in his hands.

"All right. All done. Please sit back and try to relax."

I hear the sound of wheels on linoleum, and I know that he has rolled his chair away from me. The air in front of my face is colder, empty. I am disconnected somehow.

"What is it, Doctor?" Dad's voice.

"I need to take some history from the patient first. A few more questions. And then we'll talk."

His hand is now on my wrist, light but steady pressure. I am connected again.

"Jackie, I want you to take your time, and think back over the last few days," the Specialist says slowly. "When did you first notice that you were losing the color red in your left eye?"

Suddenly, I feel sick to my stomach. I hold the handkerchief against my mouth. My left eye? My good eye?

But it's true. The beige stop signs on the way back from the neurologist. Why didn't I realize what that meant?

"Only the day before yesterday. I think. But it can't be. I can't be that . . ." It's too much for me to absorb. Ice train.

"Yes," he says softly. "I'm sorry but it's true. Your left eye is having the same problem as your right. Both optic nerves are shutting down."

"Daddy?" I call out to the gray-filled air, as if my father is lost in a sudden fog that descended between us. "Did you hear that?"

"Jackie, I'm sorry," my father says in an old man's voice, worn down and tired. "They told me that back at the other doctor's office. I didn't know how to tell you in the car, and I guess I was hoping they were wrong."

"But it's not supposed to happen in both eyes!" I protest. "The first eye doctor said that quite clearly, that he had never seen this happen in both eyes at once. He told me that!"

"Well, actually, bilateral optic neuritis of this severity is quite rare," the Specialist says. "I'm sure that other physician was telling you the truth, that he had never seen it. In fact, I've only seen a handful of cases in my career. Maybe ten, and quite frankly, none of them have lost so much vision so quickly."

"How quickly?" I burst out. "Is everything—all of it gone already?"

"No, I don't think so," he says soothingly. "Please let's stay calm."

He has kept his hand on my wrist all this time, unmoving, but the same gentle pressure. Now I feel his fingers pressing against the other side of my wrist, my pulse point. This small adjustment of his fingers touches me deeper than the skin. The hand that is around my wrist taking measure of my rising pulse is a practiced hand.

I do not know what his specialty is yet. I don't know the proper term. But I have figured out this much; this doctor has been in this room countless times with people in their darkest hour, in every sense of the word. I sensed it when I saw the other patients in his waiting room, what now seems like ages ago. Now I know. His specialty is disorders of the eye that rapidly lead to total blindness.

He is the kind of eye doctor my grandfather was, the kind that shows up just at the moment the patient is falling off the edge of the sighted world. He puts himself between the patient and that terrifying fall, the way a parent instinctively wraps fingers around the sharp corner of a table, in advance of a crawling baby.

This is how I see him, the Specialist. The only way I can keep from hysteria is to put a familiar face, a kind and loving face, on this stranger who is seeing me at my worst. I must form a mental picture of him. I can't bear the thought that he has no face, just a disconnected voice. I give him my grandfather's face, which has been so much a part of my dreams. I can close my eyes now.

"Jackie," he says after a long moment. "I know this is hard. And it will get harder, much, much harder from this moment on. But I truly believe that after some amount of time, it will also get better."

There is silence after he says this, a respectful silence, the kind that follows a public prayer. That little space when people keep their heads bowed, and clench their eyes tighter and say their own personal and private prayers.

Please let me see Kelsey's face again. Please let me see her grow up, see all the changes that each year brings to her face.

The Specialist keeps his fingers on my pulse, and I see him in my mind's eye, a younger version of my grandfather, concentrating on the second hand of his watch, counting the beats. My father has taken my other hand in his, covering it completely.

He clears his throat. "Doctor, can you tell us how much vision she will lose in her other eye?"

He wants percentages, just like Kenny.

"At the moment, it's difficult to assess functional vision due to the clouding effect of the medication," the Specialist answers, now taking his hand away. "I can't give you any more information at this point. I will see her again in the next couple of days, and we will know much more."

Clouding effect. . . . Both eyes are the same, dark blue, navy blue, the color of the water on a cloudy day.

I used to love clouds, as all children do, and since moving to Southern California, I have grown to love them more, due to their rare appearance in the relentlessly blue skies. I remember my first solo sky dive, after the free fall, after the chute opened and I floated down to earth. What struck me, what shocked me, was the silence, deepest silence unbroken by any sound, human, mechanical, or natural.

It is this silence that made me want to jump out of an airplane again and again, the addictive quality of seeing and feeling life without the sound hooked up. I wanted to possess this silence, shrink it down and take it down with me, so that I could pull it out later, like a folded poncho, and cover myself with it, retreat inside it, whenever I needed.

Then as I came closer to the ground, I drifted through a cloud. It was a smooth ride, not rough and bumpy like turbulence on an airplane. It was cold, but not wet against my face.

I was falling fast, even with the chute filled out, sifting the air above me, but the cloud was moving faster. Its mist, dry like powder, seemed to coat my skin, but not seep into it. The cloud dusted me off with its indifference, its grayness, its lack of center and substance. I did not pass through the cloud; the cloud passed through me like a ghost through a closed door, with the same horrible chilling effect. I never went skydiving again after that.

"The chemically induced blurriness should clear up within an hour," the Specialist is saying. "However, you must understand that the left optic nerve is swelling rapidly, so any recovery of vision will be temporary."

"How temporary? How much time will I have?"

"I really don't like to put a time on these things," he says, stalling.

He knows better, and so do I.

However many hours or minutes of seeing time I have left—it will never be enough.

III

GOODBYE

FIRST

SEVENTEEN

In the car on the way home, we are lost in the dark. Dad reads out the names of the signs but they don't sound familiar. He calls Kenny on the car phone, and somehow Kenny manages to guide us back to Manhattan Beach. I am keeping my left eye fixed on my father. I want his face, and not the black tunnel outside the front windshield, to be what I see first when the eyedrops wear off.

But it is Kenny's face I see first. He is opening the car door. I look up at his face. I have to look straight at him, because it is like looking through a telescope, but I can still see his face!

During dinner, I sit there not eating, but staring at the food. Then I stare at the faces around the table, at Dad and Kenny and Kelsey, stare and stare, until they turn away from my intense gaze like it's a heat lamp turned on too high. But I can't stop looking.

Later, I lock in Kelsey's soft profile, seal it into my brain, watching her sleep. I circumnavigate the house, drifting in and out of her room, breathing in the sight of her like oxygen, never quite getting my fill. I crave all the best-loved pictures of my life. I am frantic to find them. I can't go to sleep now. How could I close my eyes, as long as I can still see something with them?

I walk through the house, stumbling over toys, over the dog, anything under my feet. My visual field is narrowing—the sides were gone this morning, the top and bottom are gone now too—and what is left is dimming out. I switch on all the lights as my hands slide along the edges of the walls, but these lights do not brighten the dim shrinking telescope lens inside my left eye.

I gather all the pictures I can find, all the framed ones on the tables and desks, and all the photo albums. I pull open drawers and find old photos that didn't make it into the albums yet and grab school yearbooks from the shelves. I spread these out on the floor of the living room in a close circle around me.

As I crouch over these piles of pictures, my knees curled under my chest, I am comforted. This is my foxhole position, the last defense. Whenever I get really anxious about a project that is due under a tight deadline, I take the piles of papers off the desk and move them all to the floor, and kneel there with them. I learned this as a child. I still believe that all serious work should be done this way. My parents used to read the daily newspapers at the breakfast table, but the Sunday papers, the magazine sections, the essays, and the book reviews, covered the floors of our house like multicolored carpet. After we came home from church, we would all hover over the papers, locked in this position of prayer, worshipping the written word for the rest of the day.

Kenny and Dad have pleaded with me to go to sleep early. They said it would only make things worse if I lost any more sleep. I just stared back at them. I didn't have to say anything. Even they knew how ridiculous it sounded. How could things get worse?

"Maybe the prednisone is keeping you awake," Kenny says.

Fear is keeping me awake, not drugs, just as fear made me wet the bed a few nights ago. He knows that, but he can't bear to watch it take its course.

"Prednisone has lots of side effects, remember?" he says.

I do remember. It was the same medication Kelsey was given for her asthma. So that was the pill I took earlier. "Here, take this," the Specialist had said. I'd spilled the water down my chin as he held the glass to my lips. I thought it was a tranquilizer.

"This might help," he'd said as he handed me another handkerchief to wipe my face.

Might help. Maybe. No promises. No guarantees.

I can still see a few colors. Blues and grays mostly, some kinds of green. I know what color *maybe* is. It's gray. I look straight at the lamp with my left eye and then at the wall. No difference. Same gray mist. I hold the picture up to the light and it is no easier to see.

I feel Kenny's arms around me.

"Jackie, you need to go to bed and go to sleep."

"What time is it?" I asked him that question when he came up before. I know I keep asking, but I can't see the numbers on the clock, and I have to know what time it is. I have to know when it will be light outside again, so I can go look at the ocean.

"It's late," he says. "It's time for you to get some sleep."

"I don't want to go to sleep. I want to stay here with my pictures."

I look up at him. He is one of my most loved pictures. I look closely at his face. It's gray, like everything else. I can still tell it is Kenny's face and not anyone else's, but it's shadow against shadow. It's like looking at the negative instead of the print, a bad copy of a good original.

He kneels down and pulls me into his arms, but I pull back so that I can get another good look at his face. I can't let this picture escape before I capture it. He closes his eyes, but does not turn away from me.

He would never turn away.

It was eighteen years ago that I fell in love with him, my first year of college.

What does Kenny look like? my mother asked. *Is he tall and blond? What color are his eyes? Is he handsome?*

My two high school boyfriends had been blond and blue-eyed, golden boys. Kenny was a mirror opposite, his coloring sultry and rich.

I don't know how to describe him, but I love the way he looks.

Later she told me that she had cried when I told her that. She knew that this time I had fallen in love for good.

I cried because you were so young, and the odds were against it lasting. You were so unprepared for what might happen, how the picture might change, when the haze of lust cleared, and you got a better look at the person underneath.

But it didn't change. The picture got clearer, and I loved what I saw more and more with each year. I reminded her about this.

That's luck, not wisdom, because nobody knows anything about true love at eighteen. Kenny is the luckiest thing that ever happened to you.

Up until these last few days, I have always felt lucky. I knew that I was born lucky, simply because I was not born the way Robin was. I saw each of us in my family in our own boats, and luck seemed to hit us in different waves. All this time, for thirty-six years, I have been holding my breath, riding the crest of my huge good fortune, knowing it had to end, but not knowing exactly when the tide would turn against me. It lasted through my own child's healthy birth, her first surgery. Or was that Kelsey's luck? In that storm-tossed sea, is it possible to determine where one person's luck ends and another's begins?

I hold Kenny's face in my hands, a still photograph, my thumbs under his chin, the tips of my index fingers above his forehead. I can save that face as it is right now, safe inside my memory.

I let go of Kenny's face and look down at the picture that has fallen in my lap. It's an old family picture—my sisters and I and Robin, together, some special holiday. It's a color picture, I remember that, but it is no longer showing any of its colors. I look carefully at my brother's eyes.

Robin's real name was Arthur, but we always called him by his nickname, because his eyes were the exact color of a robin's eggs in spring. But they are not blue in this photograph anymore. They are gray, like the rest of the picture, all of us in shades of gray. I've lost all the colors now. I've lost the color blue.

Why didn't I pace myself better? Why didn't I look at the recent color photographs first, and reserve the older black-and-white photographs of my childhood for later?

I lean over the picture, put it so close to my face that my eyelashes and nose skim its cool, smooth surface. I close my eyes. I don't want to look anymore. I don't want to watch my family vanish into this cloud that has descended upon me. I want to remember them in living color.

"Kenny, I'm tired now. Please help me go to bed."

Kenny pulls the covers up over me and sits next to me. He strokes my face, slowly and carefully, as if memorizing it by touch, as if he is the one losing his sight. I can feel his body shaking beside me, but I can't cry with him, because then I would have to open my eyes to release the tears. And I have to keep my eyes shut tight so that I won't have to see his disappearing face.

EIGHTEEN

I wake up to the smell of bacon cooking. My father must be making breakfast, just as he did every Saturday morning of my childhood. I can hear the sound of footsteps coming down the hall. I sit up and fall sideways and down, right off the bed. I'm lying facedown on the floor. My forehead burns from sliding hard across the carpet. I roll over on my back. Jake is licking my face. I open my eyes, but I can't see anything. I can't see the dog, only feel the softness of fur against my skin.

I can smell and hear and touch. But I can't see. I have woken up blind.

I crawl toward the bed and reach for the end of the bedspread, but my hand grabs air. I fall down again. This time my right temple hits something hard, a piece of furniture. Then a book tumbles down, the corner scraping my shoulder.

"Help," I cry out.

In a few moments, Kenny's arms are around me, lifting me. His face is next to mine. It has a strong menthol scent, another morning smell. I reach toward his face. The back of my fingers feel the cool foam, that little bit of shaving cream that he never sees but I always do, stuck behind his ear. Now I can only smell and touch it.

"I thought you would never wake up," he says, his voice tight with forced cheerfulness. "You've been asleep for hours and hours, round the clock almost. Come into the kitchen. I've made you eggs and bacon."

"It's not morning?"

"No, it's later than that. But I've kept your breakfast warm. I didn't want to wake you up."

His voice is so different that if he didn't smell the same, I would not believe this man is my husband. He is speaking loudly, even though we are only inches apart, as if he's trying to make himself heard against a strong wind. It's not Kenny's voice at all. He is shouting at me the way the recovery nurses shouted at Kelsey, trying to bring her out of anesthesia.

"What is there to wake up for?" I shout back.

"Don't say that."

"Kenny, I just fell off my own bed! I can't keep falling down. I'm going to stay in this bed, until I can see well enough not to fall out of it."

"That's ridiculous. You are going to get up. Right now." He pulls me up to my feet.

I lean against him, limply, as if my legs are not able to support me anymore.

"Please," I say. "Help me back to bed."

"All right," he says, relenting, his voice softening, returning. "I'll go get a tray and bring it. Just this once."

He takes me by the shoulders and turns me around in a half-circle. I must have been crawling in the wrong direction. I must have hit the bookcase on the other wall. I got lost in my own bedroom. I retreat under the covers. I won't get out of bed until I can walk without falling down and I won't open my eyes until I can see. No exceptions.

Well, maybe just one exception.

"Kenny?"

"Yes, I'm right here."

"I need to go to the bathroom. Will you take me as far as the door?"

As we walk toward the bathroom, Kenny keeps his hands around my waist. His protective hold reminds me how dangerous this room has become, as if the walls and the floor and the ceiling are all conspiring to hurt me.

I clutch the doorknob to the bathroom and hold it for balance. Suddenly, it gives way and I stumble inside.

Kenny grabs me. "I'm sorry, honey. I was trying to help by opening the door for you."

"I can do this by myself."

"All right," he says. "But I'll stay on the other side of the door. Just knock on it when you are ready."

I hate this. My husband hovering around me. This is too humiliating for both of us.

I pound on the door with my entire arm. Kenny opens it and it smacks me in the head, making me yelp. I forgot the door swung inward, though it was just a few minutes ago that I went through this door. I'll never be able to handle this.

"Take me back to the bed," I say, leaning against him again. I am exhausted, as if I have just walked ten miles instead of a few feet.

"No," he says firmly. "Let's get you a plate of food, and take it outside on the deck. You need some fresh air."

I start to protest, and then I hear Kelsey's footsteps coming down the hallway from her room. My heart stops. No. I can't face her. Not now.

"Bed," I whisper urgently. "Tell her I am still asleep."

"Jackie, that's not right . . ."

"Mommy, are you awake yet?"

I clutch Kenny. He leads me over to the bed.

"Is Mommy sick?"

"No," Kenny says. "She's not really sick. She's having a little trouble with her eyes . . . um, her head . . . her headaches. But the rest of her is just fine." He stumbles over each word. He has no idea how to tell her. Neither do I. This is not in any of our parenting books.

"Mommy, why are you going back to sleep? You've been sleeping too long already."

"I agree," Kenny says. "You tell Mommy she can't sleep forever."

How long have I been sleeping? Is it the next day or the next night?

"What time is it?" I ask, reflexively looking to my right side where my clock is, but nothing is there.

I've got to stop looking. I've got to keep my eyes closed. It's too much to take in, all the things that should be there, but have disappeared during the night.

"The little hand is on the six . . . I think. No—the nine. Oh, I don't know."

"Circle on the bottom or top?"

"Bottom," she says. "I can see that. Circle is on the bottom."

"It's six o'clock, then," I say.

But six o'clock when? At night or in the morning? Kenny said I slept almost around the clock. But was it night or day when I fell asleep?

"Kelsey, is it light or dark outside?"

"It's sort of both, Mommy. Not quite dark and not quite light. Why don't you put your glasses on and look out the window?"

"They won't help me," I say too sharply, and then instantly re-

gret the words. What does she know? Has Kenny told her anything?

"Kelsey, do you think it's time for dinner or time for breakfast?"

"Silly Mommy," Kelsey laughs. There's the answer. She doesn't know anything yet. "It's time for dinner. Daddy's getting it right now—your favorite—eggs and bacon."

It's true. Breakfast has always been my favorite meal.

"Kenny, I don't want anything to eat. I'm not hungry," I say.

"Daddy's not here, Mommy. Didn't you see him go to the kitchen?"

No, I didn't even hear or feel him leave.

"Kenny!" I shout for him, angry this time. He can't just leave me talking to the air like a crazy person. "Kenny!" How could he leave me to explain this to Kelsey by myself?

"Mommy, *I'm* here. Are you having one of your headaches? Is that why you're keeping your eyes shut so tight?"

"Oh, Kelsey," I say, reaching my hands out for her. "I love you so much."

"I love you too, Mommy. And I can take care of you," Kelsey says. I feel her breath against my face, her hands stroking back my hair, her fingers gently pushing my eyelids open, the way she always does when I'm asleep and she wants me to wake up. But I can't open my eyes, even for her. Especially for her. I can't bear losing the sight of her too. I start to tremble all over, the way Kenny did last night. I pull the covers up to my chin.

"Are you cold, Mommy? I'll get you another blanket," Kelsey says.

"I don't need another blanket. I need you to go get Daddy," I say, my teeth chattering. But as she pulls away from me, I grab her hands, and pull her to me. I'm suddenly terrified of being left alone.

"I've got your dinner ready."

Kenny's voice.

"Kenny, why did you leave me like that? Without warning?"

"You'll feel better if you get something in your stomach. Just try a few bites." His voice has that faraway, nurse's tone again.

"I'll help you eat," Kelsey says. She sounds years older. It's a take-control voice, a parent's voice. "Let me feed you, Mommy."

I sit up. This is too much—Kelsey feeding me like an invalid mother in a rest home.

"Just give me the fork with the food on it," I say. "I can find my own mouth all by myself."

The food tastes wonderful, which surprises me. I can't remember food ever tasting this good.

"You're almost in the Clean Plate Club, Mommy," Kelsey says happily, a child again. "Good for you. Just a little bit of bread left."

I lean back against the pillows. Comfort food. Buttered toast and scrambled eggs, chicken noodle soup and popovers, baked custard or floating island. I could eat all of them right now. I don't want to let go of the plate, because I can still smell the food, even if I can't see it.

Kelsey is giggling loudly.

"What's so funny?"

"You look silly, Mommy. You've got egg stuck in your hair, and butter all over your—"

"Kelsey! Don't you ever speak to Mommy that way! She can't see herself." Kenny never screams at her. She falls against me.

"I'm sorry, I'm sorry," Kelsey sobs. "I didn't mean to laugh at you."

I start to cry with her.

Kenny holds both of us. He is breathing hard, his chest heaving. I can't tell if he is taking deep breaths to calm himself down, or if he is about to cry himself. What a sight we must be.

She can't see herself.

I pull out of Kenny's arms and finally open my eyes to look at myself. I hold out my hand in front of my face and move it slowly back and forth. Nothing. I look down at where my legs should be, touch my knees, hug them to my body. It's shocking to feel myself still here.

This is not what I imagined blindness to feel like. My concept of blindness was all mixed up with the fantasy of being invisible, from all those childhood television shows—unable to see, therefore unseen. Instead, everyone can see me but I can't see them. And I can't see myself. This is what it feels like to be blind.

"Will Mommy ever be able to see again?" Kelsey asks suddenly.

I don't know what we should tell her. The Specialist believes that I will see again. Maybe not as well as I could before, but better than nothing. Better than right now. Still, I am too afraid to believe it, and also too afraid not to believe it. I can't think of anything to say. But she has not asked me.

"Daddy, tell me now," Kelsey pleads. "Tell me if Mommy's eyes are going to get better again."

Kenny clears his throat, and to my surprise, recovers his lost voice.

"I called the doctor this morning while Mommy was asleep and I asked him that same question, asked him exactly when Mommy's eyes would start to get better."

He would do that. He would call to hear the news for himself, firsthand. And he would have the nerve to ask for numbers.

"What did he say?" Kelsey and I ask at the same time.

"He said that he believed Mommy's eyes would start to get better in about eight to ten weeks."

I gasp. This is a miracle! He didn't just get me a number—he got me a date! A real calendar date. Two months. Maybe less. It's now the middle of March. By the first of May, I might be able to see again. I need a calendar right here in bed with me, and I'll have Kelsey mark off the days as each one ends, the way prisoners do in those old movies. Two months—that's hardly any time at all.

"That's way too long a time for Mommy's eyes to be sick," Kelsey says. "If this doctor is so smart, why doesn't he just fix Mommy's eyes in the hospital? Why can't he operate on Mommy's eyes and make her see better? Just like my doctor fixed my nose, and helped me breathe better? Did you ask the doctor about that?"

I am barely listening, I'm so thrilled with this new piece of information. Only two months?

"Daddy, what about special glasses for Mommy?" Kelsey asks, impatiently. "Did you ask the doctor about that?"

"Of course I did. I asked him. And your grandfather left this morning, loaded up with notes to ask all the doctors at Johns Hopkins every possible question and thing you can imagine."

"My father's left already? He left without saying goodbye?" This alarms me.

"He didn't want to wake you up."

"He didn't want to see me."

"He wants to see you, Jackie, but he also wants to help you."

Why do I need help? Why not just wait? I am suddenly wary. Did Kenny just make up this number, this eight to ten weeks, for Kelsey? If I could just read the expression on his face while he's talking, I would know exactly what kind of meaning to attach to what he's saying.

"Listen to me, Kelsey," Kenny says firmly. "It's like this. Think of Mommy's eyes like a television screen. And the television screen has suddenly gone dark . . ." He pauses over the word "dark" and then continues. "Let's say the screen lost its picture for a little while. But we know the problem is with the main power source."

"What's that?" Kelsey asks.

"The plug," I say. I heard this yesterday from the Specialist. I hate this metaphor. My brain compared to a broken television set.

"Yes, Mommy's right. The plug. Actually, there are two plugs—optic nerves—that carry electricity to each eye."

"And both plugs got pulled out?"

"Well, yes—but it's more like the cords are swollen and twisted so they don't work."

"That's why her eyes look black? Because there's no lights on inside Mommy's head anymore?"

"The lights are still there," Kenny says quickly. "Mommy's eyes are still here, with all their parts."

Score one point for Kenny as he rushes in to erase this picture of a mommy with black holes for eyes.

"When the plug is out," he continues, "and you fiddle with the knobs on the front of the TV, it doesn't make the picture come back, does it?"

"No, Daddy," Kelsey answers. "Not if the picture is all gone."

"So, that's why putting glasses on the outside of Mommy's eyes won't help. Because the problem is on the inside."

The problem is on the inside. . . . He's got more problems than an arithmetic book. There's a bruise on his brain and nobody can make it better. Not even Doc.

"But how can the TV come back on all by itself? Without any-body plugging it back in?"

Good question. Why would everything just get better by wait-ing and wishing?

"The plugs are still connected," Kenny says. "We are waiting for the electricity to come back on, remember?"

"Just like when we were in Baltimore and there was a big thunderstorm, and all the lights went out, and we lit candles, and then the lights popped right back on? Like that?"

"Exactly. Now, you go get your nightie on, and wait for me in your room."

I hear her fast footsteps leaving the room. Now's my chance.

"Kenny?"

"Yes, honey?"

"Did he really say it would get better in two months?"

"Well, yes." He pauses for a second.

"It would only be two months before some improvement?"

"Yes."

"But definitely two months?"

"Well—about that. Maybe longer."

"Kenny, tell me exactly what he said. Tell me his exact words. Please."

"He said if it is going to get better, it will start to get better—maybe very slowly—but start to get better by then."

"If? *If* it is going to get better? So there is the chance that it won't get better at all?"

"Jackie, please. Don't even go there."

"But I *am* there, Kenny! I'm right there, in the dark, God-damn it, right here—forever!" I'm shouting and I know that Kelsey will hear me, but I can't control my voice. I can't seem to control anything about my body anymore.

"Anything's possible, Jackie. You know that. Until it happens or doesn't happen, anything's possible. I could get run over by a car tomorrow, and—"

"Stop it!" I can't believe he just said that. I can't believe he would be so thoughtless, so insensitive. "Damn it, Kenny. How dare you?"

"Oh, God, I'm sorry. That was the wrong example. Oh, God."

He is holding me now, and whispering in my ear. "I'm sorry, I'm sorry," he whispers over and over, like a prayer. I push him away and cup my hands over my ears. I curl up, my head against my bent knees, my face away from him, and rock back and forth, eyes shut tight.

Don't go there, Jackie.

But I am there.

"It was a stupid thing to say. I didn't mean it like that. I'm not thinking straight. I haven't slept in . . . God knows how long. Your father and I were up all night trying to figure out a plan. . . . I'm trying to do the best I can, Jackie. Don't do this. Please don't blame me."

He is rambling on, his words hollow, as if he is talking to me from a widening distance, as if I am falling down a deep well. This is why their voices sound different. We are light-years apart.

"Mommy? What's wrong? Does your head still hurt?"

Kelsey is pulling my hands from my ears. But I won't let her. I shake her hands off me. I don't want to pull her down here with me. I don't want to pull Kenny down either. They've got to stay safe— away from me and this dark cloud that is now a part of me, that is now all of me.

We have to preserve the rest of the family.

I lift my head up, and take my hands off my ears.

"Kenny, please take Kelsey out of here. To her room. To bed."

"Mommy doesn't feel well, sweetheart. I'm going to take you to bed, and we're all going to go to sleep. We'll all feel better in the morning."

"I want to sleep here with you and Mommy. Like a sandwich. Me in the middle. That always makes everything better."

"No, sweetheart. Not tonight. Let's go and leave Mommy alone."

"I love you, Mommy. I hope you feel better soon." Kelsey's hand is patting my back gently, and then it is gone.

I'm shaking all over now. I'm chilled to the bone. It's like the temperature in this room dropped to freezing in seconds.

How am I going to survive this? I am not brave enough. I am not strong enough.

I hear Kenny's footsteps coming toward me.

"Jackie, we are going to get through this. We are."

"How?"

"I'm not sure exactly how. But we will. Now let's go to sleep."

He gets under the covers with me, and holds me, spoon position, his chest to my back. Instant warmth.

"Kenny?"

"Yes," he says, his voice thick and sleepy. When was the last time he had a good night's sleep?

"You can turn the light off, so you can sleep better. Go ahead."

I feel his body go rigid, and then he holds me even closer.

"Oh, Jackie," is all he says.

I wait for the click of the light switch but it doesn't come. That's when I know. The lights are already off.

NINETEEN

It's been an awful day. First I woke up with a sore throat. Then Mommy and Daddy said I couldn't go over to my grandparents' house with my sisters because I was sick. I asked them why Mary couldn't take care of me and bring me hot tea and lemon, just like she always does. My mother said no. Polly told me to hush up, that Mommy was upset. She told me a secret. Doc fell down on Christmas night in an elevator that got stuck. He hurt his knee badly and now they think there is a problem with his heart.

What does his knee have to do with his heart? I asked. Polly said she was confused about that too. Anyway, Doc was sick in bed, and Mary was helping to take care of Doc. She said that it was really important that Doc didn't catch anything from me to make him sicker.

In the car on the way to their house, Polly was sad. She loves Doc more than anything. She said she was going over to read to him. Sally was going to play with our grandmother Pyee's old dolls.

"And then Mary is going to make us some tea with lots of

honey and baked biscuits!" Sally says, sticking her tongue out at me, as she skips up the path to our grandparents' house.

The door opens and Mary leans over and hugs Sally, holds her up high above her head, then puts her down. She walks toward our car.

"There's my jackpot," she says.

Mary always calls me that. "We hit the jackpot when we got you," she always says. I roll down the window.

"Mary, I can't come in," I say. My voice is all froggy.

"I know—your mother told me," she says. "We'll have our own special day, you and me, old pal," she says.

She puts her hand against my forehead and frowns. Her hands smell like lemons, but the smell makes me sad, because I know I won't have any of her lemony tea today. I hate being sick.

"I love you, Mary."

I was about to say this. I opened my mouth to say it, but Robin beat me to it. I had forgotten about him all the way in the back of the car. But now he's climbed up closer, behind me. I can feel his breath on my neck.

"Oh, my sweet boy," Mary says, smiling wider than ever.

She reaches around me, and holds Robin's face in her hands.

"I love you, Mary," he says again.

"How much?" she asks. "How much does my sweet boy love me?"

This is a game they always play.

"Bigger than the sky," Robin shouts, laughing.

"Yes." She claps her hands together.

"More than all stars," Robin shouts, jumping up and down, jostling my seat.

Mary laughs and reaches out to touch the end of Robin's nose. "And you are the brightest star of them all."

Robin settles back. This is how it always goes. No matter what, they always say this when they say goodbye.

Mary used to be Mommy's nurse. She came from Ireland and knocked on Pyee and Doc's door when my mother was a baby, asking if they needed help. As it happened, my mommy was very sick, so they took Mary on until she got well, but Mary just ended up staying. She always baby-sits us when Mommy and Daddy go out and Robin is home. She is the only baby-sitter that will watch Robin. All the others are scared of him.

Mary is not, though. She loves Robin the way Horace loves him. She knows that Robin could never hurt anybody.

We're taking Robin back to Rosewood today. I have to go with Mommy and Robin because there is nobody to watch me at home. This makes everybody mad. Polly is mad because she always wanted to see the new school, and now I get to go instead of her. Mommy is mad at Daddy because he wouldn't take Robin back so she could stay home with me. He said he had to go to work, so she said if something happened it would be all his fault.

"Don't let her out of the car," he said.

"Of course not," Mommy shouted out the window when she dropped him off at his office this morning.

My mother is coming down the walk from Pyee and Doc's house. She has a little pillow in her hands and hands it to me through the car window.

"Pshaw! That old thing," Mary says.

"It's my old baby pillow," Mommy says. "I want you to have it, and I want you to go to sleep. We have a long ride."

"Little Jackie's running hot," Mary says.

"I *know* that, Mary!"

Mary's eyes wince as if my mother is going to slap her in the face. My mother looks at Mary, then buries her face in her hands.

"I'm so sorry," she says. "I just can't do it all. I just can't. It's too hard."

"I know," Mary says softly. "Poor baby." Mary talks to my mother as if she is still her nurse. "Everything's going to be all right." She pats my mother on the back. Mommy rests her head against Mary's shoulder until Robin starts to tap on the window. Then she gets back in the car.

It is not that long a ride to Rosewood. I don't know why Robin can't come home more often. There are big gates and a sign over them that says ROSEWOOD HOSPITAL in big letters. I don't understand. I thought Robin went to a special school.

I start to ask my mother about this, but she yells at me.

"Be quiet and listen to me! I am going to leave the car here, right inside this gate. I am going to lock all the doors and windows. You'll be fine."

"No, Mommy, no Rosewood, no more," Robin is saying the whole time she is talking, but she keeps talking louder.

"Do not—I repeat—*do not* open the door or the window, not ever, until I get back."

"Can't I go with you?" I am scared. I don't know why. I have never been in the car by myself. It is light outside, but I don't like it here. There are high fences all around and a giant building up ahead, with many steps leading up to big white doors.

"No! Absolutely not! You are never going in there!"

"But, Mommy," I beg, "I want to see where Robin goes to school. I want to see his room, where his bed is—"

"NO!" she shouts at the top of her lungs.

"NO!" Robin shouts just as loud as my mother. "No Rosewood, no more!"

I put my hands over my ears. If I hold my ears tight against my head, the noise gets farther away, like it's coming from a cave.

I am not like Robin. I do everything at school exactly like the teachers tell me. If I keep doing everything right, if all my papers are up on the Perfect Board, then I will always be able to come home at night and go to Calvert School. I won't have to go to this special school that's really a hospital. But if something happens to my brain, I will be just like Robin. I hold my hands tighter, keeping my brain safe from all the screaming.

"No! No! No!" They are both screaming the same thing, fogging up the windows. Finally they run out of breath. It is quiet inside the car, soft and quiet like right after a thunderstorm. Mommy rolls down the window and sticks her head out. Robin is rocking back and forth, but he is quiet now too.

Finally she rolls the window back up and gets out of the car. She opens the back door and squats down so she is facing Robin.

"Robin, darling, listen to me."

"Yes, Mommy," he says, so softly I can barely hear him.

"Do you still want to come home for a weekend in February, like we planned?"

"Yes, Mommy, yes. I be a good boy. I promise."

"Then let's go." She takes his hand and shuts the door. She knocks on my window and points to the door button. I mash it down.

Robin makes a sound like a hiccup but he covers his mouth.

"Bye, Jackie," he says, looking back at me with his saddest face, still red from crying. "I love you."

"I love you, Robin," I say, but my voice is too soft, and he can't hear me with the windows rolled up. I want him to know that I said it. I have an idea. I crawl into the back seat. With my gloves on, I write the words I LOVE YOU, ROBIN so he will see them when he looks back. I write it in capital letters by rubbing the tip of my finger against the frost on the window.

I watch them walk up the long road and up the front steps. Suddenly they stop.

It looks like Robin is saying something. His mouth is open. He starts to run back to the car. My mother catches him by the edge of his jacket, but he squirms out of it, and she is left standing there with his empty jacket in her hands.

She runs after Robin. But he has already reached the car.

He pounds on the front window with his fists. I can see his white breath in the air. "Jackie," he is screaming. "Open!"

He must be so cold out there without his jacket. I reach over to open the door, but Mommy is there, saying, "No, Jackie, no! Don't open the door!"

I can't believe she really means this. I keep my hand on the handle, ready to pull it up.

Two men in white jackets come running to the car. They look like doctors. One of them is carrying another white jacket, a big one. Good. They probably saw how cold Robin was, so they brought him a warm jacket.

The men each grab one of Robin's arms and start to pull him off the front of the car. Robin is crying now. My mother walks away from him.

"Calm down, Arthur," the men shout at my brother.

Why are they calling him Arthur? Nobody ever calls him that.

"This won't hurt, Arthur, if you calm down."

They throw the jacket over his head like a tent. It has long sleeves which they tie around his back. He can't flap his arms.

"Mommy, help me," he screams.

Mommy stops walking and turns around to look just as one of the doctors pulls a big needle out of his pocket. He brings his arm up and stabs Robin in the back of his shoulder, right through the jacket.

Robin screams one last time, then falls forward. He would

have fallen straight down on the ice if the men hadn't been holding him by the jacket. His body is limp as the men drag him by the arms, his legs sticking out in front of him, his shoes sliding on their heels, making deep lines, like train tracks across the icy lawn.

Mommy runs and gets in the car. She sits there without moving. She keeps her head down. I can't see Robin and the men anymore.

My mother is crying in a way I have never seen or heard her cry before. She is holding Robin's jacket against her face.

"Mommy," I whisper.

My throat is on fire. I am so hot. It feels like there is no air in this car.

"Mommy, please."

She doesn't hear me. I wait and wait. It is beginning to get dark. I look up at the building they have taken my brother into. The windows on the first floor are lit. They are tall and thin, as big as doors, with big bars over them, their shadows casting dark stripes over the white lawn.

My mother takes a deep breath. She reaches out to me. I stare at her open hand for a moment. She wiggles her fingers impatiently. I don't know what she wants me to give her, so I put my own hand inside hers.

"Oh, sweetheart," she says, squeezing my hand. "I wanted a tissue from the glove compartment," she says, but not in an angry voice. She brings my hand up to her teary face. "But *this little hand* is a thousand times better."

She kisses my hand all over, leaving little red lipstick marks.

There is a knock at the window.

My insides jump—maybe it's Robin. I am hoping he got out somehow.

There is a man knocking on my side of the car, a short man

and he's not wearing a white jacket. I put my face against the car
window to make sure it's not Robin. When I see him close up, I start
to scream.

Mommy starts the car, and backs out of the gates fast.

"Don't look," she shouts. She puts the little pillow against my
eyes. I hold it there but I can still see the man's face.

It was a balloon face, all blown up full of air, about to explode,
with giant blisters ready to pop all over it. But he was smiling at me,
and his teeth were black, an ugly pumpkin face.

This balloon face was so much bigger than the rest of him. He
was even shorter than me. Now I'm thinking that he wasn't a man
at all. Maybe he was a little boy, maybe even younger than me,
maybe even seven. But his head was the size of a monster's. Monster
children are kept at Rosewood.

My brother isn't a monster! He doesn't belong there. He has to
get out, I have to think of something. He can't come home because
he has to be watched so much, and Doc thinks Robin is too dangerous to be around his sisters. And now Mary has to take care of Doc.
I keep thinking. Finally I remember.

"Mommy, I know where Robin can go."

She sighs. She has been holding my hand ever since we pulled
out of the gates. I love the feeling of her hand, her soft fingers rubbing against mine. I don't want to talk, because I'm afraid she'll stop
holding my hand, but what I have to tell her is very important. If we
hurry up, we can turn around and get Robin before we've gone too
far. I start talking as fast as I can.

"Horace once said that he had a room for Robin. Horace and
Lucy both said that. We can take Robin to Virginia and we can visit
him there. Horace and Lucy can watch him, because it's winter, and we
aren't down there now. They have lots of time, and they have a room."

She doesn't say anything at all. I hope she's thinking about it. I hope she will tell me I am the smartest little girl in the world to think of this. But a long time goes by and she doesn't say a word. She just keeps driving.

"Mommy, did you hear me?"

She squeezes my hand hard, so hard that her ring digs into my finger. The car stops. We are home.

"Jackie, darling," she starts to say, but then just stops. Her voice is tired. She takes another breath. "Jackie, I know all of this is very hard for you to understand."

I nod my head.

"The room that Horace has for Robin—it isn't in his house in Virginia."

"Then where is it?"

She looks out the window at our house. The windows on the first and second floors are lit, but the third floor is dark. Robin's room is on the third floor. He loves to be as high as possible and look out the window from way up there. He likes to see things the way birds do when they fly.

"The room that Horace and Lucy have for Robin . . ." She begins to cry again.

"Is where?"

"It's in their hearts, darling. It's in their hearts."

She takes her hand out of mine and puts it back up on the steering wheel.

"Now then, I'm going in to get Daddy, and he's going to carry you inside, and you are going to go to sleep," she says. "And with that fever, this will all be a bad dream."

I put the pillow against the dark window, lean against it and close my eyes. I can feel the cold outside air through the pillow, but it feels good against my burning face.

It makes no difference if it was a bad dream or not. I have bad dreams all the time and they are just as scary as things in real life because they feel like they are really happening when I dream them. I'd rather this awful day had been real because I am better at forgetting real things.

I can hear Robin's happy voice from this afternoon telling Mary how much he loves her. More than all the stars in the sky.

But stars die. The sun is a big star and it's going to die too. I read this in a book. The sun is the biggest star in the sky that we can see and it's going to die in billions of years.

Mary told me that a billion years is nothing to God. That God can blink his eye and a billion years is gone. So, if God blinks right now, the sun will die, and it will be night forever.

I have made a decision. I hate God. I hate Him for not fixing Robin. I hate Him for not fixing that little boy with the blown-up face. I hate Him for letting Doc fall in the elevator. I hate Him for letting those men tie down Robin's arms.

I am thinking about this so hard I say it out loud.

"I hate God."

"Oh, little lamb chop," Daddy says, as he picks me up and carries me into the house. "What are you saying?"

I'm not going to tell him. It's my secret.

He is carrying me up the stairs. I am so tired now I can't even open my eyes. My father's hand is across my forehead.

"Aspirin," he says, and then his hand is gone.

I feel something sweet, that sweet orange taste, being nudged between my lips. The bed sinks. Daddy is sitting beside me, holding my head up and giving me water. I still don't want to open my eyes. I drink and some of it dribbles down my chin.

My father stays there until he thinks I am asleep. He gets up and lets out a yelp when he hits his head on the top bunk like he always does.

I still sleep in the bottom bunk because of my nightmares. My parents think I will fall out of bed from screaming in my sleep. So I sleep on the bottom, even though I am older than Sally.

My parents are whispering outside my door. I can hear every word because they are whispering loudly.

"You go get them, Aubrey. I can't get in that car again. If they're already asleep, let them stay there. Tell Mary I'll be over first thing in the morning to see Father and to get them."

"I'm sorry," my father says. "I should have been there."

"Your seven-year-old daughter was there. She watched her brother being put in a straitjacket today."

"She's feverish. She won't remember this."

"This is the child that remembers everything."

He sighs. "Oh, God. A straitjacket. Oh, God."

"*And* an injection," she says, no longer whispering. "Two orderlies, a straitjacket, and an injection. That's what it took to get him in that place."

"Jackie saw that?"

"Every bit of it."

"You will never forgive me for this, will you?"

I am waiting to hear my mother's answer. So is my father. But she doesn't say anything else. I hear their bedroom door slam. Then I hear the bathtub running.

The door opens with a squeak. Daddy sits back down beside me on the bed. I sit up right away and put my arms around his neck. I don't care about pretending to sleep anymore, because it doesn't matter. I'm so sorry that Mommy is mad at him. I'm going to write him a note and put it on his pillow after he leaves. He is still the nicest father in the world to me.

He hugs me tight.

"Daddy," I whisper.

"Yes, Button."

"We've all got to think hard and find someplace else for Robin to go to school."

He pulls back and looks at me. A triangle of light reaches my bed from the door, shedding light on his face. His eyes are shiny as a cat's. He shakes his head.

"There is noplace else that will take him, Button."

"There must be!"

It hurts my throat to talk. I can't talk anymore. There must be a place for Robin, I want to say. If we look hard enough we will find the right place.

"Button, it's very late. We can talk about this later. You need to go to sleep and I need to go get your sisters."

"Do you have to?"

This makes Daddy laugh. He's thinking I said that because Sally and I always fight. But it's not that. It's that I have so much to think about I want the room quiet and all to myself.

"Yes. If they're awake, I will bring them home. No fighting, okay? You know that your mother can't take that, not tonight. Be quiet as little mouses, okay?"

I nod my head at him. He starts to get up. But I grab his hand.

"Daddy, I'm an awful sister."

"Because you fight with Sally?"

No—not that. She fights back. Once she bit me so hard I had to go to the hospital and get a shot because she has germs in her mouth.

"No, Sally's awful too," I say.

He laughs. "Then what have you done that makes you an awful sister?"

"Nothing."

"So, everything is fine."

"No, Daddy—*that's* the problem. I've done *nothing* for Robin. Not ever. I've never given him a Christmas present. I haven't played trains with him in a long time. I didn't open the car today and let him back in and . . ."

Daddy puts his fingers to my lips.

"Your throat is too sore for all this talking," he says. "Besides, that would mean that I'm an awful father. Am I an awful father?"

"No, Daddy, you are so nice, but . . ."

It's a long list, all the things I haven't done for Robin, too long to say in one night.

"Good night, Button. We'll talk about all this in the morning." He pulls the blanket up to my chin.

I close my eyes but I can't stop thinking about Robin. Robin is thirteen years old. Is that what's wrong? Is he like the thirteenth floor? If the number 13 is not there, Polly says, everybody forgets about it. People stop looking for it. They don't even miss it.

But I always look for that number when we get on an elevator. It's the first thing I look for. And I do miss Robin when he's not here. I miss his goofy laugh, and I miss hearing him sing, all high and squeaky, when he is in the bathtub. Robin loves baths.

Robin brings all sorts of toys into his bath. Even a swimming mask and snorkel. He flops around so much that the water splashes all over the floor. Once it leaked through the ceiling. Mommy told him no more swimming in the bathtub and Robin started to cry.

"Glasses yellow, Mommy," he said. "I need glasses yellow."

That's what he calls his swimming mask. Glasses yellow. I wonder what he can see in his bathtub with that mask on. It's not like there are crabs in the bathtub. He runs up the stairs with the mask and swimming trunks on, so happily. He has to wear swimming trunks so we won't see him naked in the hall before he gets in the bath.

I want to watch him in the bathtub. I want to see what he's looking at with his yellow glasses. I wonder if they are like the rose-colored glasses in the Alice in Wonderland story. I wonder if Robin's yellow glasses make him see only the good things. That's what I think yellow glasses should do. Yellow is the color of sunlight, so everything you see through yellow glasses should be sunny. I hope Robin remembered to take his yellow glasses to Rosewood.

TWENTY

"Jackie, I'm sorry to wake you, but I need to know what to do."
Kenny is sitting on the bed, gently shaking my shoulder. I can feel the heat of his stare on my face but I don't want to open my eyes, though I've been awake for quite some time. I heard the morning sounds—Kenny's shower, the hair dryer, a distant phone ringing, Kelsey shouting goodbye as she left for preschool, the door shutting behind her, the sound of a car pulling out of our driveway. I listened to all that without opening my eyes. This is the closest I can get to denial.

"Jackie, look at me. Please."

I open my eyes and look in the direction of his voice. I blink at the gray space where my husband must be. *Crash.* It's like walking straight into a steel wall, my face hitting the hard unforgiving surface first with only my paper-thin eyelids to shield me from its force. It makes me snap my head back against the dense grayness every time. I shut my eyes tight. *What's missing?* Everything. I need a thick black eye mask that will weigh my eyelids down so they won't open out of habit or hope.

"All right, I know you're awake now. Listen, the phone has been ringing off the hook. All of the calls are for you. Your sisters, your friends, the law firm, everybody wants to know what's happening, how they can help, what they can do. What do you want me to tell them?"

"Tell them there isn't anything they can do."

"They've offered to do things, bring food, take Kelsey places, read to you, take you to see other doctors, take you to see . . . just take you places. "

It is amazing how often the word "see" comes up in conversation. Kenny's voice dropped an octave when he said it, but it was too late.

"There isn't anyplace I want to go right now, Kenny."

"Please tell me what to say to everyone." He takes a deep breath. "Please."

"I don't know."

"Jackie, we need a plan. We need help. I've got to go back to work. I don't have any choice. I could try to take a leave of absence, but I don't know if we will be able to keep the medical coverage. Somebody has got to be here with you and Kelsey when I go back to work."

"Teresa can stay full-time and help with Kelsey."

"I'm talking about help for you."

"I don't need any help. I told you before. I'm not leaving this room until I'm ready. And I've got everything I need right here."

"So, what do you want me to do?"

"Go on with your regular life, just as you said." I didn't want that to come out the way it did, full of envy.

"People want to see you. They want to come visit."

"No." This is the one thing I am sure about. "I don't want anybody to see me when I can't see them."

"Even your sisters? They're ready to fly out here. What am I supposed to tell them?"

"Kenny, tell them not to come. Tell them that I'll talk to them on the telephone. I will."

This idea makes me feel better instantly. The telephone! It will be exactly the same. The great leveler. We can't see each other. "I'll visit with everybody over the phone. But I need one of those phones that have big raised numbers."

"All right, I'll get you one." He breathes a sigh of relief. I can hear a pencil scratching paper. He's writing this down. "I'm going to the store right now. Teresa is here. I won't leave you in the house alone. In the meantime, here is this phone, and I'll turn the ringer back on. You don't have to answer, but at least you can if you want."

He puts my hand on top of the receiver. I try to put my fingers around it, but knock it off the bed instead. He grabs the receiver and puts it back.

"I'm sorry. I'm so clumsy."

"No, listen. Once we get the telephone set up just right, there is nothing you can't do. You can call anybody, order things from the grocery store for delivery, take-out food, even do your shopping like that, order out of those catalogues you like to look at."

He is very excited but on the last phrase, again, his voice drops.

"Kenny, I can't read."

There is a pause. "I'll get you books on tape. I'll buy a tape recorder when I get the telephone." He writes this down.

"We've got a Walkman in Kelsey's room. I can listen to tapes on that. And the radio—yes. The news. Much better than television news because the radio news doesn't rely on pictures."

"Good, I'll get you that right now. But I meant a tape recorder that you can dictate into. If there is something you'd want to write down, a message, something you need, a question for the doctor, anything, you can dictate it."

That's true. He was a step ahead of me. I can't write. I can't read or write. But I can speak and hear.

"I'm a writer. I'm a lawyer. I can't write and I can't read."

"Jackie, there are other ways. But even so, it's only temporary. A few weeks."

He makes it sound so simple. He makes it sound as if it might be true.

"Do you really believe that, Kenny?" I have not dared ask him that question.

"Yes, absolutely. I do."

He answered too quickly.

"You can't be sure. The doctors aren't even sure. How can you be so sure?"

"I am sure," he says firmly. I would give anything to see his face when he says this, because he can disguise his voice, but not his face. His eyes would give him away, just like my father. "I can't explain why I'm so sure, but I am. I know what I think. And that's it. If you don't want to hear what I think, then don't ask me my opinion."

He's right, of course. What did I expect him to say? How could he answer any other way? He has no choice. He loves me too much to allow himself any doubt. I reach for him, but my hands grab air.

"Kenny?"

He's gone. Damn! He can't keep doing this. He's got to tell me when he's leaving. "Kenny!"

"I'm back," he says, breathing hard. "I just went into Kelsey's room to get the radio."

"But you didn't tell me . . ."

"Oh, God. I'm sorry. I forgot."

"You're so damn quiet. At least Kelsey always says goodbye.

And the dog has those collar tags that rattle. But you come and go like a ghost."

"I could wear bells on my shoes."

"Do that."

I hear the sound of paper rustling.

"What are you doing?"

"I'm adding that to my list."

"What did you add—bells on your toes?"

"Well, it's better than a dog collar."

"How about a long leash?"

"We've got one already. It's called marriage."

I start to laugh. It is a weird sensation. To want to laugh.

"Now, I'm leaving the house to run these errands. Got that?"

"Yes." I smile.

"Now let's try the phone again."

I put out both hands and he places the telephone in my lap.

"If you need me or think of anything, call Teresa and she will dial me in the car."

"All right."

"I'm only going to be about an hour or so."

That reminds me. "Kenny?"

"Yes."

"I need a clock. One that I can read. I mean . . . one that talks, one of those talking clocks."

"A talking clock?"

"Yes, I've seen them somewhere. You press a button and a little voice announces the time."

"Anything else?"

"No. Well, yes. Before you go, I've got to go."

"All right."

I sit up, and slide my legs over the edge of the bed. I feel wobbly, like I've been in bed with the flu for days. He pulls me up and we walk to the bathroom. I remember that the door opens to the inside.

"I can do this now. Really."

"I'll wait just in case."

I keep my hand on the doorknob the entire time, the way I do in a public rest room when the stall lock doesn't work and I don't want anyone to walk in on me. It's not hard at all. Not that different from when I get up in the middle of the night, in the dark, and go without my glasses. I find the flush handle with my free hand. Not bad. I can do this. No bedpans. Thank God, I'm toilet-trained.

As we go back to the bed, I count the steps. Bathroom to bed—eleven steps.

"Kenny, when you get back, would you take me to the sink, and get things laid out for me—my toothpaste and stuff? And a shower would be nice. No—maybe not. A bath would be better."

"Of course. But you don't have to wait. I can do that now, or I can call Teresa to come down."

"I'll wait for you to help me," I say in a small voice.

The greatness of my needs hits me full in the stomach. Everything is so hard. As Kenny leaves, the dog jumps on the bed. I give in to tears and soon I am releasing huge gasping sobs. I cry for my brother. I cry for my mother. I cry for every person who has ever been sick and felt this alone. The dog's solid weight leans against me and he begins to lick my tears away. Jake, the golden retriever–husky mix that Kenny and I have had for fifteen years, is deaf and almost blind with old age. What a pair we make. I throw my arms around him and cry into his thick fur.

TWENTY-ONE

DECEMBER 24, 1964

Tonight's a double celebration. My mother's birthday and Christmas Eve. But the whole day and night belongs to Mommy. It's a house rule. She said that when she was a little girl, everybody gave her one present on Christmas and said it was also her birthday present, just bigger. It was always wrapped in Christmas paper. She felt like she never really got to have her own birthday. So that's why we keep everything on Christmas Eve separate from Christmas.

Birthdays are very important in our family. On your birthday, you get to be Queen for a Day just like on television. You get everything you want, your favorite foods, favorite things to do, and everybody has to treat you like you are the most wonderful person on earth. I have a hard time doing this when Sally's birthday comes around. But not on Mommy's birthday. Everyone is happy anyway because it's almost Christmas, and we can hardly wait until the morning to see our presents.

My mother opened her birthday presents this morning at breakfast, after she slept as late as she wanted. We wrapped them in birthday paper, not Christmas paper. She didn't have to go in the kitchen all day long, which was one of her wishes. We fixed her tea and tiny cucumber and watercress sandwiches, her favorite.

My father fixed dinner, and now the best part—the birthday cake. We are in the kitchen making it look just right. Polly tried to bake one, from scratch, but she burned it, so Daddy ran out while Mommy was napping and got a store-bought cake. We're taking the Christmas decorations off of it. Instead of the red poinsettias, we put yellow candy roses on it that are hard like sugar cubes. We smooth chocolate icing around the sides to cover the green holly leaves.

Now we are counting the candles. Robin has the special job of putting on the candles. He has counted out the exact number for her age. We already tried to tell him that they wouldn't fit, but he said he could get them all on there. It's going to take forever, because he has to count each candle and stop at our ages. I don't know why he has to do it this way, but once Robin gets an idea in his head about how to do something, it is the only way he will ever do it.

"Okay, Robin," Polly says, taking a deep breath. "Now do the candles."

He counts to seven. "Seven for Sally!"

Sally smiles, showing her dimples. I wish I had dimples. Sally's yellow hair shines under the kitchen light, the same bright yellow as the candy roses. Everybody talks about how beautiful Sally's hair is, the same way they used to talk about the color of Robin's eyes.

Last Christmas Eve I cut all her hair off. I was tired of everyone calling her a "little Christmas angel." I still wish it hadn't grown back quite so fast. The grown-ups at our family parties still talk about how poor little Sally had to wear a ski hat for months to cover the spots where I cut too close to her head. For a long time, she looked like a doll that somebody's puppy had been chewing on. But it looks perfect again now, curving in an *S* around her face.

"Eight, nine for Jackie!" Robin shouts. I watch him plunk my candle down. He spaces the candles apart perfectly evenly.

"Ten, eleven, twelve, thirteen, fourteen. Fourteen for Polly!"

Polly nods her head solemnly. "That's right, Robin," she says. "That's a good boy."

"Fifteen for Robin!" He is screeching now, he is so excited.

His hand is wrapped tightly around his fifteenth candle. Polly taps lightly on his fist. She treats Robin like he is made of glass. She's been treating him like this since he started going to Rosewood.

Robin is shouting and carrying on about the number 15. Polly can't get him to hush up. Robin has been behaving different ever since he went to Rosewood.

He never really looks at me, even if he seems to be trying to tell me something. He scrambles up his words and acts like they should make sense to everybody else, even though they only make sense to him. It's not as funny as I used to think it was. It wouldn't be allowed at Calvert, where Polly, Sally, and I go to school, not for one second.

Everybody in our family has gone to Calvert. I rub my fingers over all their names on the metal plaques in the hallway. Five Gorman boys graduated from Calvert when they were twelve. My father was the youngest, so he was the last to graduate. I know all my uncles except Uncle Petey, who was killed in the war. His name was Arthur, too; Daddy named Robin after him. If anyone asks me where my brother goes to school, I don't answer, because nobody has ever heard of Rosewood. Polly says that there should be a very special school for very special children like Robin, and when she grows up, she's going to find one. And then, she's going to be a teacher at that school.

There are lots of things that Robin is best at, like adding numbers, catching crabs, and building things with his Lincoln Logs.

When he gets tired of his old toys, he makes new toys for himself out of junk that are better than any toy in a store.

Robin can put anything back together too. He can take apart his radio until it is a mess of metal wires, little nails, and round shiny beads, and he can put it all back together in a couple of minutes. He can put together our giant puzzles, the ones that take the grown-ups days to finish. He can put them together by looking at the backs of the pieces, the ones with no pictures.

But there are things Robin can't do right no matter how hard he tries. He can't speak well and he doesn't behave. Nobody can figure out what is going on in his head.

I don't know how to act around Robin anymore. I try to be nice to him, but somehow it comes out mean and I do mean things, like stay away from him, even when he's in the same room, even when he's trying to tell me something. He doesn't make sense. It's like he's not even trying to make sense. It bothers me. He will have to try to act like the rest of us. He can at least *try* not acting so crazy.

"Okay, Robin, we know all about it," I shout, and grab the candle out of his hand, then push it into the cake next to Polly's. "Fifteen. Big deal. That's enough candles. It's not like Mommy's going to count them or anything. She wants to eat cake, not candles."

Nobody can believe I'm yelling, because I'm always so quiet. Robin's face collapses. Then he screams, "No!"

Polly rubs his back, but he shakes her off. Then she pulls the fifteenth candle back out of the cake. It's covered with icing and it leaves a big hole. I stuck it down too far. It's messed up the lettering on the cake. Polly tries to give Robin back his candle, but he's still screaming.

"No! Robin gone! No Robin. No fifteen. No more!"

He covers his eyes with his hands and shakes his head hard.

Polly glares at me, jutting her chin out. We're all backwards, now, all mixed up, with Robin acting like the baby and Polly acting like his mother. She kicks me in the leg.

I've made an awful mistake. I stopped Robin's special way of doing things. I tried to hurry him up, that's all, but I ruined everything for everybody. I feel sick. I'm going to throw up if I look at that cake for one second longer. Everything is ruined.

Robin stops screaming but his face is still red, and he's hugging himself with his arms. He is looking at the cake as if *it* has made him mad and not me. Sally has run off to tell Mommy and Daddy, so we'll get in trouble.

Polly slaps me hard on my hand and it makes my eyes sting. I don't know what she wants me to do now. I don't know what to do. It's too late anyway: Daddy comes in, and Mommy is right behind him. Everybody freezes. Even Robin freezes, his back straight as a telephone pole.

"Stop it," Daddy says in a very soft voice, the one he uses when we have made him so angry that his voice chills to a whisper. "Stop it right now."

Robin turns around to face Daddy and holds up his hands, making a funny pointed shape with his fingers. His own stop sign. He looks ridiculous, but at least he is smiling again. It makes Sally giggle. But Daddy isn't looking at Robin. He's looking at Polly.

"How could you all start fighting like this on your mother's birthday?"

Polly's chin wobbles, but she doesn't say anything. She puts her hand over her mouth. She would never rat on me.

"All I wanted, just for one night, was for all of us to be together—all my children—happy," Mommy says.

My mother is shaking her head. She comes around and looks at the cake. She stands between Robin and Polly and reaches up to put her arm around them. She looks small standing between them. She is shorter than both of them.

"Mommy, make a wish," Robin says.

"Not until the candles are lit!" Sally shouts.

"No fire. No good," Robin says. "Mommy wish."

Robin isn't allowed to be around lighters and matches, ever since he made a fire on his windowsill by holding a magnifying glass over paper. If my mother hadn't smelled smoke he would have burned the house down.

"Right. No fire, Robin," Mommy says. "Let's each wish our own wishes."

We close our eyes.

Nobody says anything for a minute. Then Robin starts talking.

"No Rosewood. No more. No Rosewood. No more."

We open our eyes, but his eyes stay closed. He shouts out his wish, louder and louder, until finally he stops. He opens his eyes and smiles at us.

I hope his wish comes true. I hope he gets to go to a special school where everybody will treat him as nicely as Polly does. And I hope he gets double presents tomorrow. That was going to be my wish. I was going to give my wish to Robin. I was going to wish that he got the best presents, everything he has ever wanted in his whole life.

But now I'm scared our wishes won't come true because he broke the silence rule. It doesn't work if the wish isn't kept a secret. But Robin doesn't seem to know this. He's smiling, and Mommy has her arm around him. Sally reaches out and swipes the bottom of the cake with her finger. She sucks her finger noisily and it makes Robin laugh.

We sit down at the kitchen table and eat my mother's birthday cake. I sit next to Robin so I can tell him I'm sorry for taking his candle. I lean in toward his ear and my face touches his. It feels scratchy. How can he act so childish and be growing hairs on his face like a man?

"I'm sorry, Robin," I whisper. "I love you."

I can't tell if he hears me, because he just reaches forward for another piece of cake. But Mommy must have heard me. She reaches around Robin's back and grabs my hand and holds it tightly in her own.

TWENTY-TWO

How long has it been since the vision in the second eye was lost?"

"About a week, I think," Kenny says.

"Exactly nine days," I answer.

"I see," the Specialist says in his polite British accent. "Well, the clinical evidence from these tests is what I expected. You have lost all functional vision in both eyes. You may be at this plateau for several weeks. I'm going to increase the prednisone and perhaps that will increase the speed of your recovery."

"You still expect recovery, then?" Kenny asks. "I've been telling her that, but maybe she needs to hear it directly from you." Kenny's voice has a pleading quality.

"Yes, I do expect recovery. That's why I would like to put you on the maximum dose of steroids that your body can tolerate, but I know the side effects can cause significant discomfort."

Well, there's discomfort, and then there's significant discomfort. Discomfort is the water retention that has blown up my hands and feet to twice their normal size, making it hard to walk without stumbling over my own swollen toes, hard to hold things in my swollen fingers.

Then there's the emotional roller coaster that has me screaming inside, crying and laughing at the wrong times, yelling at the
dog, cutting Kelsey off midsentence with some kind of biting remark. I don't recognize myself anymore.

I try to tell the Specialist about all this. Kenny murmurs his
agreement as I speak.

"Here are some options," the Specialist is saying. "We could
decrease the prednisone and hope for the best. Or we can stay at the
same level, and see if you adapt better to the dosage. The third possibility, also the riskiest, is to increase the dosage, but attempt to
counteract the mood swings with other chemicals."

"What kind of other chemicals?"

"First, a strong antidepressant to short-circuit the emotional
highs and lows, sleeping medication to resist the stimulant effect.
And then, you can keep administering Valium for those unexpected
storms that arise, when you need something fast and effective."

"I would be a walking drugstore," I say.

"Of course, all of this would have to be cleared by your internist, and your therapist. These are just some general options."

"I don't have a therapist."

"Really? I had no idea. Maybe you would like some referrals?"

This is the first time I have heard surprise in this man's voice.
Am I the only one of his patients who is not under some kind of psychological care?

"No, I don't want any referrals," I say. I couldn't handle the
thought of another grief specialist fiasco. "I don't want to tell my
problems, all these dreams, these fears, whatever they are, to a
stranger whose face I can't see."

"Well, I can understand that. If you are not comfortable with
talking to someone, then it won't help. What about the other med-
ications?"

"I don't want to take all those chemicals," I say.

"I can respect that but it leaves us at an impasse. There is nothing more we can do medically at this point."

"I think we should get a prescription for some sleeping pills, Jackie," Kenny says. "Just in case."

Poor Kenny. He's the one that could use the sleeping pills. The prednisone keeps me—and therefore him—awake late into the night. I have been too afraid to let him sleep in another room, out of arm's reach. He has told me that when I do finally fall asleep I cry out in my dreams, and flail my arms and legs. He has to use all his strength to hold me down and keep me from falling out of bed, night after night.

I had thought that our bed would provide sanctuary from all our waking fears, a cushioned safety net that we could fall into together every night. I wanted to believe that the comfort of sleeping in his arms was one thing I would not lose. But I drift even farther away from him in my fitful sleep, as I wrestle alone with my dreams.

"If I took sleeping pills, would I stop dreaming?"

"I believe so. Are you having nightmares?"

"Not exactly. Just some sad memories."

"Yes, I've heard that from other patients who have lost their sight so suddenly."

"Really? What kind of dreams do they have?"

"They often tell me that they find themselves struggling with disturbing recollections, day and night. It seems quite unfair. One would hope that the sweeter memories would surface first, like cream rising to the top."

"Yes, exactly. I thought there was something wrong with me— that somehow I wasn't focusing on the positive things, all that."

"No, it's not you," the Specialist says, answering my implicit request for vindication in front of Kenny. "It's the nature of the illness that you are fighting against."

It *is* a fight. And that is why I feel so tired all the time, trying to storm my way out of this dark place.

"I don't think sleeping pills will help me," I say. "But more importantly, I don't know if I want to give up my dreams. They have such bright colors in them. All that light and detail is a wonderful thing. I wouldn't trade that even for a full night's sleep."

There is a long, uncomfortable silence. Finally, I hear Kenny shifting in his chair and the shuffling of papers near the Specialist's voice.

"Yes, well, that puts us right back where we started, doesn't it? I'm sorry I can't be of more help to you. Maybe in a few weeks, when I see you again, we will have some better ideas."

An aggravated sigh escapes Kenny's lips.

"Thank you for your time, Doctor," I say quickly, an attempt to cover up Kenny's obvious exasperation. "I know you are doing everything you can."

"One last thing before you leave. It's quite simple but important. I want you to wear dark glasses when you go outside."

"She doesn't go outside," Kenny snaps back. "This is the first time she's gone outside since she left your office nine days ago."

"I'm sorry. I'm sure this must be very frightening."

"That's the understatement of the century," Kenny says. I squirm at this uncharacteristic sarcasm. Has he been getting into my prednisone? Or has all this finally broken him down as well?

"I do go out to sit in the sun, out on our deck," I say, in an attempt to make light conversation, to leave the room on an upbeat note. "The sun feels so good on my face. I sit outside with my radio and my books on tape. But I keep my eyes closed."

"Well now, that explains the lovely suntan," he says. "It's ironic, I know, but your eyes may be even more sensitive to sunlight. Be careful."

"Yes, I will be careful." I am always careful, too fearful to be otherwise. I reach out my hand to shake his goodbye. His grip is strong and steady like his voice, and he pulls me to my feet, in a smooth, practiced motion.

As soon as we get home, and I am safe under the covers again, I make my calls. This is how I spend my days, telephone in one hand, radio in the other, flipping mechanical switches, alternating between taped and live voices. I call my father and my sisters first to tell them about the doctor's visit. Their disappointment is as audible as the static on the long-distance lines between us.

They had been expecting good news. They had hoped the Specialist would be able to detect my optic nerves coming back before I could, in the same way he had detected their departure before I did. I realize that Kenny must have been hoping for the same thing. I hadn't expected so much.

I close my eyes and try to sleep, but I can hear Teresa banging pots and pans in the kitchen. She keeps her distance from me, not even attempting to hide her fear. Unlike so many of my friends, who tried to disguise their initial uneasiness but soon after disappeared.

They were full of questions at first, breathlessly asking for all the gory details. Perhaps they wanted solid evidence that this illness was a freak occurrence or a genetic accident, something I have been carrying around with me a long time, my own optic nerve time bomb. They want it to be an illness custom-made for me. I can't blame them; otherwise, they would have to consider the possibility that it could happen to them.

Restless, I dial the Specialist's number. I wait for several minutes on hold, then as soon as I hear his voice, impatiently blurt out the question I wanted to ask him this morning.

"Will you tell me when it is time to give up?"

"Give up? I'm not sure I understand the question. Do you mean tell you when to give up the prednisone?"

"No. Will you tell me when to give up everything, give up waiting for my sight to return. I need you to tell me when there is no hope of any recovery. I want you to tell me when I should stop waiting and move on, so that I can do whatever it is that I need to do," I hesitate, my voice cracking, giving me away. "I want to know when I should start to learn Braille, memorize the bus schedules, apply for a guide dog, all that."

"Jackie, listen carefully. I will tell you as soon as I believe that clinically you have little or no chance of recovery. But that time is *not* now. And I still believe that time will not come, but if it does, and only if, I will be the first one to tell you."

"Right away? As soon as you know?"

"Absolutely. That is my duty and obligation."

"I thought . . . well, maybe with my husband there today, you just didn't want to spell it all out."

"You are my patient. Although I sympathize with your husband, and your family—and by the way, I have now spoken to all of them, including all those friends and relatives at Johns Hopkins—I want you to be assured that I will update you on your prognosis first. You first. Do you understand what I am saying?"

I breathe a sigh of relief into the phone. I am grateful that he has assumed this responsibility. This morning was not a waste of time.

"Yes, Doctor, thank you so much," I say.

"And, Jackie?"

"Yes."

"You must take heart. You must. Take heart."

"I understand," I say. "I will."

I flip the telephone's off switch, and get out of bed. In the last week, I have staked out the territory just outside our bedroom. I can count and remember the steps from bed to door to deck chair. Because I live in Southern California, I can count on warm sunlight to be waiting for me outside. I lie down on the chaise longue, eyes closed, sunglasses on. I lie there absorbing the sun into my skin, listening to the ocean breeze rustling the palm trees, imagining the blue of the Pacific Ocean only a few blocks away.

I try to focus on positive thoughts, try to guide the imagery of my approaching sleep toward a future full of hope. But I am stuck looking backwards, as Robin was, all those years ago leaving Virginia. He made the best of that backwards view. He had placed a piece of blue plastic over the back window, shading everything he saw in his favorite color. I have the full spectrum of colors restored when I look back in my dreams.

One would hope the sweeter memories would surface first, like cream rising to the top.

But that's it exactly. The sweetness that was my brother, in all his innocence, has made it back to the top.

I searched frantically but in vain for more pictures of him that night when I was trying to memorize my past visually. I wouldn't have looked so hard if I had known that his face would appear so clearly, so brightly in my dreams. Later that same night, I remembered something about our family. We hid the pictures we didn't want to look at anymore. We didn't throw them away, God forbid, or even take them out of their frames. We simply covered them over with a different picture, a more recent photograph, a happier memory.

The layers of pictures in these old frames reveal a history of our family, like the layers of wallpaper in an old house. When I would open up the back of the frames in my parents' home, older photographs would spill out, a Pandora's box of memories. Pictures of Robin as a little boy back in Virginia, holding up all his props, wooden numbers, sheets of colored plastic. But Robin's pictures were not the only ones to sink below the frame's matted surface. Any picture that illustrated our family's failures on a human scale was demoted to an unseen lower level.

Underneath a picture of Polly, newly divorced, with her two sons, I would find an earlier wedding picture, a relic of a ruined marriage. Underneath a color photograph of my father with his three brothers, I would find the single black-and-white picture of the brother who was killed in the war, young and dashing in his Air Force uniform. So it must be with the human brain, that no memory is ever erased, only covered over with later ones.

When I first came across those buried pictures, they hurt my eyes. The picture of my father's lost brother hurt the same way the baby picture of my own brother, at eighteen months old, did. He was a beautiful boy, with luminous eyes, blond curls, and a radiant smile full of hope.

My brother's shadow fell over so many of the pictures he took with his own camera, as he stood with his back to the sun, photographing his favorite sights. When Robin was not standing in front of the camera's lens, his shadow would be visible nonetheless—across my mother's eyes, over Mary's heart, reflected in the glass picture window behind us.

I was afraid of all the wrong things when I raced around in that panic before my vision failed. I thought blindness would obliterate the sight of everything I loved, like a giant eraser wielded by the cruel hand of a punishing God. But I was mistaken. The erasing

happens during my waking time. In my sleep, the old pictures resurface with a different light cast on them, like the eerie light that follows a fierce storm. This view of my childhood came at a terrible price, but I do not wish to give it back. I cling to these dreams now.

TWENTY-THREE

JUNE 1973

This is your perfect age—you will never look more beautiful, and you will never have such a strong hold on other people's hearts."

I've been sunbathing out in the backyard. My mother's words startle me. I sit up quickly and see that she has been standing there watching me. She holds out a towel for me, the way she used to when I was a little girl after a bath. I'm wearing a two-piece pink-and-white-checkered bathing suit, generously cut, with eyelet lace on the edges. But even in front of my mother, I feel self-conscious. I take the towel from her, and wrap it around me closely, covering myself from my knees to my chin.

"Be careful," she says, looking into my eyes. "Be careful with other people's hearts."

She reaches for my hands. We look down at our fingers interlaced together. Mom has large, warm hands, the mirror opposite of mine, which are small and always cold, even now, after baking in the sun.

"Look at that golden color of your skin," she says. "It erases ten years when I see you turn that color. It's as if you were back in Vir-

ginia—that last summer we were all together. You seemed to live in
the sun then, outside every minute with Doc or Horace or . . ."

Her voice drops off.

I clutch her hands, urging her to continue. But she can't. This
is how it always is in our family. We have a lot of trouble ending the
sentences and conversations that are the most important. Nobody in
my family can ever finish a sentence that begins with "Robin."

"What do you mean by 'perfect age'?" I ask her.

"It's just an idea I've always had," she says, sighing. "When I
was little, I wondered what people would look like when they entered heaven. Would they look the age they were when they died, or
a younger age? I wanted to believe that God would let each of us become our perfect age forever, with a face and a body as beautiful as
can be."

I think about this a few minutes as we walk up to the house
and into the kitchen.

"Mom, what was Robin's perfect age?"

I expect her to be taken aback by this question, but she turns
around and smiles at me. She has clearly thought about this before.

"I think that Robin's perfect age was eighteen months. You
know that picture of him in the living room, holding the ball? I was
so happy that he held on to it for the picture. That was such a tri-
umph, you have no idea."

Of course I know that picture. It is one of the few pictures of
Robin we display. But I say nothing because I am hungry for her
words. She never talks about Robin's childhood.

"Well, that picture is in black and white, of course," she continues, "but even so, I think you can see it. His eyes were so bright
and focused—none of that stuff they said later about not making eye
contact—they were perfect, and when he turned those eyes on me, it
was like being under two glorious spotlights." She looks out the

kitchen window. "And his hair was blond then, not dark like it is now, it was a halo of soft curls. Angel hair. People stopped me on the street, he was that beautiful—he was. And nobody could have known from looking at him. How could we have known? He was perfect then. He was."

I wait for a few seconds to see if she is going to go on, but she walks over to the refrigerator, and begins to pull out food to pack for the car ride to the shore this afternoon.

"Mom, what was it that made you realize something was wrong?"

She is turned away from me, but I see her back stiffen at the question. She shakes her head and turns around, a pained expression on her face.

"Oh, Jackie, it really wasn't until Polly came along and I had another child to compare him to, like a measuring glass. Then I started to see the differences." She sighs. "Polly was born only nine months after Robin, my Irish twins. She was so premature, and such a sickly-looking baby. Just dreadful. Long, skinny body, her wise little face as white and hairless as the sheet of her bassinet. I thought I'd given birth to a cigarette."

We both laugh out loud. Poor Polly. So tall and thin, and never, ever comfortable in her body or her skin. Polly has a model's figure and face, legs that start at her neck, high cheekbones, almond-shaped eyes, strong, photogenic features that match her elegant height. Still, she doesn't have a shred of self-confidence, not an ounce of awareness of her natural beauty. She hunches over, as if she is trying to shrink herself down to the size she feels inside.

"But there Polly was, nine months, then a year old," Mom says, "and suddenly she was doing things that her older brother couldn't do, and she was doing them as naturally as breathing—holding a spoon and feeding herself, learning new words instead of echoing ours. It was so wonderful to watch her develop, and so awful compared to Robin. Her accomplishments underlined his failures."

"Oh, Mom . . ." I pause and wait for her to continue.

"I remember one afternoon so vividly. I was trying to teach Robin to pick up a cookie and put it in his mouth. He was two years old then, and Polly was one. Over and over I would try to get him to hold the cookie, to perform that simple act of holding the cookie and getting it to his mouth. He couldn't do it. He would drop it, or crumble it in his fist, or stick it in his eyes. Finally, I gave up and put the lid on the jar."

She shakes her head and her eyes fill with tears. "And then, Polly marched over—she even walked better than he did—and she opened the cookie jar herself, took out a cookie, and popped it in her mouth. God, just like that. And that's when I knew that something was terribly wrong, and that it was getting worse and worse."

"Is that when you took him to Johns Hopkins for tests?"

"Oh, yes. He had already seen all the doctors, the medical ones. So the last one was Dr. Kanner, the world-renowned child psychiatrist. And he told me to put Robin away, and forget . . ."

"How could you stand that, Mom? What did you do?"

"Nothing, then—not in front of this famous doctor, who was doing us a favor by even looking at Robin, hopeless case that he thought he was. I waited, of course, until your father and I got home before I fell apart. Two or three martinis later, I sat down and cried so hard, just put my head down and wept like a baby." She winces, but remains dry-eyed, remembering. "Because I *was* a baby, only twenty-two years old. All I could do first was feel sorry for myself." She closes the refrigerator door, and sits down at the kitchen table. I take a seat on the other side. "I didn't know how I was going to man-

age. I couldn't be the mother to both of them, meet Robin's extraordinary needs, and Polly's blessedly ordinary ones. Just one or the
other. But not both at the same time."

"It must have been so hard, having both of them at home,
without any help."

"Yes, it was," she says, nodding her head. "Having a handicapped child like Robin, who couldn't feed himself, or get out of diapers until he was seven, or speak right. It was like Robin was four
or five children rolled into one, with four or five major problems."

"What about Polly? What was she like around Robin when
they were little?"

Mom shakes her head. "Poor Polly. She wasn't allowed to have
a problem. She had to be perfect, not a perfect child but a perfect
miniature adult. When she was three or four, she started taking care
of him—protecting him, translating his crazy noises. Polly was always his second mother, often a better one than I was."

I nodded. This was Polly, always older and wiser.

"I knew I made a lot of mistakes. But I wouldn't let him go like
that. Not at two years old. And I have always loved him."

"Of course you have," I say, surprised she would state something that has always been so obvious.

She looks up at me sharply.

"That's what the doctors tried to tell me back then, Jackie. It
was supposed to be my fault. Mothers of autistic children were
blamed. We had a label—"refrigerator mothers." And I tried so
hard to fight that, to tell that famous doctor and everybody else. I
loved my son. Yes, of course, I wanted him to be normal, but most of
all, I wanted him to be happy. But he was so disruptive. There were
no schools that would take him. He was violent to himself and de-
structive. You were too little to remember, but . . ." She puts her head
in her hands, and her shoulders jerk up and down.

"I remember," I say softly.

As I say this, my chest actually aches with the memories. All those trips my mother took to Rosewood, bringing him home for weekends, holidays, birthdays. All those midweek afternoon trips to bring him supplies, survival supplies, his cameras, film, and workbooks, cheerful blankets and bedspreads. She kept trying to make a hospital room look like home. She never gave up trying to make him happy.

"Anyway, that was a long time ago," Mom says. "We are all going to have a wonderful weekend, all of us together. Robin is doing so well in his new job. If it continues, he will be officially discharged from Rosewood. He's coming here on the bus—he's so proud of being able to get around town on the bus. And Polly is coming down from Philadelphia in the morning. All my children together."

"Are we taking two cars down today?"

"Yes. Robin should be here any minute. I'll take him and Mary Clark and then pick up Sally at school. I thought you would go later when Daddy gets home from work, in his car, with the dogs."

"Can Robin come with Dad and me?"

"Yes, I suppose, darling. If that's what you want. But Robin doesn't like the dogs in the same car with him, and I've got such a full load."

"That's okay. I'll sit in back with the dogs, and Robin can sit in front with Dad."

"All right. You can be the one to tell your father. He hates listening to Robin's music. But if it's what you want, he won't turn you down." She looks at her watch, and leaps out of the chair. "It's past noon, already. Why don't you go upstairs and get ready. Tell Mary Clark to get packed. I'll honk the horn when I'm ready for her to come out. Tell her to hurry."

I go upstairs to shower and change. My white lacy, puff-sleeved graduation dress is still hanging on the outside of my closet door where I left it yesterday. I hold it up against my body, and look at myself in the mirror. It doesn't seem as if it ever fit me, even as recently as yesterday. Nothing about my life seems to fit me anymore.

I walk into Sally's room to put the dress in her closet. She will graduate in two years. The dress will look perfect on her, like every other outfit of mine that she wears. I don't mind so much that she borrows my clothes, but I do mind that she always looks so much better in them than I do.

Her room is wallpapered in pink and white flowers, dotted swiss curtains on the window. The whole room is as feminine and sweet-looking as a candy striper. Her bed is covered with all the stuffed animals she has kept since she was a child. I look at the pink bunny and see the image of her at six, floating through our last happy summer in Virginia, her buttercup yellow hair reflecting the sunlight, her dimpled smile.

She hasn't changed much in ten years. She still doesn't enter a room like everybody else. She still has this tiny bounce in her step when she walks, like she's got less gravity around her little orbit. She makes Mom smile just by walking into the room, by spreading her happiness around, sprinkling cheerful words like fairy dust into the air with her high-pitched Tinkerbell voice. It drives me crazy most of the time, when I hear her chattering away to Mom and Dad, hear them laughing with her. Her voice is like ice-skating-rink music, always upbeat and perky, always playing, even as I fall on my face.

Yesterday, I walked off the graduation stage with an armful of academic awards—silver cups and trophies and sets of books. And even after all my classmates and teachers and other parents congratulated me, I still felt that I had failed to achieve the only thing my parents wanted me to have, all of us to have—easy happiness.

I can hear music coming from Mary Clark's room. I walk across the hall, and catch her dancing in front of the mirror to the tune of "Supercalifragilistic . . ." from *Mary Poppins*. She is making faces at herself as she sings the words, holding a pink umbrella above her head. Born six years ago, she is the happy ending to our family story, the one that began with a baby boy who came into life with forceps bruises on his head.

Mary Clark was also a beautiful baby. She was born two days before my twelfth birthday, in February 1967. I have always thought of her as an early birthday gift, special delivery, wrapped in layers of love. Polly, Sally, and I adored her. We kissed her face so much that the hair over her temples was rubbed off, leaving bare spots the size of quarters.

She smiles her goofy, lopsided grin, when she sees me in the mirror. She has strawberry-blond hair, a small delicate face, and large navy-blue eyes. Is this her perfect age?

"Hey, Gorgeous One, you need to get packed and ready. Mom will be honking the horn for you in a minute. You're going in her car."

She stops humming and turns around, frowning at me. "Aren't you coming with us too?"

"Of course. But I'm coming later, in Dad's car. We're going to wait for Robin and we'll take the dogs."

"Good," she says, smiling at me. "For once, I get to be the one to say goodbye first."

"What are you talking about?"

"I want to say it first. It's not fair. I'm the littlest and so I'm always the last one to go anywhere. I'll be the last one to go to college. So today I get to say goodbye first. And you will be the one left behind, waving at me, looking all sad."

Mom is honking the horn. I help her throw some clothes into a duffel bag, her baby pillow on top. The honking is louder now, as if Mom is leaning with both arms on the horn.

"Goodbye first!" she shouts, running down the steps.

I go down and stand in the doorway and wave at her, feeling and looking all sad. That tin-can taste that is the aftermath of saying goodbye coats the back of my throat. It doesn't make it hurt any less to be the one to say it first.

There was almost a full moon last night when I snuck out of the house. I wanted to see him one more time. I wanted to see him in the moonlight. He is staying in his empty house alone until his graduation, when he will move out of Baltimore and join the rest of his family.

He was sleeping under the window of the empty dining room. He looked exactly the way I had imagined, the lower half of his six-foot frame covered with his sleeping bag, the upper half pale and moonlit, his fair skin stretched tight and luminous across his chest. He was smiling in his sleep, like Sally does, the way all blondes must smile in their sleep. I still have nightmares.

I stood in the hallway a long time, drinking in the sight of him. When I walked into the room, I saw the note he had left for me, stuck on the catch of the zipper of the sleeping bag. Two words, all in capital letters, written in neon-green highlighter, glowed in the dark: WAKE ME!

I didn't wake him up. I sat down next to him and watched him sleep, memorizing the sight of him, my first love at his perfect age.

I remember every detail of our first date in tenth grade. We were just getting to know one another, both of us in brother-sister private schools. We quickly found the other things we had in common—weekend houses only a few miles apart on the Eastern Shore, each of us the middle child of five, two above and two below. I told him I liked that position, its steadiness, like a landing in between flights of stairs. He smiled sadly, and said that his family had a difference. His older sister was mentally handicapped—a lack of oxygen at birth—and had some severe physical problems as well. She didn't live at home with the rest of them. She lived in an institution. Rosewood? I asked. No, he said, looking at me with surprise. It was a hospital for the mentally ill, like Rosewood, but farther away.

When he told me about her, I squeezed his hand so hard that I thought I heard bones crunch, but he didn't seem to feel it. Nothing could hurt him as much as his own words. He was crying when he told me. Up until then, I had seen only two men cry. Horace and Robin. I had seen Horace cry only that one time when Robin was hurt. I had seen Robin cry hundreds of times, always when he had to say goodbye. But my first boyfriend didn't cry like either of them. He cried like me.

I remember my first real love letter. I wore the words on my body like badges of courage. I tore off the end pieces of his letters, the "I love you, Jackie" parts, and carried them around in my school uniform pocket, over my heart, letting the words sit there like a weight as warm as his hand. I would put the worn scraps of paper under my pillow at night, as if I believed that these words, written in his pointy fountain pen writing, could sink into my head and weave their magic into my dreams, chasing the nightmares away.

Did I know what love meant at sixteen? Do I know it now at eighteen? When *Love Story* first came out, I announced at breakfast that it was the best book I had ever read. I'd finally found the perfect definition of the word love. Mom pounced on my copy of *Love Story* and devoured it by dinnertime.

She read the last chapter in the kitchen, holding it up out of range of the grease from the frying pork chops. Mom has always read every book that her children read, from Mary Clark's kindergarten picture books to Polly's college textbooks. She said sometimes our books were the only windows she had left to see inside our hearts and minds.

Later at dinner that night, she said she'd hated *Love Story*. She started ranting and raving about it, about the shameless manipulation of Jenny's death scene, but the mere mention of it set me daydreaming. I was thinking about Oliver holding Jenny in that hospital bed, about how wonderful it would be to be loved like that. I wondered if anybody would ever love me like that.

I knew even then that he did not love me like that. A few months ago, he proved me right, although I didn't want to be right this time. While I was away at the shore for the weekend, working on my college applications, he went to the biggest party of the year with one of my best friends. At least I thought she was. Everyone in both schools saw them kissing passionately. The double whammy. Two blindsided hits that paralyzed me. I could not say goodbye then, because I was biting the inside of my lips, drawing blood.

They never said they were sorry.

Mom hated the book's definition of love. She said it was wrong. She banged her fork down on her plate that night at dinner.

"That is absolutely the stupidest line, the most dangerous line that I have ever read in any book anywhere," she shouted.

"'Love means never having to say you're sorry'?" I asked. "Why is it so stupid?"

"For God's sake, love means *always* having to say you're sorry! *Always*. If you really love somebody you can never say it enough."

In our family, love has always been about saying we're sorry. That's why I loved the book so much, because it portrayed a kind of love that sounded so effortless. It sounded painless, quiet, and serene, like Jenny's bloodless death.

So instead of waking him up to say goodbye, I wrote "Goodbye" on the note he had left for me. And then I added two words.

Because love means always having to say you're sorry.

I hear two male voices and look up. Dad's car has pulled into the driveway. Through my tears, I see my father and my brother walking toward the house. Dad must have given Robin a lift from the bus stop.

I run upstairs to my room and begin to throw my clothes and some books into a suitcase, so that we can beat the traffic over the Chesapeake Bay Bridge.

When I go downstairs, Dad is already putting things in the car. Megan, our golden retriever, is doing her dance in the front vestibule, leash in her mouth. She does not want to be left behind. The other golden, still a puppy, wags his tail so hard he falls over backwards. We step carefully over them as we carry loads out to the car.

"Call your brother," Dad says. "He's out back in the cold room, taking out the trash."

I call his name, but get no answer.

I go out, and there he is sitting on the cold room floor. Robin's face is pale, and he has a ski hat on. He takes the cold room quite literally, even in June. He looks up at me when the door opens, with a startled expression, as if he's been caught doing something bad.

"Robin, it's time to go."

He puts his head down, concentrating on the box in his lap.

He's looking through my old school papers and tests and notebooks that I had left down here to throw out.

"Can I have this box, Jackie?"

"Sure, Robin."

"Oh, thank you, Jackie. Going to take them down with me. Work all weekend on papers. Got to work hard."

"Well, that doesn't sound like much fun."

"No fun," he says, shaking his head. "No more wasting time."

He picks up the box, and I hold the door open. We put it in the trunk, and I ask Robin to sit up front with Dad. He seems reluctant at first, but I tell him I want to sit with the dogs.

I get in back and give the puppy a hug. His fur smells like gardenias, because he sleeps curled up on Mom's side of the bed each night, absorbing her perfume.

"So what was in the box?" My father gives me a puzzled look in the rearview mirror.

"My old school stuff," I say.

"Just can't tear yourself away, huh?"

"Robin wanted them."

Robin is bobbing his head up and down, which is what he always does when he's excited about something. It's hard for me to understand how anyone can be that excited about my old high school papers. I think they could be bottled and sold in the sleep aid section of the drugstore.

"What do you want Jackie's schoolwork for, Robin?"

"I'm not retarded anymore, Daddy," Robin says. "No more."

Dad doesn't say anything, but one eyebrow shoots up in surprise at this announcement.

"My friend Mr. Citron told me that today. No, sir. I'm not retarded no more. I'm just misunderstood. Work on Jackie's papers— graduate like Jackie. Yes, Daddy. Graduate from Rosewood. No Rosewood. No more."

Dad and I exchange glances in the rearview mirror. I look at Robin's profile in the side mirror of the passenger seat.

He pulls his ski hat off. It shocks me for a second, his new military haircut. The last time I saw him was late March, and he had this same ski hat on, but tufts of long hair stuck out on both sides. I remember watching him in the living room, where he was sitting, waiting for Mom to take him shopping. He was smiling to himself, his eyes closed, the long curled lashes casting a fanlike shadow against his pale skin, making him look for a moment like a little girl instead of a twenty-three-year-old man.

He looks completely different now. I look at his soft profile, as he looks out the car window. It contrasts so harshly with the bristled hair.

"Robin, when did you get that haircut?"

"Yesterday," he says, touching the back of his neck shyly. "Went all by my ownself."

"But why so short?"

"Got to look good for new job. Got to look sharp. I'm a dishwasher, now, Jackie. Work clean. Look clean."

A dishwasher. Our grandfather, Doc, must be turning over in his grave. He had so hoped one of his grandsons would be a doctor.

"You getting a job now too, Jackie?" Robin twists around to look at me, his face eager. "You going to be useful?"

This makes Dad and me burst out laughing, and Robin laughs with us, pleased that he made such a good joke.

"I'm going to postpone being useful for a few more years, Robin," I say, still laughing. "I'm going to college."

"College, yes," Robin says, his face now serious. "Got to be smart for college. I work hard, be smart, go to college someday too. Just like my sisters, Polly and Jackie."

"It's much better to be useful and make money, Robin."

"Yes," he agrees, but he tilts his head, looking as if he doubts it.

"What are you going to buy with your money?"

"The biggest TV in the world, Jackie," he says. "Giant color TV, just for me."

"That sounds expensive, Robin."

"Oh, yes," he says. "Lots of dishes."

I laugh at this, and look over at Dad, but he's stopped listening. He's fiddling with the radio buttons.

"Need a weather report," he mumbles.

"Hurricanes," Robin says.

"I don't think so, Robin," Dad says, shaking his head. "That would definitely get in the way of our fishing trip."

"Fishing, yes, good, good, good. Fishing."

Robin is bobbing his head up and down again and rocking back and forth. He loves fishing as much as my father does, as much as I do. I look at both of them; the backs of their necks are exactly the same, same skin tone and shape. I had never noticed this before.

"Good fishing. Good for Robin!" His voice is growing louder and higher with his excitement. Dad turns the volume up on the car radio.

Robin pulls out his transistor radio, and plugs in his headphones. After a few minutes of listening to static, Dad turns off the radio. He sighs, and then catches my eye in the mirror.

"Button," he says. "I was proud of you, yesterday. All those prizes."

"Thanks, Dad."

"You must have been so bored. You should have skipped a grade somewhere back there—in Calvert, maybe."

"I may skip a year in college. I think I've done all right on all my AP tests."

"That's even better," he says. "Less dishes for me to wash."

So he *had* been listening.

Robin is making noises now, weird sounds to the music he must be listening to, and I try to make out what the tune must be. I can hear an electric guitar. Dad glances at him, a look of irritation passing over his face like a thundercloud. But he doesn't say anything, knowing Robin doesn't realize he's bothering anybody.

"Eat a Peach," I mumble to myself.

"Eat a what?"

"It's from the Allman Brothers album *Eat a Peach,* Dad. Robin's listening to their music."

"Well, I'm glad I'm not listening to it. I hate that stuff. God-awful voices these new singers have—alley cat whines." I try to remember the words to the first song on the album, "Ain't Wasting Time No More."

My father slows down the car as he guides it into a gas station. Robin tears his headphones off and leaps out of the car. He loves gas stations. Dad begins filling up the tank, and Robin starts to clean the windshield. I look at my brother through the glass and wave at him, but he doesn't seem to see me. His face is twisted into an expression of fierce concentration.

As he leans over, rubbing at a stain with a paper towel, his fingers squeaking, I hear something on his shirt hit the glass, tapping over and over. I lean forward to look. It's a pin. A big wooden 4, painted yellow, with a happy face inside the triangle. Seeing that pin reminds me. I reach into my jeans pocket and feel the metal in my fingers.

"Nice pin, Robin," I say, as he gets in the car.

"Thanks, Jackie. Sure do like the number four," he says.

"Why do you like the number four?"

"Good number, sure do like that number four," he repeats.

He has never given anybody a different answer than this, but I keep asking in the hope that I'll solve the mystery. All Robin's obsessions are mysteries—his number pins, his pieces of colored glass, the wooden birdhouses he makes in woodshop that have glass sides and no roofs.

"In Japan, the number four is very unlucky. It stands for death," Dad says, getting in the car and starting the motor.

"Jesus, Daddy," I say, looking back at Robin, who unfortunately is listening to every word. "What a thing to say!"

Robin cocks his head to one side.

"Daddy, got to tell you something," he says.

"What is it, Robin?"

"Japan lost the war, Daddy. They lost it for no good. And you lost your brother in the war. Lost him for no good."

"Well, thanks for that news bulletin, Robin."

Robin pulls out a pencil and a piece of gray paper, and begins to write something down. I lean forward to look. "BULLETIN," he writes, in careful print, in the *B* section of his word list.

"Robin, can I see that for a minute?"

He pauses for a second, and then hands it over, his prize possession, his word list.

"Here's a present for you," I say, handing him a Maryland State Latin medal that I won and had just received in the mail.

"Yours, Jackie? A prize? Good for you," he says, smiling.

"*Yours* now, Robin," I say. "For graduating from Rosewood."

He pins it right above the big 4, near his heart, place of honor.

I look down at the paper he gave me, which is not paper but a piece of gray cardboard. It looks exactly like the cardboard that comes inside of Dad's shirts from the dry cleaners. It's covered with words, at least a hundred words, in Robin's careful print writing. Every day Robin writes down all the words he hears and reads and

doesn't know, then writes down the dictionary definitions and mem-
orizes them. He will often stay up until the middle of the night
memorizing that day's words. He won't go to sleep until he's done.

I skim it, and stop at the S's. "Supercalifragilistic" is one, with
a blank next to it where the definition should go. He must have been
listening to Mary Clark's songs.

I point to it.

"Robin, that's not a real word. It's make-believe."

"Make-believe? What's that? Is that a compound word?" He's
pulling out his pencil. "I'll put it in the *M* column, under 'misunderstood.'" He looks up at me. "Sentence: *Robin misunderstood the word
supercalifragilistic.*"

"Yes, but don't worry about the *M* column right now, Robin."
Even after all these years, he can't focus on more than one idea at a
time. "I'm talking about that supercalifragilistic word. You didn't
find it in the dictionary because it's not real. It's a magic word."

"All words are magic," he says. "Good words make good
things happen. Don't you know that already, Jackie?"

I blink at him.

"Yes, Robin. You're right."

"Better learn about good words in college," Robin says, his
head bobbing up and down. "Good words are useful, like good
numbers."

My father smiles at me in the rearview mirror.

"That's true, Robin," he says, winking at me.

We are coming into the sleepy, one-store town of Neavitt, and
in another few miles we'll be home. I can hardly wait to get there. I
love that house as much as I love any member of my family. Robin is
smiling too, holding his camera up to the window, taking pictures.
We turn onto the gravel road, and then the dirt road that leads up to
our house. Dad stops the car and holds his finger to his lips.

The great blue heron is there, that rarely seen, shy creature. We all hold our breath, but he has already spotted us. He swoops up and across the pond and the creek, his huge wings casting a prayer-like shadow on the steel-blue water. From the car I can see Sally and Mary Clark in the swimming pool and Mom and Polly out on the porch, setting the table for lunch. I take a deep breath of the salty air, look toward the water, at the dock, a duplicate of the one at my grandparents' house in Virginia, and see the fishing boat tied up to the mooring. It's a perfect day. Not a cloud in the sky.

"No hurricanes today," Robin says. "Good day for fishing."

"Yes, Robin, right again," Dad says, letting his hand rest on Robin's shoulder for a few seconds.

Robin looks at Dad's hand, and beams up at him, a smile as bright as the one he gave me when I handed him my Latin medal.

And I realize how rare it is for Dad to listen to my brother, and to listen hard enough and long enough to find something they can agree upon. It was a two-hour car ride door to door. I didn't know why I wanted the three of us to be together in the car like this, but now I do. It is my last summer at home before I go away to live. And this is the picture I wanted to take with me—all of us together on this glorious June day, and all of us happy.

IV

THE SEEING

GLASS

push the toy aside, and lie down next to her, shoulder to shoulder. I probe the contours of her face lightly with the tips of my fingers, careful not to wake her up.

She still sleeps with her mouth open. Her hair covers her eyes. How long has it been since she has had her bangs cut? I must tell Kenny to make an appointment for her. This makes me realize that I have no idea what my own hair must look like. Well, it doesn't matter. I'm not going anywhere.

Kelsey starts to mumble in her sleep, unintelligible words. I hear Kenny's footsteps coming down the hallway. Then his footsteps stop, and I hear the rattle of Jake's collar, the thump of his tail against the tile. I know that Kenny has his arms wrapped around the dog, his face buried in his neck. I hear him give a long sigh. I wonder if he knows how often he sighs, if anyone ever hears themselves sigh. His footsteps start again. I hear him stop in the doorway.

"Oh, Jackie," he says, his voice cracking.

Kelsey stirs at the sound. She is waking up. I slide off her bed, and walk toward Kenny. I walk into his open arms, knowing that they are open, and will always be open when I turn to walk in his direction, waiting to enclose me. I lean against him, take a deep breath of him.

"Kelsey needs a haircut, I can tell," I say, strangely proud that I have managed to see something about our daughter that he has not.

"She looks fine."

"Does she? What does she look like? Tell me."

"Just like always. Think of the most beautiful little girl in the world, and that's her. Just like always."

"Oh, Kenny, that's not enough. Has her face changed? Does her hair still have all those gold and copper highlights in them? Do her eyes still have those flecks of amber? Do her cheeks still look

"Please stay here with me, Mommy. I'll rub your back like you used to do with me and help you get sleepy."

It's like a knife thrust to the heart—this little voice using the past tense. *Like you used to do with me.*

"That's a great idea, Kelsey, but I'll rub your back instead, while you get sleepy, and I'll stay with you until you fall asleep."

I hear the springs of the bed squeak as she turns over on her stomach, and I start to massage her back in slow circles.

"Mommy, I don't want to go to school anymore," she says after a few moments. "I don't want to go tomorrow morning."

I had forgotten this miracle of the nightly confession, when she would tell me all of her troubles just before she fell asleep.

"Why? Is somebody teasing you at school?"

"No. My friends and the teachers are always nice. But I miss you, Mommy. I don't want you to be home all by yourself and lonely."

"I'm fine. I don't want *you* to be lonely either. You should be out and playing with your friends."

"I want you to take me to school then."

"I can't drive you to school, Kelsey. You know that."

"You don't have to drive the car, Mommy. You can sit in the car with me, in the back seat, right beside me, can't you?"

"Is that what you really want?"

I hear her turn over, and feel both her arms around my neck, her gentle breathing against my cheek.

"Yes, Mommy. That's what I want. You right beside me, always."

I can stay beside her. I can move with her though I can't see her moving. This is the hardest part, losing the moving pictures that make up our present. Suddenly, I ache with remorse remembering the time my silence conspired to deny that right to another mother. All those years ago, I looked at these things as a hospital lawyer, not as a mother, and certainly not as a woman who would someday lose her sight.

A deformed, terminally ill newborn baby was about to be taken off life support, and the parents wanted to take a video of the last day of the infant's brief, tragic life. Another lawyer for the hospital was concerned that the movie could be used in a later lawsuit as evidence of malpractice. He did not think any picture taking should be allowed. I disagreed with him and argued on behalf of the parents. He listened to me patiently, then reached a compromise with the parents.

He told the nurses in the neonatal unit to allow the parents to bring in a camera but not a camcorder. They could only take still photographs of their child. I knew what my mother would have given for moving color pictures of her only son at his perfect age. But I did not argue the point any further. I still regret that silence. The lawyer had called it a reasonable compromise. I would argue differently now, knowing what I know now. Life is always a compromise, I would argue, but witnessing death, the death of a child, without the chance to record that child's life, is a compound tragedy.

I shudder at this memory, as if a sudden draft has entered the room. I hold Kelsey close in my arms, and listen to her quiet, even breathing. She lifts up her head, suddenly, knocking my chin.

"Mommy?"

"I thought you were asleep already."

"Almost. But I remembered something I wanted to tell you. We got a present in the mail, from one of your sisters, a picture book. You need to get Daddy to read it to you."

"What's it called?'

"That's the best part. It's called *If You're Afraid of the Dark, Remember the Night Rainbow.* You'll love this book, Mommy."

"All right, Kelsey. We'll get Daddy to read it to both of us tomorrow."

"I love you, Mommy."

"I love you too."

She settles back in my arms. In a few moments, she is asleep.

I have my own night rainbow. Seeing it has not made me any less afraid of the dark, but I am less afraid of the night. I've been seeing a kaleidoscope before I fall asleep. The colors are brilliant and mesmerizing, rolling across the inside of my eyelids—undulating waves of color in a psychedelic waterfall, washing over me, cleansing me of all the day's dirty grayness.

I close my eyes and wait for the night rainbow to herald my Technicolor dreams.

TWENTY-FIVE

My sisters and I are sitting in the family waiting area while Dad talks to Mom in her hospital room. We each have our own notepads we carry around with us. Sally is looking over her pad of paper. It is lined blue stationery, letter-sized, with a print of pansies across the top, so much like the ones in the wallpaper of her old room in the house we grew up in, which is now long since sold.

Tomorrow morning, Mom will leave this hospital for the last time.

"I can get some of these things from the pharmacy in the morning. Supplies that the home nurse will need," Sally explains, glancing at Polly. "The plastic bowl, the bedpan, disposable gloves, skin lotion, and all that. I can also fill the take-home medicine prescriptions."

Polly nods and looks down at her pad, a lined yellow legal pad, with the days of the week written in seven columns across the page.

"I've got a schedule of all the nurses in the area who do this kind of home care. I've got the next several days set up," she says, her voice dropping. "I've got backups if any of these don't work out or Mom doesn't like them."

"I'm going to go down to the shore early in the morning," says Mary Clark, the baby of the family, just graduated from college, although she missed the ceremony to stay with Mom during the last session of chemotherapy. "And I'll have her bed ready with her favorite sheets and pillows. I'll put flowers from her cutting garden on her nightstand, at eye level, where she won't have to sit up to see them." She looks up at all of us, her face pale. "And I'll fill the refrigerator with food, for Mom and for us, so we don't have to go to the grocery store. I'm going to bake some custards—maybe her stomach can handle that."

There is a long silence, during which they stare down at their own handwriting. I search in my purse for my pen and paper. I pull out my little three-ring assignment notebook. "What can I do?" I ask as I finally locate a broken crayon at the bottom of my purse.

They look at me with surprise. I must have been told, but I wasn't paying attention, as usual.

"What?"

"Didn't you know?" Sally asks. "Mom told us that you were going with her. She wants you to be in the ambulance with her."

"She does?"

"Yes," Polly says.

"But why?"

They shrug their shoulders.

"Just me?"

"Only one family member allowed, according to hospital policy," Polly says.

I get up and walk down the hallway and knock on my mother's door, announcing myself. I wait for a few seconds. Then, I hear both Mom's and Dad's voices say that I can come in.

"I'm going to make some calls," Dad says, getting up from the empty bed next to Mom's. "You can keep your mother company for a few minutes."

I walk over to her and pull up a chair as close to her bed as possible. I would sit at the foot of her bed if I could, just like Danny, our golden retriever, and curl up right at her feet, but I know that the slightest wrong movement could hurt her, especially when she is still connected to all those tubes.

She smiles at me, and reaches out her hand. Her fingers are cold at the tips, and this stuns me, my mother's always warm hands, suddenly cold.

"Mom, do you really want me to go with you in the ambulance tomorrow?"

"Yes, but only if you want to."

"Of course. I just . . ." I don't want to complain or appear ungrateful, so I stop speaking and rub her hands between my own, trying to warm us both.

"What's wrong, darling?"

"I've been feeling so useless, Mom. I wish I had a nursing degree instead of a law degree, and at least I could help, by doing all the stuff . . . you know . . ."

"I don't want that," she says. "I want you to be my daughter, not my nurse."

"But how can I help you as a daughter? I'll just let you down, tomorrow. If something happens . . ." I hesitate.

I am the absolute worst person to have around in an emergency. I panic. I scream. I freeze. I can't think clearly or even follow directions. Not me. I am the last person my mother needs in that two-hour ambulance ride tomorrow.

"You have never let me down," she says.

I stare at her. Of course I have let her down, too many times to count. Of all of us, I am always the one who never pays enough attention to details, who forgets things, who still doesn't know how to cook a decent meal or find the way to the doctor's office or order the right size curtains. I have messed up each of these simple tasks in the last few weeks, when doing simple things right was so important— particularly when it was for someone as unerringly competent and efficient at taking care of people as my mother.

"But, Mom, I don't know what to do if something goes wrong."

"The paramedics will be there. They will take care of everything."

"Then why do you need *me* to be in the ambulance with you?"

"Just to be there, darling. To sit there and let me look at your sweet face. You can tell me things."

"What things?"

"Everything! Describe all the things you see. Tell me what you see out the window that I can't look out of myself. I want you to tell me every detail of the scenery. As soon as the water comes into view, when we are going over the Bay Bridge, tell me how many boats are out on the water, if there are waves, and what color the water is, and the sky. Paint the pictures for me, with those big eyes that see everything . . . You always painted pictures with your words. Even when you were very little, you would come up with the right words."

"What words? My silly little compositions at Calvert?"

"Yes, all those too. But I was just thinking of something else. I was thinking about that time, that dreadful day we took Robin back. Do you remember?"

"Yes, Mom. I do."

I am the one who always remembers. She knows this better than anyone. This is the first time she has ever spoken to me about that day, about seeing those words I wrote for Robin. I wanted *him* to see them, to know that I was thinking about him. I had just learned to write those words. It was freezing cold. I scratched the tip of my finger into the frost on the back windshield as my mother and brother walked away from the car.

I LOVE YOU, ROBIN. Big letters, big enough for him to see from far away.

I thought that he would look back at the car. Robin was always looking back, always taking one last look.

"Mom, I never knew you saw those words."

"I know, darling," she says, closing her eyes, as if she still can't bear the sight. "I knew that you wrote them for your brother. But he couldn't read them anyway because they were backwards. From outside the car, they were backwards."

I shake my head. Not until this moment had I realized that. It's true. I would have had to write them in mirror writing, in reverse, and at seven, I wouldn't have known how to do that.

"I was a goofy kid, Mom, always messing things up."

"No, Jackie—you didn't mess it up!" She is gripping my hand now and her eyes are wide open, looking at me. "Don't you understand, Jackie? *I could see them!* I got back in the car, and I put the car in reverse, and there they were, your words. I saw the words in the mirror, but I couldn't read them. So I turned around and looked directly at them." She winces in pain, and takes one hand away from mine. Holding it against her right side, she continues. "I was looking at that place I had to leave my son, looking at it through your eyes. It was that last look back that somehow gave me the strength to turn the car around and go forward—to go home without . . ."

Without him. The strength to go home without him. She doesn't need to speak these words. We both know what happened that day.

"You were so little, and scared. But you gave me those words, and that is your gift, your strength," she says.

"I see now, Mom. But I inherited that gift from you."

"No," she says, shaking her head.

"Yes, Mom. You did that for me, when I thought that no words could possibly help me, you found the words nine years ago, when Robin died."

She opens her eyes to look at me. I expect to see pain there, but I don't.

"I am so glad," she says. "You were so alone and so sad, crying into that public telephone, with nobody around to help you."

I was in Atlanta, finishing up my first year of law school, when I got the news. Kenny had already moved to California for a new job. I was living in a rented room, with only a few days before I would join him. There was an emergency message for me taped to the blackboard of my last constitutional law class. CALL YOUR HUSBAND ASAP.

When I finally got through, Kenny was crying.

"Robin's been in a car accident," he sobbed.

I didn't understand at first. I thought he must have been mistaken. Robin didn't have a driver's license. He walked or took buses everywhere.

"No," I said. "He doesn't drive. He couldn't have gotten into a car accident."

"Jackie—he was hit by a car."

I couldn't breathe then. I crumpled to the floor of the lobby outside the law library. I sat there on the floor, screaming *NO* over and over again into the phone.

"I'm sorry, I'm so sorry," Kenny kept saying, and I let the handset drop, but I could still hear him repeating, "I'm sorry, I'm so sorry," like a whispered prayer.

"Just another first-year student freaking out over exams," was the next thing I heard, and that's when I realized that there were people in line behind me, waiting to use the phone. A hand reached over my head for the receiver, but I grabbed it first. I pulled myself up by the metal cord and draped my arms protectively around the phone. Then I hung up on Kenny, the first and only time I have ever done so.

I dialed home, person-to-person, collect, for my mother.

"Mom," was all I could say before I became hysterical.

"Hold on to this, Jackie. I know you will remember. He's safe now. He's where he was happiest, back in Virginia again—down on the end of the dock, first thing in the morning, down there with Horace, and he's got his crab net all ready. And nothing can hurt him anymore. He is finally safe and out of all danger."

Her voice had been so sure and so calm. I wrapped that voice and that image around me when I flew home for Robin's memorial service.

My brother was thirty-one years old when he died; twelve of those years had been spent in a mental institution. But it was standing room only in that church, filled with his friends and admirers, all crying their hearts out for him. The one person smiling was Mary, even as the tears rolled down her cheeks.

"Do you remember what Mary said when Robin died?" I ask my mother.

"No, darling, I don't. What did she say?"

"You know how Robin loved his trains. She said that he was on the express train to heaven, and that he was so happy, traveling so fast, zooming by all the stars in the sky."

And you are the brightest star of them all.

Mom smiles, her eyes closed.

"Oh, yes, dear old Mary. She would have believed that. Her Irish Catholic faith was so strong, so comforting. She believed that the innocents, the suffering children, the handicapped, they all had special seating in heaven."

"I believe that too, Mom," I whisper, leaning close. "Don't you?"

She smiles again, but doesn't answer, still keeping her eyes closed.

"Jackie, do you remember how much Robin loved colors?"

"Yes, Mom, I do remember."

"Of course you do," she says, nodding her head, a faint smile crossing her still-beautiful face.

What is my mother's perfect age? Right this moment, at the end of her struggle, she is ageless, looking both impossibly young and impossibly old at the same time. She is so still, barely breathing now.

"Mom?"

"Yes, darling. I'm still here. I'm just so tired. But I wanted to tell you what I believe about heaven. I believe that heaven is full of the most beautiful colors. And I know Robin is there, feasting his eyes. It is an idea that I have clung to ever since we lost him."

"Yes, Mom," I whisper. "And you'll be right beside him."

She squeezes my hands, and they are finally warm again.

"Stay here with me," she says at last. "Stay until I fall asleep."

"I will, Mom. And I'll be there for you tomorrow."

She says softly, "I know you will."

TWENTY-SIX

That's very interesting," the Specialist says after I finish giving him an elaborate description of my night rainbows over the phone.

I can tell by the even tone of his voice that he did not find this at all interesting and certainly not remarkable. But I persist.

"Doesn't it mean anything—this burst of color before I go to sleep?"

"No," he says. "It doesn't have any real clinical importance. Is there any change in your vision during the day, when your eyes are open?"

"No," I answer, my voice now deflated, sounding as flat as his.

"I'm sorry. Then, do you have any other questions?"

He always asks me this before he says goodbye, even when I can hear the intercom and telephone lines ringing in the back-ground, and I always decline politely, but this morning the unasked question that has been waiting impatiently, like a frantic hand wav-ing in the front row, bursts out of me.

"Doctor, do you think I might be going crazy? Because I've been so afraid that all of this—that it's all in my head." I stumble over the words. "If you know what I mean," I add, hoping he does know what I mean, even though I'm not making any sense, which is my point exactly.

"Are you asking me whether this might be some kind of hallucination? Are you worried that you might be delusional?"

"Yes," I say. "I'm not sure where the dividing line is—between a dream and a hallucination, between delusional and crazy."

I don't know whether I am scared out of my mind, or just plain scared. And I don't know if anyone knows any better than I do.

"In other words, you are concerned that your optic nerve disorder might be psychosomatic in origin?"

"Yes," I sigh heavily, not realizing until this moment that I have been holding my breath. "Yes, that's it. That's what I've been trying to say."

"Well, I can assure you that your loss of vision is not a figment of your imagination. It's a definite neurological deficit."

"How can you be so sure? Aren't you always basing your medical opinion upon what I tell you, what I think I am seeing? And what if I don't know what I'm talking about? Like right now . . ." I start to laugh awkwardly, hearing how ridiculous I sound, but as I laugh, my eyes fill up with tears—another thin dividing line that is always shifting.

He does not say anything for a moment. I try to contain a sob in the silence that follows.

"I understand now exactly what is frightening you," he says finally, his voice both strong and tender at the same time, his finger in the dam, sounding the way my father sounds when he knows that I am about to flood the telephone lines.

"You do?" I choke this question out. Then I hold the receiver so close to my cheek it hurts, but I don't want to miss a word of his answer.

"Yes, I do. But let me respond to your questions first. I did not base my diagnosis of your condition solely upon your inability to read out the letters and numbers on the wall chart. When I first saw you, I examined your dilated eyes and that is when I detected objective medical evidence of severe optic neuritis."

"Objective evidence?"

"Obvious clinical findings of a neurological failure were present. There are more complex ways to describe it, in medical terminology, but basically I observed a loss of color of your optic nerve discs."

"So what color were they? What color are they supposed to be?"

"Healthy optic nerve discs in someone your age should be pink. Your right optic nerve had already turned a pale yellow by the time you presented in my office. And your left optic nerve was an in-between color, beige, still some pink left but distinctly fading. If I had not seen that evidence, then I would have tested you with different equipment."

"Like what?"

"We can discern with a machine whether or not the patient's eyes—the entire ophthalmological system, rather—is healthy but the patient still cannot see."

"You mean like a kind of vision lie detector test?"

He laughs. "Well, I wouldn't call it that—particularly in front of the patient. But it does determine whether or not the brain is deceiving the body. The receptors in the brain may be blocked from absorbing any further visual information."

"But how is this blockage different from a neurological blockage like mine? Isn't it another electrical shortage to the television screen?"

"No, these cases are different. These are total blackouts without any mechanical explanation. All the wires and cables are connected, but no messages are coming through."

"But why?"

"Massive emotional trauma." He says these three words as if they should always go together, as if they are hyphenated. "Some patients here—Asian war refugees, mostly old women—have lost their vision. Their surviving relatives say that the visual loss occurred shortly after they saw their families tortured and killed."

I ponder this for a moment, trying to fit it into his television metaphor. "It's as if a thick black curtain suddenly crashed down, covering the screen. The pictures may still be playing, but it is impossible to see through that curtain. Is that it?"

"Yes, that's one way of looking at it."

"Do they ever see again?"

"Not in my experience. Since it's not a medical problem, there is no medical solution. You see, in these cases, psychological health is very closely connected with physical health—"

"Isn't it always?" I interrupt. "Remember—you suggested that I see a therapist when I lost my vision. Why wouldn't intense psychotherapy help these women?"

Even as I ask this, I know the answer. I imagine an army of grim, black-coated grief specialists marching around these pseudo-blind women, trying to get them to talk about their memories. It would be futile. If some things are so terrible to see that they blind the witness, they would likely render them mute as well. Unspeakable acts. Hideous sights. In law school you learn that the one airtight case of emotional distress damages is the fatal injury of a child right before the mother's eyes.

I think about my own mother's eyes. They were never quite the same color after losing Robin to Rosewood, fading faster still with each passing year after his death. The massive emotional trauma named Robin still bleeds, but it does not bleed out words, only silences. Our family wound does not bleed out the color red, but blue, the color of blood from the inside.

I shut my eyelids tight, but I can't hold the tears back any longer.

"Jackie—are you still there?"

I am startled by his voice. "Yes, I'm sorry. I was just thinking about those women and how awful it must be for them." My voice gives way, and I sob into the phone like a child.

"I'm so sorry," he whispers. "I have made quite a mess of all this. I did not tell you this story to make you feel badly, or even worse than you do already."

"I know," I sniffle into the telephone. "It's not your fault. I'm sorry to behave this badly."

"No apologies necessary. Listen, you must understand that your own illness was *not* precipitated by witnessing an unbearable event or suffering extreme psychological stress."

Here we go again, right back to my original question. *Circle tracks*.

"But I'm not so sure, Doctor." I'll ask it again, a different way. "Our little girl had been very sick, even at one time misdiagnosed with cystic fibrosis, and I had been losing a lot of sleep. I was so afraid that she would not get better, that something would go wrong with her surgery. Maybe it brought all this on."

"Those are the fears of every mother. Sleep deprivation and anxiety over a child's illness. Fatigue and worry do explain why you did not notice the visual losses in that right eye—the color red, the peripheral, the depth perception—but they're not the cause."

"But, it's not just that. I've always been terrified of the dark—

always had nightmares, had to keep the light on in my room, even when I grew up. Did I bring my own worst fear upon myself, some-how—created my own darkness, even though it was the last thing I would have wanted?"

"Blindness has been one of your greatest fears?"

"Yes," I whisper into the phone. I am momentarily stunned by his use of the word blindness. He has never used it in our conversations until now. "Yes. Going blind *was* my biggest fear."

"You are in good company," he says emphatically. "Most every person, myself included, will place blindness at the very top of the list of terrors. This doesn't make you crazy, just human."

"And still terrified."

"Yes. But it is an understandable terror. Anyone in their right mind would be terrified to find themselves where you have found yourself."

There is a long silence as I mull over his choice of words. He has been extraordinarily generous with his time. Unlike lawyers, who can bill for telephone consultations, this is nonreimbursable. Yet I can't seem to say goodbye first, even though I know that is what he's waiting in silence for me to do.

"When there is a change in your daylight vision, you must call me right away."

"Yes," I respond dutifully. But I still have one more question. "What kind of change?" I ask. "What will I see first?"

"I'm glad you asked," he says, his voice lifting. "First, put your glasses on—then look for a shade of color moving."

"What shade? I see everything now in the same monotone gray. What color will come through first? Red?"

"No," he says. "Red will be the last to return. Blue. Look for blue."

"Blue?"

"Yes. A strong, bracing shade of blue will move out of the grays. Look for that. Keep your eyes focused on anything that is blue."

"The ocean? The waves? I live near the beach."

"No. That's not blue enough."

"The sky?"

"Too pale. This will be a darker blue. More like the color of your eyes. Look at your own eyes. Look in the mirror. When that shade of blue comes back, then call me."

"You're kidding, aren't you?"

"No," he says. "I'm quite serious. Also, it would help if you wore blue clothes that match your eyes. And have everyone around you do the same."

"Really?"

"Yes, really," he says firmly. "I do have to go give a lecture now. I'm sorry. But please call me later if you have questions. Until then, put on your glasses, and keep looking."

As soon as I hang up the phone, I power-walk to the bathroom, sixteen steps reduced to nine or ten. I lean over the sink until the end of my nose touches the glass. Then I pull back a few inches. I stare straight ahead. Nothing.

Of course, I don't have my glasses on. I have to wait until Kenny gets home to find them. But I keep staring.

When I start to see my own eyes, it will mean that my eyes are starting to see. This seems so impossibly simple.

I reach for the earphones that are always around my neck and turn to the classical music station, as if to put my thoughts on hold. I keep staring at the mirror, blinking and waiting, and I am still there when Kenny comes home for lunch.

TWENTY-SEVEN

I tell Kenny every word of the conversation with the Specialist and ask for my glasses, which he presses into my hand. I put them on. The weight of them on my face is like a shot of adrenaline. They make me feel like a seeing person again. I lean forward into the mirror, my hands against the glass for balance. There is no change.

"Kenny, why don't you go put on a bright blue shirt," I say, turning toward the spot where I last heard his voice. "Then move back and forth in front of me and maybe I will see you moving around me."

I feel his hand on my shoulder and the other gently touching my cheek, turning my head to the right of where I was looking, to where he must have been standing all along.

"Jackie, I have to tell you something." I take a long breath. His next sentence can't possibly be something I want to hear. "You're the one who should be moving."

"What?"

"It's time for you to get out. Not just out of bed, but out of your pajamas, and out of the house. You need to move around. I would love to take you walking down by the beach. Please."

"Now?"

"Yes, right now."

I don't want to go out. I want to stay here and keep staring in the mirror, so I don't say anything. I feel Kenny's arms around me, encircling me from behind, his chest pressed against my back, his chin resting on my right shoulder. I try to visualize his face next to mine in the mirror, but I can't. We have never stood in front of a mirror looking at ourselves. Neither one of us has ever spent any more time than necessary looking at our reflections.

I have regarded mirrors as necessary, unpleasant invasions of my constitutional right to privacy, like sobriety checkpoints or metal detectors in airports. A mirror forces me to look at myself as other people see me. I glance in them before going out in the world, to make sure I don't look ridiculous, with my skirt caught up in my panty hose or an ink smudge on the end of my nose. But right now I would give anything to see myself in the mirror.

Even if the Specialist had not suggested it, I would be looking for my eyes first when I looked in the mirror. I have never thought my eyes were particularly memorable, although women at the cosmetic counters who make these judgments all day long tell me with certainty that my eyes are my best feature. In fact, I always wished I had green eyes, Scarlett O'Hara eyes, the same color as those of my childhood friend Ann, the color of youth and spring and hope. I thought blue eyes were boring, at least on me anyway. My parents and my siblings all had blue eyes and I wanted to be different and exotic. If I couldn't have green eyes, then I wanted to have dark brown eyes like Doc and Horace and Lucy, because I thought they were thinking deep important thoughts with their dark eyes.

And yet Robin's eyes were the exception to the dullness of blue. I was unwavering in my belief that he had the most beautiful color eyes in the world. Yet blue is the color that fades the fastest, and even then, even at the age of six, I knew that the bright blue light that was my brother would be the first to go out.

I remember the day when we were little that a friend of my grandmother's came over to lunch at my grandparents' house in Baltimore and exclaimed that "little Jackie" had the most extraordinary eyes.

"There's nothing at all extraordinary about her eyes," Doc grumbled, loudly enough for me to hear every word. "She's myopic and astigmatic, which amounts to the bad vision of an old lady in a young girl. The only difference is that she has large eye openings, which make them more prominent, with more of those same watery-blue irises that every one of my grandchildren have. More color showing, that's all. Nothing extraordinary about her eyes."

I absorbed these words deep into my brain and waited until the following summer to take them out in the sunlight and look at them again.

"What does Doc mean when he says we all have watery-blue eyes?" I asked Horace one day when we were alone on the dock crabbing.

He didn't laugh. He never laughed at my questions, which is why I was always saving them up to ask him. Horace took his time before answering, let the question sit between us, like a loose fishing line, waiting for the big fish, the big thought, to come along and pull it taut.

"Well, I think what your grandfather means is that there are all different kinds of blue," he said. "And water—salt water anyway, the kind of water in this river, the kind of water in tears—well, that kind of water changes its blue with the weather, because it's like a mirror of the sky."

"Then having watery-blue eyes is a good thing?"

"Yes, that's how I see it," he said, smiling at me. "Watery blue is the best blue because it is *all* kinds of blue. Like that dark blue you and your brother have in your eyes, that's the color of this river just before a storm is coming, that blue means something serious is happening real soon."

That dark blue you and your brother have in your eyes.

But Robin and I didn't have the same color eyes—or did we?

I need to call my sisters, my three-way mirrors. I start to move out of Kenny's embrace, but he holds me closer.

"Jackie, please. Will you take a walk down along the beach with me?"

"Yes, but later, when it's dark."

"Why?"

"I don't want to be around people yet. I don't want people seeing me when I can't see them."

"I can see you and I think you look fine. You do. I'll make sure your clothes are all right . . . Please."

I squirm around to talk to him face-to-face. "I was planning on calling my sisters, and giving them an update—to tell them to send me any of their old blue clothes," I say, stalling until I think of a better excuse. "You know how long that could take. It would be much better if you go back to work, and we'll take a walk tonight. I promise."

He pulls away so suddenly I lose my balance and bang against the edge of the tile counter.

"Fine," he says. "I'll go back to work. You stay here and talk on the telephone. Just go ahead and do that. Let life just move on right past you, let it go."

There is red in his voice.

"Kenny, please don't do this." I hear his footsteps walking away. I call out to him. "Kenny, please don't do this."

"Do what?" he snaps. "I'm not doing anything. I *can't* do anything. It is so hard just watching you and not being able to help you—just watching you do nothing. Do you have any idea how that feels?"

"No," I say, cautiously, "I have no idea."

"No, you don't. And I don't have any idea how *you* feel."

"But you can see how I feel."

"Yes. But, Jackie, I'm not seeing the same person anymore."

"What do you mean you're not seeing the same person?" I cry out. "What do you mean? How do I look different to you?"

It can't really be that bad. I know I'm clean. Every morning and evening, I have walked into the bathroom with Kenny and we have gone through the basic hygienic routine together. He has taken baths and showers with me so that I don't slip. He has put soap in my hands and toothpaste on my toothbrush . . .

Suddenly, I remember all the other things that I used to do, all the little maintenance details that most men, Kenny included, don't notice unless they are *not* done. And for the past few weeks, they have not been done. I must look neglected and unkempt— unplucked eyebrows, unshaven legs, unmoisturized skin, the gray seeping out of my hair follicles.

"Oh, God, I must look awful. How can I possibly go outside?"

"Jackie, listen to me. You don't look awful. No. But you do look different. I hate telling you this, but I have never lied to you. You look blind."

I walk toward him, my hands outstretched, and as soon as I feel his hands, I stop walking, and stand there. We hold each other carefully, at arm's length, as if we are about to dance.

"Tell me the truth," I say, deliberately holding my head up, straightening my spine, my chin thrust forward, trying to look as if I can take whatever he says next. "Tell me what you see now when you look at me, and how I look different."

He sighs deeply. I do feel very sorry for him. I know that if this were happening to someone else, one of his closest friends or one of his sisters, he would have been talking to me about it all along. Instead, it's happening to me. He can't speak to anyone else without feeling as if each word is a betrayal of confidence. He has been raised by the same rules of family silence, where unsightly handicaps or illnesses were not mentioned, let alone discussed in graphic detail. But from my dreams I have learned that silences can be deafening and all the more hurtful for leaving things unsaid.

"Kenny, please. Tell me what looking blind means."

He pulls me toward him.

"Jackie, when I came home to find you staring into the mirror, trying so hard to see yourself, it just finished me."

"Is that what you meant when you said I looked blind? That I looked pathetic with my nose against the glass?"

"No, not really. Look, let's not talk about that now. Let's go."

"No, Kenny. Finish what you were saying."

"This is so hard. It's something different about your eyes," he says. "It wasn't true those first few weeks of your blindness, but it is now."

"How have my eyes changed? Are they a different color?"

"No, not that. They are still that pretty blue—really, it's just that . . . It's that your eyes don't move anymore. It's so eerie, and sad. In the beginning, you still *looked*—you would look at me when I spoke to you, or at least look in my general direction. Now your eyes stay fixed, staring straight ahead, no matter what is going on around you. Your eyes don't follow sound, whether it's me or the television."

"My eyes don't move? They look like a dead person's eyes, is that it?"

"No, it's not like that. I can't explain it. It's just that I know you can't see, but you need to keep trying, keep looking."

THE SEEING GLASS   227

"But, I am still looking! It's all I think about nowadays, Kenny—seeing and looking. I'm trying so hard. See? I'm even wearing my glasses."

"I know—it helps. It makes a big difference in how you look. A blind person doesn't wear regular glasses."

I have to laugh. "It is the height of optimism for a blind person to wear prescription glasses."

"Yes," he says, his tone of voice upbeat once again. "And so is getting into regular clothes and going outside. Don't give up."

"Okay, I'll go walking with you."

Kenny picks out my clothes and helps me get dressed, zipping and buttoning me up tight, like a child about to encounter snow for the first time.

I fall down within seconds of going through the front door.

"I never did get an exact count of the front steps," I whimper, my right knee throbbing from its unintentional slide into our cement planter.

"Oh, God, I'm sorry." Kenny is out of breath, each word coming with a short burst of air, with urgency. He must have leaped over the stairs, onto the landing, trying to break my fall. "Are you all right?"

"Fine," I say with what is, for me, enormous restraint. "We'd better keep moving before I change my mind."

"You don't take another step without holding on to me. Not one more step, do you hear me?"

We walk down the block without any more falls. I hold him stiffly and follow his instructions.

"Step down off the curb. We're in the crosswalk."

I step down and forward one step and then I hear the sound of a car speeding by. I clutch Kenny around the neck with both arms, as if drowning.

"It's all right," he says, trying to pry my fingers loose from their death grip. "Calm down. Don't panic."

"The car!"

He yanks me back up onto the curb, but still I cling to him.

"Jackie, the car was going in the opposite direction. It had already passed us by the time we started crossing the street."

"I didn't know that! I couldn't possibly know that!" I sob.

"But I could see it. I would never have walked into the street with you and put you in danger. Never. Don't you know that?"

Yes, I know that. But a car could hit him too. Maybe he would be paying too much attention to me, to my stepping off the curb, to all these little things that we now have to pay attention to, and he would not see the car that hit us. People die in crosswalks. My brother died in one. Robin never saw the car that hit him.

Polly, a lawyer then, handled everything. She reviewed the accident report and spoke to the witnesses. They all said the same thing, saw it the same way, from different directions, different vantage points. They said a young man anxious to catch a bus ran into the street, into oncoming traffic. He never even looked for cars.

They all remember him flailing his arms, trying to get the bus driver to see him, to stop for him. But the bus kept moving and the cars kept moving, the drivers catching sight of him too late. His body hit one windshield, cracking it, and was flung by the force of that impact several feet away, onto the hood of another car. He was pronounced dead at the scene, in the crosswalk of one of Baltimore's busiest intersections.

Over ten years later, my sisters still avoid driving through this intersection. They take the circuitous route around it, long winding side streets, often adding more than a half hour to their commutes.

I ask Kenny to take me home so I can call my sisters.

TWENTY-EIGHT

As soon as we get home, I assume my crash landing position. I get back into my pajamas, into bed, my hands on the raised-number buttons of my telephone.

I start dialing.

"Sally, do I have the same color eyes as Robin did?"

"Jesus," she sighs. "Don't you ever say hello anymore?"

"Well, I figure that you know my voice by now."

"Well, yes, but I need a minute to collect my thoughts. What did you ask me?"

"About the color of my eyes—and Robin's eyes."

"I'm not sure, Jackie. I'm not sure I understand your question. Why are you asking about all this now, of all times?"

Her voice is still high-pitched, and goes up an octave when she's worried. She's in the soprano range now.

"I've been thinking about him a lot, dreaming about him."

"What kinds of dreams? What kinds of thoughts?" Her voice deepens down to its professional baritone. Sally is a psychologist. Dreams and thoughts are the currency of her trade.

"Mostly memories—happy childhood ones."

"Happy ones? Are you sure? And they are about Robin and

you?" She rapid-fires these questions at me, not waiting for an answer before launching another barrage. "I don't think you should be doing this, Jackie. We are all so worried about you getting lost in the past, all this looking back."

"I'm fine, Sally, really. Tell everybody that."

"Are you taking any antidepressants?"

"No," I say. "I've always trusted my mind and my feelings, and I don't want them to be chemically altered just when I need them most."

"Yes, I understand that, Jackie, but it's the comforting thoughts that you need the most, not the disturbing ones."

"I know. I'm trying to focus on those. Honestly, I'm trying."

"Do you want to know what I think?"

"Yes."

"Are you sure?"

"Yes," I say again. "I really do want to know."

I not only want to know what she thinks, I want to think the way that she does, look the way that she looks, my blond dimpled sister. I want to share her sunnier view of everything.

"All right then," she says. "Here's the story. You are at a very low point. It's perfectly natural for you to linger in this valley, and reflect upon every other sad memory and low point in your life."

"Right. It's natural but not necessarily healthy."

"Exactly. So, you have to refocus your concentration. You lift up your head—literally lift up your thoughts—in order to climb out."

"But how do I do that?"

"Well, each time a sad image comes to you, visualize your hand reaching in to take it away and replacing it with a happier picture."

"Sally, I understand all about that. We've been doing this as a family for years. But don't you ever wonder what happens to the other pictures? Where do they go?"

"You don't have to worry about that right now."

"But that's *all* I worry about—everything that's been hidden and missing and covered up. It's come back to me now for a reason, I have to believe this. It would be wrong to discard these thoughts now."

"I think we're going around in circles here." I can hear her little boy calling for her in the background. "It must be my fault. Let me think of another idea."

"No, don't worry. I'm *fine*. Listen, I can hear this is a bad time. I'll call you tomorrow, all right?"

I hang up the phone and dial the next number.

"Polly, did Robin and I have the same color blue eyes?"

"Oh, Jackie. Let me think."

I can see Polly hunched over the telephone, her eyes closed, analyzing my question as if it is a final exam. "I think so, yes. I do," she says at last. "I mean, both of you as children had such haunting eyes. Maybe yours are larger—or maybe they just look larger because your face is smaller, but the same blue. Yes. I would have to conclude that it is the same blue."

"Really? It never occurred to me to ask before."

"Does it help to know that you and Robin were similar in this way, or does it make it worse?"

"I'm not sure," I say.

"When you asked me that, I tried to think of what Mom might have said."

"And?"

"Well, I was remembering how much she used to worry about you both. Her soft-shell crabs—that's what she called you and Robin."

"What exactly do you think she meant by that?"

"Well, I think it was that you were similar in your vulnerability to being hurt. You both were so sensitive and trusting."

"Yes, but all children are like that."

"No, you and Robin were always wrapped in your own worlds. And even as adults, both of you walked around in a kind of trance. It worried Mom so, because she thought you were magnets for all the bad people out there."

"Polly, do you remember when Robin was beaten up by that gang of kids, my freshman year of college?"

"Oh, Jackie, there were so many times that he was hurt like that. No, that particular incident I don't remember."

I tell Polly what I remember. It was October of 1973, and I had just met Kenny at college. I was home for a long weekend, talking to a high school friend on the phone—talking, I'm sure, about Kenny. It was one of those sparkling fall afternoons, chilly enough for a sweater, and I was in the kitchen, looking out the window, thinking how perfect everything was, me included, in that self-absorbed way particular to an eighteen-year-old girl in love.

I heard knocking at the front door and finally got off the phone to answer it. It was our neighbors down the street. They had tried to call, but the line was busy. They told me they had my brother at their house and he had gotten hurt. I remember thinking it had been an accident. Somehow, even then, it was my biggest fear for him. But they said it was no accident, that he had been "roughed up." Some kids from another neighborhood had followed him, teasing him; they knocked him down, stole his wallet and his radio. Our neighbors' son had found him, chased the boys away, and brought him home.

I went over to their house, and there was Robin, holding a washcloth against his face. It hurt to look at him. His face was swollen up like a boxer's coming out of the ring, our brother who never raised his fist against a soul, yet seemed always to be on the receiving end. The neighbors' son told me that a pack of kids had gone after him, kids no older than eleven or twelve. He had seen them from the top of the street, throwing things at Robin, calling him names. Robin didn't respond, just tried to walk faster. Then they knocked him down, took his things, kicked him in the head.

Polly doesn't say anything after this last detail. She has been listening carefully, the way she has always listened to me ever since we were children.

"God, Jackie, it's hard for me to picture Robin's face without some kind of bruise or cut or scar. All those years in Rosewood, he would get beaten up all the time by the other patients, usually in some kind of struggle over his things—his camera or his radio, which Mom and Dad were always replacing. But I somehow thought that out in the real world, he would be more protected."

"No, Polly. He had even *less* protection on the outside."

"But he was so big and strong. Why didn't he ever fight back?"

We both stay silent, thinking about this fact for a moment. It was true that he was well over six feet tall and not physically disabled in any way. But his mental handicap showed—in his posture, his haunted eyes, his clothing choices. He looked strange. His size alone was not enough to intimidate a mugger, not even children half his age. With their vicious eyes, those children saw in this soft and sweet man an easy target, and they smashed him into the street.

I break the silence first. "I've had a difficult time remembering him without his head being hurt in some way too," I confess. "From that first memory in Virginia, when he was banging his head into the dock, all the way to just a few moments ago, when Kenny took me out for a walk, and I thought about the end of his life."

"Oh, God, Jackie. Don't think about all that now."

"Sally said that I should try to focus on other images, happier memories."

"Mom would have said the same thing."

"You know something, though, Polly? Recently, even in my dreams, it has been easier to see the happier pictures. I've been seeing Robin in a different light."

"What do you mean?"

"Well, he's in my dreams but without the worry that seemed to be etched on his face. He looks peaceful. His presence in my dreams brings me a kind of stillness, as if he is trying to calm me down."

Speaking these thoughts to Polly confers a weight to them, something substantial for me to hold on to. It's been eleven years since Robin died.

"Polly," I begin in a quiet voice. "If I ever recover my sight, I want to look through his things. The bag he was carrying that day. I don't know what I'd be looking for—I just want to see his things."

"Oh, Jackie, I've never found the strength to do it myself. When your eyes get better—and they *will*—we'll do it together. Maybe we'll find out what he's trying to tell you."

Polly's other line rings and she puts me on hold. I can guess who it is, and when Polly comes back on the line, she confirms my hunch.

"That was Mary Clark. She's already spoken to Sally."

"All right, you tell her everything I just told you, and then have her call me if she has any brilliant insights. All right?"

"Sure."

I wait by the phone. Do they burn up the telephone wires talking to each other after each conversation with me, comparing notes, trying to come up with a better strategy to pull me through this darkness, the way we did when Mom was dying? I wonder how close to getting on an airplane to Los Angeles each one of them has been in these last few weeks.

I keep begging them not to leave their jobs, not to take time away from their lives. I have made Kenny promise to reinforce this in the conversations that I know he must be having with each of them from his office. They have respected my decision, although I know how hard it is for them to stay away.

The telephone rings and I know it is Mary Clark, calling in her answers to all my questions. We all have our roles, quite dependent upon our birth order, and she is the problem-solver of the family.

Polly, the oldest girl, is the questioner, trying to get at the answers by finding the right question. The classic middle child, I am the mediator, looking at both sides of every question, finding the balance. Although it seemed she was always talking when we were little, Sally is now the listener, listening until the person talking figures it out on their own. Mary Clark, the fourth and youngest sister, is the clean-up batter. She takes a huge swing at the problem and almost always hits it out of the park.

"Jackie, I've heard all about your dreams. And I know what he's trying to tell you. It's quite simple."

"What? No, wait—first take a deep breath. Take your time. I want you to speak in nice full sentences, no shortcuts, all right?"

Mary Clark, once notified by Johns Hopkins that she had achieved a genius score in the math pre-SATs at the age of nine, is now in the banking industry, and still juggling numbers. To avoid a moment's boredom, she is working toward her master's in computer sciences at night. She talks as fast as her fingers move on the keyboard, faster even, stringing sentences together like long-division calculations. I'm always telling her to slow down, so that I can have time to think about each word she is saying; it drives her crazy.

"All right. Whenever I'm in trouble, Mom comes to me—in dreams, in visions, whatever—and she's always got that worried look on her face, carrying her pad of paper, the one she wrote on in the hospital all the time. Anyway, she gives me advice that way."

"Really? You never told me this before."

"Well, there didn't seem to be a reason to talk about it before."

After all this time some things never change—we still need permission to talk about the most important things in our family.

"Anyway, I agree that he is trying to tell you something by appearing so clearly in your dreams. But you'll figure out what it is that Robin is trying to tell you on your own."

"That's it? You said before that you knew what it was! I was counting on you to have figured it all out for me. What good is a baby sister if not to do all the toughest work?"

"Well, all right, if you insist. I'll tell you my first guess, which is always the one to go with, at least on those standardized exams. I do think I know. But you were much closer to him, are now much closer to him, so I may not be getting the same message."

"What message are you getting?"

"Well, for what it's worth, I think he's trying to tell you to be brave. To hold on. He's telling you that you are going to make it through this, make it through to the other side."

"The other side?" I don't bother to disguise the alarm in my voice.

"God, no—not *that* other side!" She laughs out loud. "Jackie, you have been living in California way too long—you really have."

"Mom always said that when she thought I'd said something incredibly stupid, but was too polite to say so. All right, genius, then what *did* you mean by the other side?"

"Simply that you are on your way to getting better, to seeing again. That old light at—"

I rush in to finish her sentence, a few words ahead of her for a change. "I know, that old light at the end of the tunnel, and not the one that is the headlight of the approaching train."

She laughs again. "Now that we have solved all your problems, please put my favorite person on the phone. I want to know if she got the book I sent her."

I call out for Kelsey and put the receiver back in its cradle as soon as I hear her voice chirping away to my sister.

I lie back in bed, my eyes closed, and put Mom's baby pillow under my neck. I try to summon happier images.

One picture comes to me from all the ones I memorized that last night I could see. It was taken by a professional photographer and appeared on the front page of the *Baltimore Sun*'s Life Section, one Sunday in April 1959, underneath the headline "The Rites of Spring." It is a photo of Mom and Polly and Sally and me trying on Easter hats in a store. We are dressed in our Sunday outfits; back in those days we dressed up to go shopping downtown.

My dress matched Polly's and I was thrilled to look as much like her as possible. Sally was about eighteen months old, a porcelain baby doll, framed in pink organdy and white silk ribbons, sitting at Mom's feet, her cherub face turned away from the mirror. We are all hovering within inches of our mother in front of a three-way looking glass. Mom is smiling into the mirror at us, and Polly and I are smiling back at her image in the mirror. If you look carefully at the photograph, as carefully as I have, you notice that not one of us was actually looking at our own reflection.

I thought my mother was the most beautiful woman in the world. We all did, and that adoration is reflected in our faces. Her looks were soft and dreamy, and even when she was angry, her lovely, even features kept their serene expression. It was an enigma throughout my childhood, how she stayed so picture-perfect, even when she was screaming-mad. Her lips would maintain their rose-bud shape, her thick hair swept smooth as honey from her heart-shaped face.

I wanted to be just like her, and I tried to mimic her pose, but instead the elastic strap under my chin snapped, sending my hat backwards. Just as I reached with my left hand to keep it from falling off, the photographer took the shot. Later when the photo editor from the newspaper called to get permission to run the photo, he told Mom that he had chosen this one, where one of her children was taking off her hat, because it looked so natural. If it hadn't been for that hat falling off, it would have looked too much like a fairy tale family, too good to be true.

When Mom told us this, her face bright, I still wasn't sure whether I had done a good thing or a bad thing by taking my hat off. Had I messed up by doing something real, something a make-believe perfect child would not do? I asked Mom about this, and she took me in her arms for a good long hug. She reminded me that I didn't have to be perfect, and our family wasn't perfect, but all we had to do was love each other as perfectly as possible. And didn't we all do that? Even when our Easter hats were uncomfortable and too tight, she said, teasing me, and tickling me under my chin until I dissolved into giggles.

"Yes, we all love each other as perfectly as possible," Dad said, and I can remember how he looked at all of us that night, how he still looks at us. "Each one of my girls is beautiful to me," he always said. "Because each of them, in their own way, looks like their mother."

I have never thought of myself as beautiful, and I doubt at this point in my life I ever will. But the closest I ever come to believing such a thing is when someone tells me I look like my mother.

I dial one more number.

"Dad. Did Robin and I have the same color eyes?"

"Hello, Button. Well, let me think. Yes. You do. Of course, they were the exact same color as my father's. He had the best eyes in our family. Royal-blue eyes. Yes. You and your brother had that color."

"Dad, how come you never told me that before?"

"I didn't? Well, I probably didn't want to make your sisters jealous."

"No. I mean the part about your father's eyes."

"Well, he died before you were born, before any of my children were born, but I was so happy when I first saw that Robin's eyes were his color."

"But, Dad, if they were a dark blue, then why was he nick-named Robin, after the color of a robin's eggs?"

"Oh, that was your mother's idea. I think she saw more light in his eyes than anybody else did. Or more light than I did. Anyway, they were a wonderful blue, whatever shade you want to call it, and yours are just the same shade as your brother's. Yes, I'm quite sure."

When we hang up, I close my eyes again and try to imagine Robin and me, side by side as children, down in Virginia. All the pictures I have of this time are in black and white, but I try to add color to them now.

I remember the colors of that summer, the dark yellow of Robin's crab-finding glass, the shades of blue of my grandparents' house through the back window of our car as we pulled away, and the colors of our hands, holding crab nets and fishing rods over the water, the hot sun baking our skin.

Robin's hands were two-toned, sheer ivory with splotches of sunburned pink peeling on the wrists and knuckles. Horace's hands shone like polished mahogany. They were streaked with scars from the work of boat tending and fishing and crabbing. The scars crisscrossed his long, nimble fingers, slashes of light against dark. Doc's hands were light brown and crusty-looking, like the top of Lucy's biscuits right out of the oven in the morning.

And my hands, like the rest of me that summer, were basted with baby oil a deep golden brown. I can see the plump roasted chicken wing of my arm where it crooked out of my white sailor's shirtsleeve. I measured the passage of time by the color of my skin. When I saw my skin turn as brown as Doc's, and then browner still, I knew summer vacation was nearing its end. I would hold my fore- arm against Horace's, annually doomed to disappointment that I had not managed to stay in the sun long enough to turn as dark as him.

I believed that darker meant stronger. Horace and Lucy were so strong they could pick Sally and me up together when they first saw us running toward the house. They would swing us high above their heads, and keep laughing as they swung us until we were giddy with laughter, and yet they never seemed to run out of breath.

I figured that if my skin grew that dark, then I would be so strong that I wouldn't have to wear a life preserver anymore. Noth- ing, not even a fast river current, could overpower me. If I got darker than darkness itself, the night of my nightmares could never swallow me up and take me away. Like they took my pale brother away.

In a sense, I was right about Horace being strong. He lived to be ninety-three years old, and my mother visited him just before he died. He sat up in bed and told her that if his own mother had flown down from heaven to see him, he could not have been happier. He told Mom that his Robbie was waiting up there for him, keeping a spot warm for him out on the fishing boat.

With all my heart I wish there were more happy pictures of my brother to summon. I had so many plans for making it all up to him, all the lost, sad years. When I got out of college and started working, I wrote his name in the blank beside the beneficiary designation for my life insurance. I wrote him a letter that would go with it, that would tell him I wanted him to spend the money on a trip that he had always dreamed about. It was my way of making up to him all those family vacations we took without him. The last time I saw him, at Christmas, we talked about how I would buy him a ticket to Los Angeles and we would go to Disneyland together. His lifelong dream had been to go to there.

He died before I moved to California, and the first time I went to Disneyland, I could almost feel him beside me, riding all the rides over and over, and shaking hands with his favorite cartoon characters in life-sized versions. He would have taken hundreds of pictures. Under that perennially sunny cloudless sky, there would be no shadows hovering over our images. I seize this picture that was never taken, and rescue it from oblivion, if only to prize it in the black-light of my blind dreams.

TWENTY-NINE

We live in an upside-down house. The main living areas are upstairs to take advantage of our panoramic ocean view—a view that is often obscured in the early morning by fog or smog or a combination of the two, leaving a beige soupy mist outside our windows. But on those days when an offshore wind blows in a westerly direction, it unveils a postcard-perfect stretch of the Pacific.

The bedrooms are on the lower level of the house. I must climb the staircase—five steps to the middle landing, nine more to the top—for my first cup of coffee of the day. A few weeks ago, Kenny stopped bringing my coffee downstairs. He didn't have to tell me why, although he mumbled something about missing me sitting there with him during breakfast. As an additional incentive, he reads the newspaper to me out loud. I don't mind this routine at all; I've been getting up earlier anyway, so that I will have more daylight time to look for blue.

It's been ten and a half weeks since my gray fog descended, past the eight-to-ten-week range the Specialist had forecast.

"It could take longer for some people," the Specialist said when I called him at the end of the fifty-sixth day. "I still believe that your sight will improve, but don't expect a dramatic moment. It will be subtle. That's why you must concentrate on looking carefully."

I reach the top of the stairs now, and stand there for a moment, looking straight ahead to the picture window. Still nothing.

I reach for the counter to guide me the seven steps to the breakfast table where my cup of coffee will be waiting. I know Kenny is sitting there already; I can hear the rustle of papers.

My hand hits something hard as it slides across the tiles, and then there is a loud crash, something shattering into pieces at my feet.

"Damnit, *please* don't leave anything at the edge of these counter tops! It's like you've laid a booby trap for me."

"Good morning," Kenny says.

"What did I break this time?"

"A little clay something that Kelsey made for you in school."

"Oh, no. A little clay something?"

"It's all right," Kenny says. "We forgot about that tabletop rule. It's our fault." I hear him get up from the breakfast table. "Stay there, Jackie—I don't want you to cut your bare feet on the pieces. I'm coming over to clean it up."

I look at his voice now, when he speaks, because I have been working hard at all those things that now require deliberate concentration, lifting and turning my head toward sound, putting on my glasses when I wake up, assuming expressions on my face other than frozen expectation and imminent despair.

So it happens then, when I least expect it, just when I lift my head to my husband's voice.

The grayness moves.

"Kenny!" I shout.

The gray shape gets larger and takes on a blue tone as it moves closer and faster toward me.

"What!" he screams. "Did you hurt yourself?"

"Kenny—I think I see you!"

He grabs me and pulls me into his arms, pressing me against his body, but I pull back out of his embrace. I want to see more.

"Kenny, what are you wearing?"

"That blue terry-cloth bathrobe you gave me years ago. I've been wearing it every minute that I'm around you."

"Move around, move around! Let me see you move, Kenny!" I am shouting.

"Mommy, Daddy, what's going on?"

Kelsey! I want to see her—the shape of her moving! I reach for Kelsey, but I can't see her, can't even see her shape.

I hear Kenny whispering to her.

"But, Daddy, I've been wearing that same blue dress every day since you bought it for me—it's in the dirty clothes bag now."

"Go get it!" Kenny and I call out at the same time, and then collapse into laughter. Finally, together, we are laughing out loud.

Later, I have Kenny dial the Specialist's number. When he gets on the line and I announce my news, he tells me he's delighted. Not surprised, but delighted. "You've turned a corner," he says.

Circle tracks, Jackie. Heading back home.

The Specialist reminds me that he had assured me it would get better, and it did.

"So even great doctors indulge in I-told-you-so's," I say, and he laughs.

It may take months before I have any functional vision, he

cautions, and that's going to be hard. In the meantime, I must keep looking.

I am the first to say goodbye in this conversation. I grab Kenny's hand and lead him out to the deck. I look toward the sound of the Pacific and wait for its watery blue depths to overtake the brilliance of my dreams.

THIRTY

MARCH 1995

I can see all the colors now. It took me over a year to get them back, with Kelsey's help. We went to places where I could feast my eyes on color—art museums, fabric stores, flower nurseries. My favorite discovery was the tropical fish stores, where I could watch colors swim before my hungry eyes like tantalizing morsels of food.

Always the store clerks would ask if we wanted to buy something.

"Just looking," Kelsey would say, smiling.

Finally, after several months of hard looking, I could see the whole color wheel, the blues returning first, reds and pinks straggling in later, the bright red of a stop sign last of all. Though the brightness sense, the Specialist had told me, might never come back.

I remembered so many things about color during the siege of blindness. I remembered that each color has its place on the spectrum of natural light. We learn that as children, of course, when we learn how to draw a rainbow, before we grow up and move on to more sophisticated relationships with color and light. But Robin never forgot its magic. And when I had no choice but to look back, I saw the dramatic play of light on every color, every moment, every person in my life.

As a little girl, when my father first told me that his Uncle Ogden was a poet of light verse, I was thrilled. I thought that he was writing poetry about all the different kinds of light—sunlight, moonlight, firelight, starlight, twilight, and candlelight. I remember being disappointed to learn that he was famous for his poetry because it was lighthearted. I thought being lighthearted was a weakness, a lacking of heart.

I know better now. It is very difficult to be lighthearted, and even more difficult to write poetry that makes readers feel that way. Dear old Ungle Og knew quite a bit about light. I know from my family that he worked very hard to take the sadness out of his verse, to put rhyming walls of glass around it, to take off the roof of convention, like Robin's birdhouses, so that the bird could fly away, with a full wingspan, free again. For light is a moving force.

Light moves the darkness. During my blindness, I forgot this lesson, not because I had stopped seeing, but because I had stopped moving. I had stopped living in the present, and the light that propels all life had moved on without me. In the end, it was the light of my family's love—the love from those in heaven above and those still with me on earth—that guided me and moved me forward.

It took some time after my sight returned to work up the courage to go through Robin's things, but Polly and I did as we'd promised each other. We sat side by side and unzipped the bag he was carrying when he was hit by the car he never saw thirteen years earlier.

I made my big sister reach inside first. She pulled out a handful of papers. The Baltimore Metro bus schedule. A library card. A Maryland voter's card—Robin was the first mentally handicapped person to register to vote in the state. His community college ID and a transcript of his grades. He got a satisfactory in Money Management. Business cards and receipts. Banking statements. Newspaper clippings, mostly weather-related—hurricane and flash-flood reports, killer bees and falling meteors.

We looked through a folder that contained his word lists and some of Mary Clark's old homework and a list of snow days he recorded from 1962 to 1973. The Rosewood years. He must have listened for Calvert closings on his little transistor radio. I had a ghostly image of Robin with his face pressed against his radio, looking at the falling snow through barred windows, listening for the announcements that told him his sisters would be spending their day sledding and playing in the snow. I closed my eyes tightly.

Polly must have been thinking the same thing, because she began to zip the duffel bag closed. "I think that's quite enough for one morning," she said. I gently took the bag from her and told her I was ready to see everything it contained.

I felt around and pulled out rolls and rolls of undeveloped film. My Latin medal. A hand-carved number 4, painted bright yellow, with a happy face carved inside the triangle. I leaned back and closed my eyes again.

Sure do like the number four, Jackie.

I took a deep breath and reached in the bag, searching each corner until something sharp pricked my finger. I pulled out a dark yellow, almost amber piece of glass with dangerous jagged edges. The crab-finding glass. How on earth had he managed to keep it with him all those years?

"You're right," I told Polly. "Enough for one day."

Later I took the rolls of film to be developed and then studied the photographs Robin had taken, trying to understand what images he wanted to preserve, trying to see the world through his eyes. I was reminded of one of my brother's great heroes, Miss Simons, who wrote a book, *The Hidden Child*, about teaching children with autism. In it, she advises the teacher to walk behind the child and do exactly what the child does, over and over, until the teacher understands it. Harry Citron, my brother's most beloved teacher—the man who taught him he wasn't retarded, just misunderstood—had told us the only way another human being can fully understand the autistic mind is to go through the existentialist door, to experience a sense of alienation from your own world.

I put down the photos and picked up Robin's crab-finding glass. I walked upstairs to catch the last rays of sunset through the yellow glass. I held it before my eyes and it made the colors outside almost too bright. I turned around and wandered through the house, up and down the hallways, pacing the floors as I had those nights I was revved up on prednisone.

I hadn't recovered the ability to distinguish a darker color against a lighter shade. This meant I couldn't read any monochromatic screens—on a computer, a digital thermometer, even the car radio—and it made reading difficult. The dark words on white paper would tax my eyes to the point that I was unable to read for more than five minutes before the letters blurred out.

But with Robin's glass before my eyes, I saw things I hadn't been able to see before. Shadows appeared, colors sharpened. I walked over to Kelsey. She was playing on a monochromatic computer Kenny had bought me, but I had never been able to see the letters on the screen. The elusive brightness sense. Holding up the glass, I could now see every word.

I took Robin's glass straight to the optometrist's office and asked if he could make me a pair of reading glasses to match this shade of amber. He held the glass up to the light and turned it over. I would indeed have yellow glasses and be able to read at length again. He told me this part of the yellow spectrum had been in research and development for fifteen years and was used by many people with varying visual disabilities. My brother had discovered it nearly thirty years before, using it to find crabs in the salty water, to see shadow moving against shadow.

Ben and I are playing his favorite game of hide-and-seek. I kneel down behind the couch, out of his sight.

"Where are you, Mommy?"

"Here," I whisper.

He follows my voice, walks around the couch and finds me.

"Peekaboo! I see you!" he shouts, falling over backwards like an overeager puppy. He rolls to his feet, still laughing, his blond curls flopping all around his dimpled face.

"Good for you, Ben. Now it's your turn to hide."

"Yes," he says, his blue eyes darkening with intent. "My turn."

But he doesn't move. He covers his eyes with his hands, sure that he is completely hidden. Like most children at eighteen months, he believes his eyes are two-way windows that when shuttered block out not only his view of the world, but the world's view of him.

With each successive turn, I hide farther and farther away from him. He gets impatient waiting for me to pop out, so he begins to roam the house, searching for me. He is learning how to look with his whole body, not just his eyes.

Some children never learn to look, and they turn into adults who cannot see. It takes an early loss—something that had always been there, and was supposed to be there forever. Something very important and very loved must be snatched away suddenly, unexpectedly, for this lesson to be imprinted permanently on a child's mind.

For me, it was my brother, taken away in the darkness, right before my eyes. The next morning I woke up looking for him, and every morning afterward. I cried for my brother from that day forward, and even now I cry for him, as much for the sadness of his life as for the sadness of his death. But grief is a cleansing force. Love washes through the pain, like sunlight through clear water.

In my blindness, I found my brother again and I followed him in his childhood footsteps. I stood inside his shadow and occupied its darkness. In the azure sanctuary of memory, I could restore his face at his perfect age, all the scars from his violent birth and the wounds from his violent death healed. He had the skin of a baby, as smooth and soft as my son's appears to me at this moment. And this is how I see him still.

GRATITUDE LIST

This book would not have made it into print without the constant emotional support of family and friends. Thus, my list of people to thank is as huge as the generosity of their hearts.

The center of this story pivots on the lessons taught to me by my family in Heaven, whose memories light all my dark hallways here on earth.

My mother, Jacquelin Woods Gorman, who taught me how to love.

My brother, Arthur "Robin" Gorman, who taught me how to look.

I must also thank my living family, for their understanding of my need to write this story and their gracious permission in allowing it be published.

My sisters, Polly, Sally, and Mary Clark, who always hold me close, across the space of time and distance.

My children, Kelsey and Benjamin, who, like all children, have not forgotten how to see with their hearts.

Very special thanks to another generation of family members who sustained me during my illness with comfort calls and visits—

my maternal aunt, Anne Byrd Nalle, my maternal uncle, Dr. Alan Churchill Woods, Jr., and my dear father-in-law, Len.

I must also thank my writing group, who over the course of many years together have become my writing family, sisters and brothers in our shared love of words: Jan Bramlett, Russel Lunday, Joy Martin, Peter Nason, Vickie Pynchon, Birute Pitrius Serota, Kathleen Wakefield, Rita Williams, and special thanks to Jonathan Aurthur, who gave this book its final title and copy-edit.

I am deeply grateful for the patience and diplomacy of the following first readers of drafts of the work in progress: Marilyn and Austin Anderson, Kathryn and Alfred Checchi, Joyce and Aubrey Chernick, Alice Gorman, Jill Cherneff and Rocky Laverty, Roberta Berg Moller, Karen Ray, and Ann Whitman Hurd.

I must apologize yet another time to those friends, too many to name here, who forgave rude lapses of manners and communication and late appearances and no-shows at important events and celebrations during the process of writing and re-writing this book. I can never say it enough. I'm sorry, I'm sorry, I'm sorry.

I owe an incalculable debt to the following people who kept me nurtured in body, mind, and spirit during the writing binges: The Lucha Family—Gladis, Victor, Kike, and Marcela, sweet souls; the terrific staff at The Lodge at Lionshead, Vail, Colorado; Margaret Stoll, Ph.D., a true Grief Specialist; Dr. William Lang and Dr. Alfredo Sadun, Marvelous Medicine Men; Reverend John Calhoun, Rabbi Leon Kahane, and Dr. Barbara Fine, gifted spiritual counselors of Manhattan Beach Community Church.

This book was illuminated brilliantly by the following literary lights in very human form:

Julie Grau, editor extraordinaire, who helped me weave a solid book from the gossamer threads of dreams and memory; Nicole Wan and the staff at Riverhead Books and the Putnam Publishing

Group for their enthusiasm and talent; Jim Levine and Arielle Eckstut, of James Levine Communications, Inc., agents and friends, who had the clear-eyed vision to see the importance of telling this story and never stopped believing in my ability to make it into a book.

I am very thankful to Isabel Nash Eberstadt and Linell Nash Smith, cousins and writers, for their kind permission to quote portions of their father's wonderful poetry in this book.

Although I have not yet laid eyes upon them, I send my most heartfelt appreciation and admiration to two remarkable teachers, Harry Citron and Jean Simons, who continued to teach my brother when there was no school for him, and who have kept his memory alive in their hearts all this time.

FINALLY, FOREVER, FOR KENNY, FOR EVERYTHING.

ABOUT THE AUTHOR

Jacquelin Gorman manages Aequilibris Trust, a private foundation that funds nonprofit emotional-support groups for people with debilitating physical or mental illnesses and their families. She lives with her husband and two children in Manhattan Beach, California, and is at work on her first novel.

TWENTY-FOUR

APRIL 15, 1991

I listen to the eleven o'clock news reports about the lines of cars near the airport filled with desperate people trying to get their tax returns stamped at the last open post office. It is a comforting image in a misery-loves-company kind of way. Tonight there are a whole lot of people as nervous, scared, frustrated, and rigidly awake as I have been for the past four weeks.

I hear the rustle of a newspaper. Kenny is reading the news, while I am listening to it. I wish I could ask him to read it to me, but I already feel like the never-ending favor.

I get up and walk slowly, arms outstretched, to Kelsey's room. This is when I spend my time with her, when she is asleep. I still can't hear her sweet voice without my heart breaking because I can't see that face, so I visit her when she is silent.

My knuckles, now covered with Band-Aids, graze the walls of the hallway. I stub my toe on the half-open door. Damn.

Six steps to her bed. I reach toward her and I feel the velvet fur of her enormous stuffed bunny rabbit, the one Mom sent her for her second birthday, the last present she got from her grandmother. I

dusky rose when she wears bright yellow? Tell me those things." I
know that my voice is rising, but I can't control its pitch.

"Mommy?"

I almost jump out of my skin. I pull from Kenny, silently, but
he does not let me go. He pulls me in the other direction, toward our
daughter's bed. Then he lets go.

"Mommy, will you stay and tell me a bedtime story. Please?"

"Daddy's here, darling," I answer. "He can read you a story."

"No he's not, Mommy. He left. And you don't have to read me
one, you can just lie beside me and make one up."

I get under the covers with her, press my face into her curls and
breathe in the smell of her hair, the honey-apricot scent of her sham-
poo. I hear her sniffle and feel her shudder against me. When I reach
down to touch her face, my fingers slide across her wet cheeks.

"What's wrong, darling?"

"You don't ever want me around you anymore, Mommy. You
don't want to play with me. I miss you."

Not this. Where is Kenny?

"I want to play with you, Kelsey, but I can't see the games. I
can't read you stories."

"But you don't have to *do* anything, Mommy. Just let me stay
near you, and we can talk, and we can just be together like always."

I hold her close against me, and she clings to me. How can I explain all this to her? Where are the words?

"I know it's hard to understand. It's so hard for me too, Kelsey.
I hear your sweet voice and I want to see you, and it makes me so
much sadder when I think about how much I want to see you."

"But you *can* see me, Mommy."

"No, I *can't*." Her denial is an insult, insinuating that I can't see
because I'm not trying hard enough or I don't want it badly enough.

"You can see me that other way, Mommy. Not with your eyes. You can see me with your heart."

"Kelsey, what are you talking about? Who told you this?" Now I'm angry. Who has been filling her little head with these fuzzy words and saccharine ideas, as insubstantial as puffs of cotton candy? "Who told you this?"

"You did, Mommy," she says, squeezing my hands. "You told me that story right after Grandmommy died, and I was crying because I couldn't see her in heaven and you said that I could always see her with my heart."

"Yes, now I remember. I did say that, but, Kelsey, this is different."

"But it's the same. You said that I could close my eyes and see Grandmommy smiling at me. And that's what you can do. You can always see me with your heart even when your eyes don't work. You *can*."

"Kelsey, I'm not sure that I can do that, I—"

"Yes you can. You told me that, and you wouldn't ever lie to me."

"No . . ."

"No, you can't see me with your heart?"

I sigh. "No, I would never lie to you. And yes, Kelsey, you're right. I can see you with my heart—I can see you very clearly, even in the dark."

I turn over on my side, facing her. I blink into the darkness, stare straight ahead, where I think her face must be.

"Can you see me smiling right now, Mommy?"

"Yes," I lie.

Then I close my eyes. I can't do this.

"Kelsey, I'm really tired. I need to go back to my bed."